Faint heart ne'e

Locklear had patrolled the ravine at midmorning bow, and an arrow-filled quiver, when he first scream. He knew that Kit, with her short lance, had gone in the opposite direction on her patrol, but the repeated kzin screams sent gooseflesh up his spine. Perhaps the tabbies had surrounded Boots, or Puss. He notched an arrow, half climbing to the lip of the ravine, and peered over low brush. He stifled the exclamation in his throat.

They'd found Puss, all right—or she'd found them. She stood on all-fours on a level spot below, her tail erect, its tip curled over, watching two hated familiar figures in a tableau that must have been as old as kzin history. Almost naked for this primitive duel, ebony talons out and their musky scent heavy on the breeze, they bulked stupefyingly huge and ferocious. The massive gunner, Goon, and engineer Yellowbelly circled each other with drawn stilettoes. What boggled Locklear was that their modern weapons lay ignored in neat groups. Were they going through some ritual?

They were like hell, he decided. No telling how long they'd been there, but Goon's right forearm dripped blood, and Yellowbelly's thigh was a sodden red mess. Swaying drunkenly, Puss edged nearer to the weapons. As Yellowbelly screamed and leaped, Goon screamed and parried, bearing his smaller opponent to the turf. What followed then was fast enough to be virtually a blur in a roil of Kzersatz dust as two huge tigerlike bodies thrashed and rolled, knives flashing, talons ripping, fangs sinking into flesh.

THE MAN-KZIN WARS

Larry Niven

with

Poul Anderson

and

Dean Ing

BAEN BOOKS

THE MAN-KZIN WARS

This is a work of fiction. All the characters and events portrayed in this book are fictional, and any resemblance to real people or incidents is purely coincidental.

A Baen Books Original

Baen Publishing Enterprises
260 Fifth Avenue
New York, N.Y. 10001

First printing, June 1988
  Second printing, July 1988

ISBN: 0-671-65411-X

Cover art by Steve Hickman

Printed in the United States of America

Distributed by
SIMON & SCHUSTER
1230 Avenue of the Americas
New York, N.Y. 10020

CONTENTS

Introduction

Larry Niven

"The Warriors" wasn't just the first tale of the kzinti. It was the first story I ever offered for sale. I was daydreaming in math class, as usual, and I realized that I'd shaped a complete story. So I wrote it down, and bought some magazines to get the editorial addresses, and started it circulating.

It was years before anyone bought it. By then I'd rewritten it countless times, trying out what I was learning from my correspondence writing course. Fred Pohl (editor of *Galaxy* and *Worlds of If* in those days) saw it often enough that he eventually wrote, "I think this can be improved . . . but maybe you're tired of reworking it, so I'll buy it as is . . ." It was probably his title, too.

The kzinti look a little blurred here, don't they? I mean, if you've known them elsewhere. Subsequently they changed in several ways.

I learned to answer John W. Campbell's challenge: "Show me something that thinks as well as a man, or better, but not like a man." The kzinti took on more detail, gained greater consistency and lost some of their resemblance to humanity. They were born as one of a thousand catlike aliens in science fiction. As I learned how to make an alien from basic principles, body and mind and soul, the kzinti became more themselves.

At the same time they were changing in another way, evolving over several centuries. The Man-Kzin Wars changed them far more than they changed mankind, because the wars killed off the least intelligent and most aggressive.

This book was conceived in a casual encounter.

Marilyn and I were driving to a Nebula Awards banquet with Jim Baen in the back seat. She drove, we talked . . .

I knew about franchise universes. Jim and I had edited *The Magic May Return* and *More Magic*, tales set in the *Magic Goes Away* universe but written by friends whom we had invited in. I had played in neighbors' playgrounds, too. "A Snowflake Falls" used Saberhagen's "Berserkers," by invitation. I'd written a tale set at Lord Dunsany's "edge of the world," and a report on the year the Necronomicon hit the college campuses in paperback, and a study of Superman's fertility problems.

I've never been in a war, nor in any of the armed forces. Wars have happened and may happen again in most of my series universes, including known space, but you'll never *see* them. I lack the experience. Here are a couple of centuries of known space that are dark to me.

By the time we parked, Jim and I had agreed to open up the Man-Kzin Wars period of known space.

Any writer good enough to be invited to play in my universe will have demonstrated that he can make his own. Would anyone accept my offer? I worried also that intruders might mess up the playground, by violating my background assumptions.

But I did want to read more tales of Known Space . . . and I hadn't written any in years.

For the Warlock's era I had written a "bible," a set of assumptions, list of available characters, backgrounds, a few story ideas. For the Man-Kzin Wars the "bible" was already written, by John Hewitt for the Chaosium role-playing game, "Ringworld." I photocopied the appropriate pages, with his permission and Chaosium's.

I did not anticipate what happened.

I had to turn down one story outline and one completed story. It didn't matter. Poul and Dean both turned in 40,000-word novellas! And now they're talking about sequels.

It's as if you can't say anything *short* in the Known Space universe

I guess I'm flattered. And I surely got my wish. These stories read like good Poul Anderson, and good Dean Ing, and good Niven; and Niven couldn't have written them.

THE WARRIORS

Larry Niven

"I'm sure they saw us coming," the Alien Technologies Officer persisted. "Do you see that ring, sir?"

The silvery image of the enemy ship almost filled the viewer. It showed as a broad, wide ring encircling a cylindrical axis, like a mechanical pencil floating inside a platinum bracelet. A finned craft projected from the pointed end of the axial section. Angular letters ran down the axis, totally unlike the dots-and-commas of Kzinti script.

"Of course I see it," said the Captain.

"It was rotating when we first picked them up. It stopped when we got within two hundred thousand miles, and it hasn't moved since."

The Captain flicked his tail back and forth, gently, thoughtfully, like a pink lash. "You worry me," he commented. "If they know we're here, why haven't they tried to get away? Are they so sure they can beat us?" He whirled to face the A-T Officer. "Should *we* be running?"

"No, sir! I don't know why they're still here, but they can't have anything to be confident about. That's

7

one of the most primitive spacecraft I've ever seen." He moved his claw about on the screen, pointing as he talked.

"The outer shell is an iron alloy. The rotating ring is a method of imitating gravity by using centripetal force. So they don't have the gravity planer. In fact they're probably using a reaction drive."

The Captain's catlike ears went up. "But we're lightyears from the nearest star!"

"They must have a better reaction drive than we ever developed. We had the gravity planer before we needed one that good."

There was a buzzing sound from the big control board. "Enter," said the Captain.

The Weapons Officer fell up through the entrance hatch and came to attention, "Sir, we have all weapons trained on the emeny."

"Good." The Captain swung around. "A-T, how sure are you that they aren't a threat to us?"

The A-T Officer bared sharply pointed teeth. "I don't see how they could be, sir."

"Good. Weapons, keep all your guns ready to fire, but don't use them unless I give the order. I'll have the ears of the man who destroys that ship without orders. I want to take it intact."

"Yes, sir."

"Where's the Telepath?"

"He's on his way, sir. He was asleep."

"He's always asleep. Tell him to get his tail up here."

The Weapons Officer saluted, turned, and dropped through the exit hole.

"Captain?"

The A-T Officer was standing by the viewer, which now showed the ringed end of the alien ship. He pointed to the mirror-bright end of the axial cylinder. "It looks like that end was designed to project light. That would make it a photon drive, sir."

The Captain considered. "Could it be a signal device?"

"Urrrrr . . . Yes, sir."

"Then don't jump to conclusions."

Like a piece of toast, the Telepath popped up through the entrance hatch. He came to exaggerated attention. "Reporting as ordered, sir."

"You omitted to buzz for entrance."

"Sorry, sir." The lighted viewscreen caught the Telepath's eye and he padded over for a better look, forgetting that he was at attention. The A-T Officer winced, wishing he were somewhere else.

The Telepath's eyes were violet around the edges. His pink tail hung limp. As usual, he looked as if he were dying for lack of sleep. His fur was flattened along the side he slept on; he hadn't even bothered to brush it. The effect was far from the ideal of a Conquest Warrior as one can get and still be a member of the Kzinti species. The wonder was that the Captain had not yet murdered him.

He never would, of course. Telepaths were too rare, too valuable, and—understandably—too emotionally unstable. The Captain always kept his temper with the Telepath. At times like this it was the innocent bystander who stood to lose his rank or his ears at the clank of a falling molecule.

"That's an enemy ship we've tracked down," the Captain was saying. "We'd like to get some information from them. Would you read their minds for us?"

"Yes, sir." The Telepath's voice showed his instant misery, but he knew better than to protest. He left the screen and sank into a chair. Slowly his ears folded into tight knots, his pupils contracted, and his ratlike tail went limp as flannel.

The world of the eleventh sense pushed in on him.
He caught the Captain's thought: ". . . sloppy civilian get of a sthondat . . ." and frantically tuned it out. He hated the Captain's mind. He found other minds aboard ship, isolated and blanked them out one by one. Now there were none left. There was only unconsciousness and chaos.

Chaos was not empty. Something was thinking strange and disturbing thoughts.

The Telepath forced himself to listen.

Steve Weaver floated bonelessly near a wall of the radio room. He was blond, blue-eyed, and big, and he could often be seen as he was now, relaxed but completely motionless, as if there were some very good reason why he shouldn't even blink. A streamer of smoke drifted from his left hand and crossed the room to bury itself in the air vent.

"That's that," Ann Harrison said wearily. She flicked four switches in the bank of radio controls. At each click a small light went out.

"You can't get them?"

"Right. I'll bet they don't even have a radio." Ann released her chair net and stretched out into a five-pointed star. "I've left the receiver on, with the volume up, in case they try to get us later. Man, that feels good!" Abruptly she curled into a tight ball. She had been crouched at the communications bank for more than an hour. Ann might have been Steve's twin; she was almost as tall as he was, had the same color hair and eyes, and the flat muscles of conscientious exercise showed beneath her blue falling jumper as she flexed.

Steve snapped his cigarette butt at the air conditioner, moving only his fingers. "Okay. What have they got?"

Ann looked startled. "*I* don't know."

"Think of it as a puzzle. They don't have a radio. How might they talk to each other? How can we check on our guesses? We assume they're trying to reach us, of course."

"Yes, of course."

"Think about it, Ann. Get Jim thinking about it, too." Jim Davis was her husband that year, and the ship's doctor full time. "You're the girl most likely to succeed. Have a smog stick?"

"Please."

Steve pushed his cigarette ration across the room. "Take a few. I've got to go."

The depleted package came whizzing back. "Thanks," said Ann.

"Let me know if anything happens, will you? Or if you think of anything."

"I will. And fear not, Steve, something's bound to turn up. They must be trying just as hard as we are."

Every compartment in the personnel ring opened into the narrow doughnut-shaped hall which ran around the ring's forward rim. Steve pushed himself into the hall, jockeyed to contact the floor, and pushed. From there it was easy going. The floor curved up to meet him, and he proceded down the hall like a swimming frog. Of the twelve men and women on the *Angel's Pencil*, Steve was best at this; for Steve was a Belter, and the others were all flatlanders, Earthborn.

Ann probably wouldn't think of anything, he guessed. It wasn't that she wasn't intelligent. She didn't have the curiosity, the sheer love of solving puzzles. Only he and Jim Davis—

He was going too fast, and not concentrating. He almost crashed into Sue Bhang as she appeared below the curve of the ceiling.

They managed to stop themselves against the walls. "Hi, jaywalker," said Sue.

"Hi, Sue. Where you headed?"

"Radio room. You?"

"I thought I'd check the drive systems again. Not that we're likely to need the drive, but it can't hurt to be certain."

"You'd go twitchy without something to do, wouldn't you?" She cocked her head to one side, as always when she had questions. "Steve, when are you going to rotate us again? I can't seem to get used to falling."

But she looked like she'd been born falling, he thought. Her small, slender form was meant for flying; gravity should never have touched her. "When I'm sure we won't need the drive. We might as well stay ready 'til then. Because I'm hoping you'll change back to a skirt."

She laughed, pleased. "Then you can turn it off. I'm not changing, and we won't be moving. Abel says the other ship did two hundred gee when it matched courses with us. How many can the *Angel's Pencil* do?"

Steve looked awed. "Just point zero five. And I was thinking of chasing them! Well, maybe we can be the ones to open communications. I just came from the radio room, by the way. Ann can't get anything."

"Too bad."

"We'll just have to wait."

"Steve, you're always so impatient. Do Belters always move at a run? Come here." She took a handhold and pulled him over to one of the thick windows which lined the forward side of the corridor. "There they are," she said, pointing out.

The star was both duller and larger than those around it. Among points which glowed arc-lamp blue-white with the Doppler shift, the alien ship showed as a dull red disk.

"I looked at it through the telescope," said Steve. "There are lumps and ridges all over it. And there's a circle of green dots and commas painted on one side. Looked like writing."

"How long have we been waiting to meet them? Five hundred thousand years? Well, there they are. Relax. They won't go away." Sue gazed out the window, her whole attention on the dull red circle, her gleaming jet hair floating out around her head. "The first aliens. I wonder what they'll be like."

"It's anyone's guess. They must be pretty strong to take punishment like that, unless they have some kind of acceleration shield, but free fall doesn't bother them either. That ship isn't designed to spin." He was staring intently, out at the stars, his big form characteristically motionless, his expression somber. Abruptly he said, "Sue, I'm worried."

"About what?"

"Suppose they're hostile?"

"Hostile?" She tasted the unfamiliar word, decided she didn't like it.

"After all, we know nothing about them. Suppose they want to fight? We'd—"

She gasped. Steve flinched before the horror in her face. "What—what put that idea in your head?"

"I'm sorry I shocked you, Sue."

"Oh, don't worry about that, but *why?* Did—shh."

Jim Davis had come into view. The *Angel's Pencil* had left Earth when he was twenty-seven; now he was a slightly paunchy thirty-eight, the oldest man on board, an amiable man with abnormally long, delicate fingers. His grandfather, with the same hands, had been a world-famous surgeon. Nowadays surgery was normally done by autodocs, and the arachnodactyls were to Davis merely an affliction. He bounced by, walking on magnetic sandals, looking like a comedian as he bobbed about the magnetic plates. "Hi, group," he called as he went by.

"Hello, Jim." Sue's voice was strained. She waited until he was out of sight before she spoke again.

Hoarsely she whispered, "Did you fight in the Belt?" She didn't really believe it; it was merely the worst thing she could think of.

Vehemently Steve snapped, "No!" Then, reluctantly, he added, "But it did happen occasionally." Quickly he tried to explain. "The trouble was that all the doctors, including the psychists, were at the big bases, like Ceres. It was the only way they could help the people who needed them—be where the miners could find them. But all the danger was out in the rocks.

"You noticed a habit of mine once. I never make gestures. All Belters have that trait. It's because on a small mining ship you could hit something waving your arms around. Something like the airlock button."

"Sometimes it's almost eerie. You don't move for minutes at a time."

"There's always tension out in the rocks. Sometimes a miner would see too much danger and boredom and frustration, too much cramping inside and too much room outside, and he wouldn't get to a psychist in time. He'd pick a fight in a bar. I saw it happen once. The guy was using his hands like mallets."

Steve had been looking far into the past. Now he turned back to Sue. She looked white and sick, like a novice nurse standing up to her first really bad case. His ears began to turn red. "Sorry," he said miserably.

She felt like running; she was as embarrassed as he was. Instead she said, and tried to mean it, "It doesn't matter. So you think the people in the other ship might want to, uh, make war?"

He nodded.

"Did you have history-of-Earth courses?"

He smiled ruefully. "No, I couldn't qualify. Sometimes I wonder how many people do."

"About one in twelve."

"That's not many."

"People in general have trouble assimilating the facts of life about their ancestors. You probably know that there used to be wars before—hmmm—three hundred years ago, but do you know what war is? Can you visualize one? Can you see a fusion electric point deliberately built to explode in the middle of the city? Do you know what a concentration camp is? A limited action? You probably think murder ended with war. Well, it didn't. The last murder occurred in twenty-one something, just a hundred and sixty years ago.

"Anyone who says human nature can't be changed is out of his head. To make it stick, he's got to define human nature—and he can't. Three things gave us our present peaceful civilization, and each one was a technological change." Sue's voice had taken on a dry, remote lecture-hall tone, like the voice on a teacher tape. "One was the development of psychistry beyond the alchemist stage. Another was the full development of land for food production. The third was the Fertility Restriction Laws and the annual contraceptive shots. They gave us room to breathe. Maybe Belt mining and the stellar colonies had something to do with it, too; they gave us an inanimate enemy. Even the historians argue about that one.

"Here's the delicate point I'm trying to nail down." Sue rapped on the window. "Look at that spacecraft. It has enough power to move it around like a mail missile and enough fuel to move it up to our point eight light—right?"

"Right."

"—with plenty of power left for maneuvering. It's a better ship than ours. If they've had time to learn how to build a ship like that, they've had time to build up their own versions of psychistry, modern food production, contraception, economic theory, everything they need to abolish war. See?"

Steve had to smile at her earnestness. "Sure, Sue, it makes sense. But that guy in the bar came from our culture, and he was hostile enough. If we can't understand how he thinks, how can we guess about the mind of something whose very chemical makeup we can't guess at yet?"

"It's sentient. It builds tools."

"Right."

"And if Jim hears you talking like this, you'll be in psychistry treatment."

"That's the best argument you've given me," Steve grinned, and stroked her under the ear with two fingertips. He felt her go suddenly stiff, saw the pain in her face; and at the same time his own pain struck, a real tiger of a headache, as if his brain were trying to swell beyond his skull.

"I've got them, sir," the Telepath said blurrily. "Ask me anything."

The Captain hurried, knowing that the Telepath couldn't stand this for long. "How do they power their ship?"

"It's a light-pressure drive powered by incomplete hydrogen fusion. They use an electromagnetic ramscoop to get their own hydrogen from space."

"Clever . . . Can they get away from us?"

"No. Their drive is on idle, ready to go, but it won't help them. It's pitifully weak."

"What kind of weapons do they have?"

The Telepath remained silent for a long time. The others waited patiently for his answer. There was sound in the control dome, but it was the kind of sound one learns not to hear: the whine of heavy current, the muted purr of voices from below, the strange sound like continuously ripping cloth which came from the gravity motors.

"None at all, sir." The Kzin's voice became clearer; his hypnotic relaxation was broken by muscle twitches. He twisted as if in a nightmare. "Nothing aboard ship, not even a knife or a club. Wait, they've got cooking knives. But that's all they use them for. They don't fight."

"They don't fight?"

"No, sir. They don't expect us to fight, either. The idea has occurred to three of them, and each has dismissed it from his mind."

"But why?" the Captain asked, knowing the question was irrelevant, unable to hold it back.

"I don't know, sir. It's a science they use, or a religion. I don't understand," the Telepath whimpered. "I don't understand at all."

Which must be tough on him, the Captain thought. Completely alien thoughts . . . "What are they doing now?"

"Waiting for us to talk to them. They tried to talk to us, and they think we must be trying just as hard."

"But why?—never mind, it's not important. Can they be killed by heat?"

"Yes, sir."

"Break contact."

The Telepath shook his head violently. He looked

like he'd been in a washing machine. The Captain touched a sensitized surface and bellowed, "Weapons Officer!"

"Here."

"Use the inductors on the enemy ship."

"But, sir! They're so slow! What if the alien attacks?"

"Don't argue with me, you—" Snarling, the Captain delivered an impassioned monologue on the virtues of unquestioning obedience. When he switched off, the Alien Technologies Officer was back at the viewer and the Telepath had gone to sleep.

The Captain purred happily, wishing that they were all this easy.

When the occupants had been killed by heat he would take the ship. He could tell everything he needed to know about their planet by examining their life-support system. He could locate it by tracing the ship's trajectory. Probably they hadn't even taken evasive action!

If they came from a Kzin-like world it would become a Kzin world. And he, as Conquest Leader, would command one percent of its wealth for the rest of his life! Truly, the future looked rich. No longer would he be called by his profession. He would bear a *name* . . .

"Incidental information," said the A-T Officer. "The ship was generating one and twelve sixty-fourth gee before it stopped rotating."

"Little heavy," the Captain mused. "Might be too much air, but it should be easy to Kzinform it. A-T, we find the strangest life forms. Remember the Chunquen?"

"Both sexes were sentient. They fought constantly."

"And that funny religion on Altair One. They thought they could travel in time."

"Yes, sir. When we landed the infantry they were all gone."

"They must have all committed suicide with disintegrators. But why? They knew we only wanted slaves. And I'm still trying to figure out how they got rid of the disintegrators afterward."

"Some beings," said the A-T Officer, "will do anything to keep their beliefs."

Eleven years beyond Pluto, eight years from her destination, the fourth colony ship to We Made It fell between the stars. Before her the stars were green-white and blue-white, blazing points against nascent black. Behind they were sparse, dying red embers. To the sides the constellations were strangely flattened. The universe was shorter than it had been.

For awhile Jim Davis was very busy. Everyone, including himself, had a throbbing blinding headache. To each patient, Dr. Davis handed a tiny pink pill from the dispenser slot of the huge autodoc which covered the back wall of the infirmary. They milled outside the door waiting for the pills to take effect, looking like a full-fledged mob in the narrow corridor; and then someone thought it would be a good idea to go to the lounge, and everyone followed him. It was an unusually silent mob. Nobody felt like talking while the pain was with them. Even the sound of magnetic sandals was lost in the plastic pile rug.

Steve saw Jim Davis behind him. "Hey, Doc," he called softly. "How long before the pain stops?"

"Mine's gone away. You got your pills a little after I did, right?"

"Right. Thanks, Doc."

They didn't take pain well, these people. They were unused to it.

In single file they walked or floated into the lounge. Low-pitched conversations started. People took couches, using the sticky plastic strips on their falling jumpers. Others stood or floated near walls. The lounge was big enough to hold them all in comfort.

Steve wriggled near the ceiling, trying to pull on his sandals.

"I hope they don't try that again," he heard Sue say. "It hurt."

"Try what?" Someone Steve didn't recognize, half-listening as he was.

"Whatever they tried. Telepathy, perhaps."

"No. I don't believe in telepathy. Could they have set up ultrasonic vibrations in the walls?"

Steve had his sandals on. He left the magnets turned off.

". . . a cold beer. Do you realize we'll never taste beer again?" Jim Davis' voice.

"I miss waterskiing." Ann Harrison sounded wistful. "The feel of a pusher unit shoving into the small of your back, the water beating against your feet, the sun . . ."

Steve pushed himself toward them. "Taboo subject," he called.

"We're on it anyway," Jim boomed cheerfully. "Unless you'd rather talk about the alien, which everyone else is doing. I'd rather drop it for the moment. What's your greatest regret at leaving Earth?"

"Only that I didn't stay long enough to really see it."

"Oh, of course." Jim suddenly remembered the drinking bulb in his hand. He drank from it, hospitality passed it to Steve.

"This waiting makes me restless," said Steve. "What are they likely to try next? Shake the ship in Morse code?"

Jim smiled. "Maybe they won't try anything next. They may give up and leave."

"Oh, I hope not!" said Ann.

"Would that be so bad?"

Steve had a start. What was Jim thinking?

"Of course!" Ann protested. "We've got to find out what they're like! And think of what they can teach us, Jim!"

When conversation got controversial it was good manners to change the subject. "Say," said Steve, "I happened to notice the wall was warm when I pushed off. Is that good or bad?"

"That's funny. It should be cold, if anything," said Jim. "There's nothing out there but starlight. Except—" A most peculiar expression flitted across his face. He drew his feet up and touched the magnetic soles with his fingertips.

"Eeeee! Jim! Jim!"

Steve tried to whirl around and got nowhere. That was Sue! He switched on his shoes, thumped to the floor, and went to help.

Sue was surrounded by bewildered people. They split to let Jim Davis through, and he tried to lead her out of the lounge. He looked frightened. Sue was moaning and thrashing, paying no attention to his efforts.

Steve pushed through to her. "All the metal is heating up," Davis shouted. "We've got to get her hearing aid out."

"Infirmary," Sue shouted.

Four of them took Sue down the hall to the infirmary. She was still crying and struggling feebly when they got her in, but Jim was there ahead of them with a spray hypo. He used it and she went to sleep.

The four watched anxiously as Jim went to work. The autodoc would have taken precious time for diagnosis. Jim operated by hand. He was able to do a fast job, for the tiny instrument was buried just below the skin behind her ear. Still, the scalpel must have burned his fingers before he was done. Steve could feel the growing warmth against the soles of his feet.

Did the aliens know what they were doing?

Did it matter? The ship was being attacked. His ship.

Steve slipped into the corridor and ran for the control room. Running on magnetic soles, he looked like a terrified penguin, but he moved fast. He knew he might be making a terrible mistake; the aliens might be trying desperately to reach the *Angel's Pencil*; he would never know. They had to be stopped before everyone was roasted.

The shoes burned his feet. He whimpered with the pain, but otherwise ignored it. The air burned in his mouth and throat. Even his teeth were hot.

He had to wrap his shirt around his hands to open the control-room door. The pain in his feet was unbearable; he tore off his sandals and swam to the control board. He kept his shirt over his hands to work the controls. A twist of a large white knob turned the drive on full, and he slipped into the pilot seat before the gentle light pressure could build up.

He turned to the rear-view telescope. It was aimed at the solar system, for the drive could be used for messages at this distance. He set it for short range and began to turn the ship.

The enemy ship glowed in the high infrared.

"It will take longer to heat the crew-carrying section," reported the Alien Technologies Officer. "They'll have temperature control there."

"That's all right. When you think they should all

be dead, wake up the Telepath and have him check."
The Captain continued to brush his fur, killing time.
"You know, if they hadn't been so completely help-
less I wouldn't have tried this slow method. I'd have
cut the ring free of the motor section first. Maybe I
should have done that anyway. Safer."

The A-T Officer wanted all the credit he could get.
"Sir, they couldn't have any big weapons. There isn't
room. With a reaction drive, the motor and the fuel
tanks take up most of the available space."

The other ship began to turn away from its tor-
mentor. Its drive end glowed red.

"They're trying to get away," the Captain said, as
the glowing end swung toward them. "Are you sure
they can't?"

"Yes, sir. That light drive won't take them anywhere."

The Captain purred thoughtfully. "What would
happen if the light hit our ship?"

"Just a bright light, I think. The lens is flat, so it
must be emitting a very wide beam. They'd need a
parabolic reflector to be dangerous. Unless—" His
ears went straight up.

"Unless what?" The Captain spoke softly, demand-
ingly.

"A laser. But that's all right, sir. They don't have
any weapons."

The Captain sprang at the control board. "Stupid!"
he spat. "They don't know weapons from sthondat
blood. Weapons Officer! How could a telepath find
out what they don't know? WEAPONS OFFICER!"

"Here, sir."

"Burn—"

An awful light shone in the control dome. The
Captain burst into flame, then blew out as the air left
through a glowing split in the dome.

* * *

Steve was lying on his back. The ship was spinning again, pressing him into what felt like his own bunk.

He opened his eyes.

Jim Davis crossed the room and stood over him. "You awake?"

Steve sat bolt upright, his eyes wide.

"Easy." Jim's gray eyes were concerned.

Steve blinked up at him. "What happened?" he asked, and discovered how hoarse he was.

Jim sat down in one of the chairs. "You tell me. We tried to get to the control room when the ship started moving. Why didn't you ring the strap-down? You turned off the drive just as Ann came through the door. Then you fainted."

"How about the other ship?" Steve tried to repress the urgency in his voice, and couldn't.

"Some of the others are over there now, examining the wreckage." Steve felt his heart stop. "I guess I was afraid from the start that alien ship was dangerous. I'm more psychist than emdee, and I qualified for history class, so maybe I know more than is good for me about human nature. Too much to think that beings with space travel will automatically be peaceful. I tried to think so, but they aren't. They've got things any self-respecting human being would be ashamed to have nightmares about. Bomb missiles, fusion bombs, lasers, that induction injector they used on us. And antimissiles. You know what that means? They've got enemies like themselves, Steve. Maybe nearby."

"So I killed them." The room seemed to swoop around him, but his voice came out miraculously steady.

"You saved the ship."

"It was an accident. I was trying to get us away."

"No, you weren't." Davis' accusation was as casual

as if he were describing the chemical makeup of
urea. "That ship was four hundred miles away. You
would have had to sight on it with a telescope to hit
it. You knew what you were doing, too, because you
turned off the drive as soon as you'd burned through
the ship."

Steve's back muscles would no longer support him.
He flopped back to horizontal. "All right, you know,"
he told the ceiling. "Do the others?"

"I doubt it. Killing in self-defense is too far outside
their experience. I think Sue's guessed."

"Oooo."

"If she has, she's taking it well," Davis said briskly.
"Better than most of them will, when they find out
the universe is full of warriors. This is the end of the
world, Steve."

"What?"

"I'm being theatrical. But it is. Three hundred
years of the peaceful life for everyone. They'll call it
the Golden Age. No starvation, no war, no physical
sickness other than senescence, no permanent mental sickness at all, even by our rigid standards. When
someone over fourteen tries to use his fist on someone else we say he's sick, and we cure him. And now
it's over. Peace isn't a stable condition, not for us.
Maybe not for anything that lives."

"Can I see the ship from here?"

"Yes. It's just behind us."

Steve rolled out of bed, went to the window.

Someone had steered the ships much closer together. The Kzinti ship was a huge red sphere with
ugly projections scattered at seeming random over
the hull. The beam had sliced it into two unequal
halves, sliced it like an ax through an egg. Steve
watched, unable to turn aside, as the big half rotated
to show its honeycombed interior.

"In a little while," said Jim, "the men will be coming back. They'll be frightened. Someone will probably insist that we arm ourselves against the next attacks, using weapons from the other ship. I'll have to agree with him.

"Maybe they'll think I'm sick myself. Maybe I am. But it's the kind of sickness we'll need." Jim looked desperately unhappy. "We're going to become an armed society. And of course we'll have to warn the Earth . . ."

IRON

Poul Anderson

1

The kzin screamed and leaped.

In any true gravity field, Robert Saxtorph would have been dead half a minute later. The body has its wisdom, and his had been schooled through hard years. Before he really knew what a thunderbolt was coming at him, he had sprung aside—against the asteroid spin. As his weight dropped, he thrust a foot once more to drive himself off the deck, strike a wallfront, recover control over his mass, and bounce to a crouch.

The kzin was clearly not trained for such tricks. He had pounced straight out of a crosslane, parallel to Tiamat's rotation axis. Coriolis force was too slight to matter. But instead of his prey, he hit the opposite side of Ranzau Passage. Pastel plastic cracked under the impact; the metal behind it boomed. He recovered with the swiftness of his kind, whirled about, and snarled.

For an instant, neither being moved. Ten meters

from him, the kzin stood knife-sharp in Saxtorph's awareness. It was as if he could count every redorange hair of the pelt. Round yellow eyes glared at him out of the catlike face, above the mouthful of fangs. Bat-wing ears were folded out of sight into the fur, for combat. The naked tail was angled past a columnar thigh, stiffly held. The claws were out, jet-black, on all four digits of either hand. Except for a phone on his left wrist, the kzin was unclad. That seemed to make even greater his 250 centimeters of height, his barrel thickness.

Before and behind the two, Ranzau Passage curved away. Windows in the wallfronts were empty, doors closed, signs turned off; workers had gone home for the nightwatch. They were always few, anyway. This industrial district had been devoted largely to the production of spaceship equipment which the hyperdrive was making as obsolete as fission power.

There was no time to be afraid. "Hey, wait a minute, friend," Saxtorph heard himself exclaim automatically, "I never saw you before, never did you any harm, didn't even jostle you—"

Of course that was useless, whether or not the kzin knew English. Saxtorph hadn't adopted the stance which indicated peacefulness. It would have put him off balance. The kzin bounded at him.

Saxtorph released the tension in his right knee and swayed aside. Coming upspin, his speed suddenly lessening his weight, the kzin—definitely not a veteran of space—went by too fast to change direction at once. As he passed, almost brushing the man, the gingery smell of his excitement filling the air, Saxtorph thrust fingers at an eye. That was just about the only vulnerable point when a human was unarmed. The kzin yowled; echoes rang.

Saxtorph was shouting too, "Help, murder, help!"

Somebody should be in earshot of that. The kzin skidded to a halt and whipped about. It would have been astounding how quick and agile his bulk was, if Saxtorph hadn't seen action on the ground during the war.

Again saving his breath, the man backed downspin, but slantwise, so that he added little to his weight. Charging full-out, the kzin handicapped himself much more. The extra drag on his mass meant nothing to his muscles, but confused his reflexes. Dodging about, Saxtorph concentrated first on avoiding the sweeps of those claws, second on keeping the velocity parameters unpredictably variable. From time to time he yelled.

One slash connected. It ripped his tunic from collar to belt, and the undershirt beneath. Blood welled along shallow gashes. As he jumped clear, Saxtorph cracked the blade of his hand onto the flat nose before him. It did no real harm, but hurt. The kzin's eyes widened. The pupil of the undamaged one grew narrower yet. He had seen the scars across his opponent's chest. This human had encountered at least one kzin before, face to face.

But Saxtorph was 15 years younger then, and equipped with a Gurkha knife. Now the wind was gusting out of him. His gullet was afire. Sluggishness crept into his motions. "Ya-a-ah, police, help! Ki-yai!"

A whistle skirled. The kzin halted. He stared past Saxtorph. The man dared not turn his head, but he heard cries and footfalls. The kzin turned and sped in the opposite direction, upspin. He whirled into the first crosslane he came to and disappeared.

And *that* wasn't like his breed, either. Saxtorph sagged back against a wallfront and sobbed breath into his lungs. Sweat was cold and acrid on him. He felt the beginnings of the shakes and started calling calm down on himself, as the Zen master who helped train him for war had taught.

One cop waved off a score or so of people whom the commotion had drawn after him and his companion. The other approached Saxtorph. He was stocky, clean-shaven, unremarkable except for the way he cocked his ears forward—neither aristocrat nor Belter, just a commoner from Wunderland. "*Was ist hier los?*" he demanded somewhat wildly.

Saxtorph could have recalled the Danish of his childhood, before the family moved to America, and brushed the rust off what German he'd once studied, and made a stab at this language. The hell with it. "Y-y-you speak English?" he panted.

"*Ja*, some," the policeman answered. "Vat is t'is? Don't you know not to push a kzin around?"

"I sure do know, and did nothing of the sort." Steadiness was returning. "He bushwhacked me, completely unprovoked. And, yes, this sort of thing isn't supposed to happen with kzinti, and I can't make any more sense of it than you. Aren't you going to chase him?"

"He's gone," said the policeman glumly. "He vill be back in Tigertown and t'e trail lost before ve can bring a sniffer to follow him. How you going tell vun of t'ose *Teufel* from anot'er? You come along to t'e station, sir. Ve vill give you first aid and take your statement."

Saxtorph drew a long breath, grinned lopsidedly, and replied, "Okay. I'll want to make a couple of phone calls. My wife, and—it'd be smart to ask Commissioner Markham if I can put off my appointment with him."

2

Tiamat is much less known outside its system than it deserves to be. Once hyperdrive transport has become readily available and cheap, it may well be receiving tourists from all of human space: for it is a curious object, with considerable historical significance as well.

Circling Alpha Centauri A near the middle of those asteroids called the Serpent Swarm, it was originally a chondritic body with a sideritic component giving it more structural strength than is usual for that kind. A rough cylinder, about 50 kilometers in length and 20 in diameter, it rotated on its long axis in a bit over ten hours; and at the epoch when humans arrived, that axis happened to be almost normal to the orbital plane. Those who settled on Wunderland paid it no attention; they had a habitable planet. The Belters who came later, from the asteroids of the Solar System, realized what a treasure was theirs. Little work was needed to make the cylinder smooth, control precession, and give it a centrifugal acceleration of one g at the circumference. With its axial orientation, the velocity changes for spacecraft to dock were minimal, and magnetic anchors easily held them fast until they were ready to depart. The excavation of rooms and passages in the yielding material went rapidly. Thereafter, spaces just under the surface provided Earth-weight for such activities as required it, including the bringing of babies to term; farther inward were the levels of successively lower weight, where Belters felt comfortable and where other undertakings were possible.

Everywhere around orbited members of the Swarm, their mineral wealth held in negligible gravity wells. Tiamat boomed. It became an industrial center, devoted especially to the production of things associated with spacefaring.

When the kzinti invaded, they were quick to realize its importance. Their introduction of the gravity polarizer changed many of the manufacturing programs, but scarcely affected Tiamat itself; one seldom had any reason to adjust the field in a given section, since one could have whatever weight was desired simply by going to the appropriate level.

Out of the years that followed have come countless stories of heroism, cowardice, resistance, collaboration, sabotage, salvage, ingenuity, intrigue, atrocity, mercy. Some are true. Certainly, when the human hyperdrive armada entered the Centaurian System, Tiamat might well have been destroyed, had not the Belter freedom fighters taken it over from within.

So ended its heroic age. The rest is anticlimax. More and more, new technologies and new horizons are making it a relic.

However, it is still populous and interesting. Not least of its attractions, though a mixed blessing, are the kzinti. Of those who stayed behind at this sun, or actually sought there, after the war—disgraced combatants, individuals who had formed ties too strong to break, Kdaptist refugees, eccentrics, and others less understandable—a goodly proportion have their colony within Tiamat. Tigertown is well worth visiting, in a properly briefed tour group with an experienced guide.

Tiamat also contains the headquarters of the Interworld Space Commission, which likewise is not as much in the awareness of the general public as it ought to be. Now that the hyperdrive has abruptly opened a way to far more undertakings than there are ships and personnel to carry out, rivalry for those resources often gets bitter. It can become political, planet versus planet at a time when faster-than-light travel has made peace between them as necessary as peace between nations on Earth had become when humankind was starting its outward venture. Until we have created enough capability to satisfy everyone, we must allocate. Alpha Centauri—Wunderland, parts of the Serpent Swarm—alone among human dwelling places, suffered kzin occupation, almost half a century of it. Alpha Centaurian men and women endured, or waged guerrilla warfare from remote and desolate bases, until the liberation. Who would question *their* dedication to our species as a whole?

At least, it was an obvious symbolism to make them the host folk of the Commission; and Tiamat, not yet into its postwar decline, was a natural choice for the seat.

3

"Good evening," replied Dorcas Glengarry Saxtorph. The headwaiter had immediately identified her as being from the Solar System and greeted her in English. "I was to meet Professor Tregennis. The reservation may be in the name of Laurinda Brozik." You didn't just walk into the Star Well; it was small and expensive.

Very briefly, his smoothness failed him and he let his gaze linger. Ten years after the end of the war, when outworlders had become a substantial fraction of the patronage, she was nonetheless a striking sight. A Belter, 185 centimeters in height, slender to the point of leanness, she was not in that respect different from those who had inhabited the Swarm for generations. However, you seldom met features so severely classic, fair-skinned, with large green eyes

under arching brows. The molding of her head was
emphasized by the Sol-Belter style, scalp depilated
except for a crest of mahogany hair that in her case
swept halfway down her back. A shimmery gray gown
folded and refolded itself around carriage and gestures which, even for a person of spacer ancestry,
were extraordinarily precise.

The headwaiter regained professionalism. "Ah, yes,
of course, madame." Dorcas didn't show her forty
Earthyears much, but nobody would take her for a
girl. "This way, please."

The tables were arranged around a sunken transpar-
ency, ten meters across, which gave on the surface of
Tiamat and thus the sky beyond. Nonreflecting, in
the dim interior light it seemed indeed a well of
night which the stars crowded, slowly streaming.
The table Dorcas reached was on the bottom tier,
with a view directly down into infinity. A glowlamp
on it cast softness over cloth, silver, ceramic, and the
two people already seated.

Arthur Tregennis rose, courtly as ever. A Plateaunian of Crew descent, the astrophysicist stood as tall
as she did and still more slim, practically skeletal.
He had the flared hook nose and high cheekbones of
his kindred; the long nail on his left little finger
proclaimed him an aristocrat of his planet, never
subject to manual labor. Dorcas sometimes wondered
why he kept that affectation, when he admitted to
having sympathized with the democrats and their revolution, 33 years ago. Habit, perhaps. Otherwise he
was an unassuming old fellow.

"Welcome, my lady," he said. His English was
rather flat. Since the advent of hyperdrive and
hyperwave, he'd been to so many scientific confer-
ences, or in voice-to-voice contact with colleagues,
that native accent seemed to have worn off—except,

maybe, when he was with his own folk on top of Mount Lookitthat. "Ah, is Robert detained?"

"I'm afraid so," Dorcas let the waiter seat her. She'd reacquired a little sophistication since the war. "He had a nasty encounter, and the aftermath is still retro on him. He told me to come alone, give you his regrets, and bring back whatever word you have for us."

"Oh, dear," Laurinda Brozik whispered. "He's all right, isn't he?"

The English of Tregennis' graduate student was harder for Dorcas to follow than his. It was from We Made It.

The young woman was not a typical Crashlander—is there any such thing as a typical anything?—but she could not have been mistaken for a person from anywhere else. Likewise tall and finely sculptured, she seemed attenuated, arachnodactylic, somehow both awkward and eerily graceful, as if about to go into a contortion such as her race was capable of. She belonged to the large albino minority on the planet, with snowy skin, big red eyes, white hair combed straight down to the shoulders. In contrast to Tregennis' quiet tunic and trousers, she wore a gown of golden-hued fabric—an expert would have identified it as Terrestrial silk—and an arrowhead pendant of topaz; but somehow she wore them shyly.

"Well, he survived, not too upset." Glancing at the waiter, Dorcas ordered a dry martini, "—and I mean *dry*." She turned to the others. "He was on his way to talk with Markham," she explained. "Late hour, but the commissioner said he was too busy to receive him earlier. In fact, the meeting was to be at an auxiliary office. The equipment at the regular place is all tied up with—I'm not sure what. Well, Bob was passing through a deserted section when a kzin came out of nowhere and attacked him. He kept himself alive, without any serious damage, till the noise drew the police. The kzin fled."

"Oh, dear!" Laurinda repeated. She looked appalled.

Tregennis had a way of attacking problems from unexpected angles. "Why was Robert on foot?" he asked.

"What?" said Dorcas, surprised. She considered. "The tubeway wasn't convenient for his destination, and it's not much of a walk. What of it?"

"There have been ample incidents, I hear. Kzinti with their hair-trigger tempers; and many humans bear an unreasoning hatred of them. I should think Robert would take care." Tregennis chuckled. "He's too seasoned a warrior to want any trouble."

"He had no reason to expect any, I tell you." Dorcas curbed her irritation. "Never mind. It was doubtless just one of those things. He has a ruined tunic and four superficial cuts, but he gave as good as he got. The point is, the police are in an uproar. They were nervous enough, now they're afraid of more fights. They've kept him at the station, questioning him over and over, showing him stereograms of this or that kzin—you can imagine. When last he called, he didn't expect to be free for another couple of hours, and then, on top of having nearly gotten killed, he'll be wrung out. So he told me to meet you on behalf of us both."

"Horrible," Laurinda said. "But at least he is safe."

"We regret his absence, naturally," Tregennis added, "and twice so when we had invited you two to dinner here in celebration of good news."

Dorcas smiled. "Well, I'll be your courier. What is the message?"

"It is for you to tell, Laurinda," the astrophysicist said gently.

The girl swallowed, leaned forward, and blurted, "This mornwatch I got the word I'd hoped for. On the hyperwave. My father, he, he'd been away, and afterward I suppose he needed to think about it, because that is a lot of money, but—but if necessary, he'll give us a grant. We won't have to depend on the Commission. We can take off on our own!"

"Wow-oo," Dorcas breathed.

Though it made no sense, for a tumbling few seconds her mind was on Stefan Brozik, whom she had never met. He had been among those on We Made It quickest to seize the chance when the Outsiders came by with their offer to sell the hyperdrive technology. For a while he was an officer in one of the fleets that drove the kzin sublight ships back and back into defeat. Returning, he made his fortune in the production of hyperdrives for both government and private use; and Laurinda was his adored only daughter—

"It will take a time," came Tregennis' parched voice. "First the draft must clear the banks, then we must order what we need and wait for delivery. The demand exceeds the supply, after all. However, in due course we will be able to go."

His white head lifted. Dorcas remembered what he had said to Markham, when the commissioner declared: "Professor, this star of yours does appear to be an interesting object. I do not doubt an expedition to it would have scientific value. But space is full of urgent work to do, human work to do. Your project can wait another ten or fifteen years."

Iron had been in Tregennis' answer: "I cannot."

"Wonderful!" exclaimed Dorcas. Her jubilation was moderate merely because she had expected this outcome. The only question had been how long it would take. Stefan Brozik wouldn't likely deny his little girl a chance to go visit the foreign sun which she, peering from orbit around Plateau, had discovered, and which could make her reputation in her chosen field.

Nonetheless, Dorcas' gaze left the table and went off down the well of stars. Alpha Centauri B, dazzling bright, had drifted from it. She had a clear view toward the Lesser Magellanic Cloud. In yonder direction lay Beta Hydri, and around it swung Silvereyes, the most remote colony that humankind had yet planted. Beyond Silvereyes—But glory filled vision. Laurinda's sun was a dim red dwarf, invisible to her. Strange thought, that such a thing might be a key to mysteries.

Anger awoke. "Maybe we won't need your father's money," Dorcas said. "Maybe the prospect will make that slime-bugger see reason."

"I beg your pardon?" asked Tregennis, shocked.

"Markham." Dorcas grinned. "Sorry. You haven't been toe-to-toe with him, over and over, the way Bob and I have. Never mind. Don't let him or a quantum-headed kzin spoil our evening. Let's enjoy. We're going!"

4

The office of Ulf Reichstein Markham was as austere as the man himself. Apart from a couple of chairs, a reference shelf, and a desk with little upon it except the usual electronics, its largeness held mostly empty space. Personal items amounted to a pair of framed documents and a pair of pictures. On the left hung his certificate of appointment to the Interworld Space Commission and a photograph of his wife with their eight-year-old son. On the right were his citation for extraordinary heroism during

the war and a portrait painting of his mother. Both
women showed the pure bloodlines of Wunderland
aristocracy, the older one also in her expression; the
younger looked subdued.

Markham strove to maintain the same physical
appearance. His father had been a Belter of means,
whom his mother married after the family got in
trouble with the kzinti during the occupation and
fled to the Swarm. At age 50 he stood a slender,
swordblade-straight 195 centimeters. Stiff gray-blond
hair grew over a narrow skull, above pale eyes, long
nose, outthrust chin that sported the asymmetric
beard, a point on the right side. Gray and close-
fitting, his garb suggested a military uniform.

"I trust you have recovered from your experience,
Captain Saxtorph," he said in his clipped manner.

"Yah, I'm okay, aside from puzzlement." The space-
man settled back in his chair, crossed shank over
thigh. "Mind if I smoke?" He didn't wait for an
answer before reaching after pipe and tobacco pouch.

Markham's lips twitched the least bit in disdain of
the uncouthness, but he replied merely, "We will
doubtless never know what caused the incident. You
should not allow it to prey on your mind. The resi-
dent kzinti are under enormous psychological stress,
still more so than humans would be in comparable
circumstances. Besides uprootedness and culture
shock, they must daily live with the fact of defeat.
Acceptance runs counter to an instinct as powerful in
them as sexuality is in humans. This individual, whoever he is, must have lashed out blindly. Let us hope
he doesn't repeat. Perhaps his friends can prevail on
him."

Saxtorph scowled. "I thought that way, too, at first.
Afterward I got to wondering. I hadn't been near any
kzinti my whole time here, this trip. They don't min-

gle with humans unless business requires, and then they handle it by phone if at all possible. This fellow was way off the reservation. He lurked till I arrived, in that empty place. He was wearing a phone. Somebody else, shadowing me, could have called to tell him I was coming and the coast was clear."

"Frankly, you are being paranoid. Why in creation should he, or anyone, wish you harm? You specifically, I mean. Furthermore, conspiracy like that is not kzin behavior. It would violate the sense of honor that the meanest among them cherishes. No, this poor creature went wandering about, trying to walk off his anger and despair. When you chanced by, like a game animal on the ancestral planet passing a hunter's blind, it triggered a reflex that he lost control of."

"How can you be sure? How much do we really know about that breed?"

"I know more than most humans."

"Yah," drawled Saxtorph, "I reckon you do."

Markham stiffened. His glance across the desk was like a levelled gun. For a moment there was silence.

Saxtorph got his pipe lit, blew a cloud of smoke, and through it peered back in more relaxed wise. He could afford to; somatic presence does make a difference. Barely shorter than the Wunderlander, he was hugely broader of shoulders and thicker of chest. His face was wide, craggy-nosed, shaggy-browed, with downward-slanted blue eyes and reddish hair that, at age 45, was getting thin. Whatever clothes he put on, they soon looked rumpled, but this gave the impression less of carelessness than of activity.

"What are you implying, Captain?" Markham asked low.

Saxtorph shrugged. "Nothing in particular, Commissioner. It's common knowledge that you have quite a lot to do with 'em."

"Yes. Certain among the rabble have called me 'kzin-lover.' I did not believe you shared their sewer mentality."

"Whoa, there." Saxtorph lifted a palm. "Easy, please. Of course you'd take a special interest. After all, the kzin empire, if that's what we should call it, it's still out yonder, and we still know precious little about it. Besides handling matters related to kzin comings and goings, you have to think about the future in space. Getting a better handle on their psychology is a real service."

Markham eased a bit. "Learning some compassion does no harm either," he said unexpectedly.

"Hm? Pardon me, but I should think that'd be extra hard for you."

Markham's history flitted through Saxtorph's mind. His mother had apparently married his commoner father out of necessity. Her husband died early, and she raised their son in the strictest aristocratic and martial tradition possible. By age 18 Markham was in the resistance forces. As captain of a commando ship, he led any number of raids and gained a reputation for kzin-like ruthlessness. He was 30 when the hyperdrive armada from Sol liberated Alpha Centauri. Thereafter he was active in restoring order and building up a Wunderland navy. Finally leaving the service, he settled on the planet, on a restored Reichstein estate granted him, and attempted a political career; but he lacked the needful affability and willingness to compromise. It was rumored that his appointment to the Space Commission had been a way of buying him off—he had been an often annoying gadfly—but he was in fact well qualified and worked conscientiously.

The trouble was, he had his own views on policy.

With his prestige and connections, he had managed in case after case to win agreement from a voting majority of his colleagues.

Saxtorph smiled and added, "Well, Christian charity is all the more valuable for being so rare."

Markham pricked up his ears. The pale countenance flushed. "Christian!" he snapped. "A religion for slaves. No, I learned to respect the kzinti while I fought them. They were valiant, loyal, disciplined—and in spite of the propaganda and horror stories, their rule was by no means the worst thing that ever happened to Wunderland."

He calmed, even returned the smile. "But we have drifted rather far off course, haven't we? I invited you here for still another talk about your plans. Have I no hope of persuading you the mission is wasteful folly?"

"You've said the same about damn near every proposal to do any real exploring," Saxtorph growled.

"You exaggerate, Captain. Must we go over the old, trampled ground again? I am simply a realist. Ships, equipment, trained crews are in the shortest supply. We need them closer to home, to build up interstellar commerce and industry. Once we have that base, that productivity, yes, then of course we go forward. But we will go cautiously, if I have anything to say about it. Was not the kzin invasion a deadly enough surprise? Who knows what dangers, mortal dangers, a reckless would-be galaxytrotter may stir up?"

Saxtorph sighed. "You're right, this has gotten to be boringly familiar territory. I'll spare you my argument about how dangerous ignorance can be. The point is, I never put in for anything much. For a voyage as long as we intend, we need adequate supplies, and our insurance carrier insists we carry

double spares of vital gear. The money Professor
Tregennis wangled out of his university for the charter won't stretch to it. So we all rendezvoused here
to apply for a government donation of stuff sitting in
the warehouses.

"It just might buy you a scientific revolution."

He had rehashed this with malice, to repay Markham
for the latter's own repetition. It failed to get the
man's goat. Instead, the answer was, mildly, "I saw
it as my duty to persuade the Commission to deny
your request. Please believe there was no personal
motive. I wish you well."

Saxtorph grinned, blew a smoke ring, and said,
"Thanks. Want to come wave goodbye? Because we
are going."

Markham took him off guard with a nod. "I know.
Stefan Brozik has offered you a grant."

"Huh?" Saxtorph grabbed his pipe just before it
landed in his lap. He recovered his wits. "Did you
have the hyperwave monitored for messages to members of our party?" His voice roughened. "Sir, I
resent that."

"It was not illegal. I was . . . more concerned than
you think." Markham leaned forward. "Listen. A
man does not necessarily like doing what duty com-
mands. Did you imagine I don't regret choking off
great adventures, that I do not myself long for the
age of discovery that must come? In my heart I feel a
certain gratitude toward Brozik. He has released me.

"Now, since you are inevitably going, it would be
pointless to continue refusing you what you want.
That can only delay, not stop you. Better to cooperate, win back your goodwill, and in return have some
influence on your actions. I will contact my colleagues. There should be no difficulty in getting a
reversal of our decision."

Saxtorph sagged back in his chair. "Judas . . . priest."

"There are conditions," Markham told him. "If you are to be spared a long time idle here, prudent men must be spared nightmares about what grief you might bring on us all by some blunder. Excuse my blunt language. You are amateurs."

"Every explorer is an amateur. By definition."

"You are undermanned."

"I wouldn't say so. Captain; computerman; two pilots, who're also experienced rockjacks and planet-siders; quartermaster. Everybody competent in a slew of other specialties. And, this trip, two scientists, the prof and his student. What would anybody else *do?*"

"For one thing," Markham said crisply, "he would counsel proper caution and point out where this was not being exercised. He would keep official policy in your minds. The condition of your obtaining what you need immediately is this. You shall take along a man who will have officer status—"

"Hey, wait a minute. I'm the skipper, my wife's the mate as well as the computerman, and the rest have shaken down into a damn good team. I don't aim to shake it back up again."

"You needn't," Markham assured him. "This man will be basically an observer and advisor. He should prove useful in several additional capacities. In the event of . . . disaster to the regular officers, he can take command, bring the ship back, and be an impartial witness at the inquiry."

"M-m-m." Saxtorph frowned, rubbed his chin, pondered. "Maybe. It'll be a long voyage, you know, about ninety days cooped up together, with God knows what at the end. Not that we expect anything more than interesting astronomical objects. Still, you're right, it is unpredictable. We're a close-knit crew, and the scientists seem to fit in well, but what about this stranger?"

"I refer you to my record," Markham replied. When Saxtorph drew a sharp breath, the Wunderlander added, "Yes, I am doubtless being selfish. However, my abilities in space are proven, and—in spite of everything, I share the dream."

5

In her youth, before she became a tramp, *Rover* was a naval transport, UNS *Ghost Dance*. She took men and matériel from their sources to bases around the Solar System, and brought some back for furlough or repair. A few times she went into combat mode. They were only a few. The kzinti hurled a sublight fleet out of Alpha Centauri at variable intervals, but years apart, since one way or another they always lost heavily in the sanguinary campaigns that followed. *Ghost Dance* would release her twin fighters to escort her on her rounds. Once they came under attack, and were the survivors.

Rover might now be less respectable, maybe even a bit shabby, but was by no means a slattern. The Saxtorphs had obtained her in a postwar sale of surplus and outfitted her as well as their finances permitted. On the outside she remained a hundred-meter spheroid, its smoothness broken by airlocks, hatches, boat bays, instrument housings, communications boom, grapples, and micrometeoroid pocks that had given the metal a matte finish. Inboard, much more had changed. Automated as she was, she never needed more than a handful to man her; on a routine interplanetary flight she was quite capable of being her own crew. Most personnel space had therefore been converted for cargo stowage. Those people who did travel in her had more room and comfort than formerly. Instead of warcraft she carried two Prospector class boats, primarily meant for asteroids and the like but well able to maneuver in atmosphere and set down on a fair-sized planet. Other machinery was equally for peaceful, if occasionally rough use.

"But how did the Saxtorphs ever acquire a hyperdrive?" asked Laurinda Brozik. "I thought licensing was strict in the Solar System, too, and they don't seem to be terribly influential."

"They didn't tell you?" replied Kamehameha Ryan. "Bob loves to guffaw over that caper."

Her lashes fluttered downward. A tinge of pink crossed the alabaster skin. "I, I don't like to . . . pry—ask personal questions."

He patted her hand. "You're too sweet and considerate, Laurinda. Uh, okay to call you that? We are in for a long haul. I'm Kam."

The quartermaster was showing her around while *Rover* moved up the Alpha Centaurian gravity well until it would be safe to slip free of Einsteinian space. Her holds being vacant, the acceleration was several g, but the interior polarizer maintained weight at the half Earth normal to which healthy humans from every world can soon adapt. "You want the grand tour, not a hasty look-around like you got before, and who'd be a better guide than me?" Ryan had said. "I'm the guy who takes care of inboard operations, everything from dusting and polishing, through mass trim and equipment service, on to cooking, which is the real art." He was a stocky man of medium height, starting to go plump, round-faced, dark-complexioned, his blue-black hair streaked with the earliest frost. A gaudy sleeveless shirt bulged above canary-yellow slacks and thong sandals.

"Well, I—well, thank you, Kam," Laurinda whispered.

"Thank *you*, my dear. Now this door I'd better not open for you. Behind it we keep chemical explosives for mining-type jobs. But you were asking about our hyperdrive, weren't you?

"Well, after the war Bob and Dorcas—they met and got married during it, when he was in the navy and she was helping beef up the defenses at Ixa, with a sideline in translation—they worked for Solar Minerals, scouting the asteroids, and did well enough, commissions and bonuses and such, that at last they could make the down payment on this ship. She was going pretty cheap because nobody else wanted her. Who'd be so crazy as to compete with the big Belter companies? But you see, meanwhile they'd found the real treasure, a derelict hyperdrive craft. She wasn't UN property or anything, she was an experimental job a manufacturer had been testing. Unmanned; a monopole meteoroid passed close by and fouled up the electronics; she looped off on an eccentric orbit and was lost; the company went out of business. She'd become a legend of sorts, every search had failed, on which basis Dorcas figured out where she most likely was, and she and Bob went looking on their own time. As soon as they were ready they announced their discovery, claimed salvage rights, and installed the drive in this hull. Nobody had foreseen anything like that, and besides, they'd hired a smart lawyer. The rules have since been changed, of course, but we come under a grandfather clause. So here we've got the only completely independent starship in known space."

"It is very venturesome of you."

"Yeah, things often get precarious. Interstellar commerce hasn't yet developed regular trade routes, except what government-owned lines monopolize. We have to take what we can get, and not all of it has been simple hauling of stuff from here to there. The last job turned out to be a lemon, and frankly, this charter is a godsend. Uh, don't quote me. I talk too much. Bob bears with me, but a tongue-lashing from Dorcas can take the skin off your soul."

"You and he are old friends, aren't you?"

"Since our teens. He came knocking his way around Earth to Hawaii, proved to be a good guy for a *haole*, I sort of introduced him to people and things, we had some grand times. Then he enlisted, had a real yeager of a war career, but you must know something about that. He looked me up afterward, when he and Dorcas were taking a second honeymoon, and later they offered me this berth."

"You had experience?"

"Yes, I'd gone spaceward, too. Civilian. Interesting work, great pay, glamor to draw the girls, because not many flatlanders wanted to leave Earth when the next kzin attack might happen anytime."

"It seems so romantic," Laurinda murmured. "Superficially, at least, and to me."

"What do you mean, please?" Ryan asked, in the interest of drawing her out. Human females like men who will listen to them.

"Oh, that is—What have I done except study? And, well, research. I was born the year the Outsiders arrived at We Made It, but of course they were gone again long before I could meet them. In fact, I never saw a nonhuman in the flesh till I came to Centauri and visited Tigertown. You and your friends have been out, active, in the universe."

"I don't want to sound self-pitying," Ryan said, unable to quite avoid sounding smug, "but it's been mostly sitting inboard, then working our fingers off, frantic scrambles, shortages of everything, and moments of stark terror. A wise man once called adventure 'somebody else having a hell of a tough time ten light-years away.' "

She looked at him from her slightly greater elevation and touched his arm. "Lonely too. You must miss your family."

"I'm a bachelor type," Ryan answered, forbearing to mention the ex-wives. "Not that I don't appreciate you ladies, understand—"

At that instant, luck brought them upon Carita Fenger. She emerged from a cold locker with a hundred-liter keg of beer, intended for the saloon, on her back, held by a strap that her left hand gripped. High-tech tasks were apportioned among all five of *Rover's* people, housekeeping chores among the three crewmen. This boat pilot was a Jinxian. Her width came close to matching her short height, with limbs in proportion and bosom more so. Ancestry under Sirius had made her skin almost ebony, though the bobbed hair was no longer sun-bleached white but straw color. Broad nose, close-set brown eyes, big mouth somehow added up to an attractive face, perhaps because it generally looked cheerful. "Well, hi," she hailed. "What's going on here?"

Ryan and Laurinda halted. "I am showing our passenger around the ship," he said stiffly.

Carita cocked her head. "Are you, now? That isn't all you'd like to show her, I can see. Better get back to the galley, lad. You did promise us a first-meal feast." To the Crashlander: "He's a master chef when he puts his mind to it. Good in bed, too."

Laurinda dropped her gaze and colored. Ryan flushed likewise. "I'm sorry," he gobbled. "Pilot Fenger's okay, but she does sometimes forget her manners."

Carita's laugh rang. "I've not forgotten this night-watch is your turn, Kam. I'll be waiting. Or shall I seduce Commissioner Markham—or Professor Tregennis?" To Laurinda: "Sorry, dear, I shouldn't have said that. Being coarse goes with the kind of life I've led. I'll try to do better. Don't be afraid of Kam. He's harmless as long as you don't encourage him."

She trudged off with her burden. To somebody born to Jinx gravity, the weight was trifling. Ryan struggled to find words. All at once Laurinda trilled laughter of her own, then said fast, "I apologize. Your arrangements are your own business. Shall we continue for as long as you can spare the time?"

6

The database in *Rover* contained books as well as musical and video performances. Both the Saxtorphs spent a considerable amount of their leisure reading, she more than he. Their tastes differed enough that they had separate terminals in their cabin. He wanted his literature, like his food, plain and hearty; Dorcas ranged wider. Ever since hyperwave made transmission easy, she had been putting hundreds of writings by extrasolar dwellers into the discs, with the quixotic idea of eventually getting to know most of them.

The ship was a few days into hyperspace when she entered the saloon and found Tregennis. A couple of hours' workout in the gym, followed by a shower and change of coverall, left her aglow. The Plateaunian sat talking with Markham. That was unusual; the commissioner had kept rather to himself.

"Indeed the spectroscope, interferometer, the entire panoply of instruments reveals much," Tregennis was saying. "How else did Miss Brozik discover her

star and learn of its uniqueness? But there is no
substitute for a close look, and who would put a
hyperdrive in an unmanned probe?"

"I know," Markham replied. "I was simply inquir-
ing what data you already possess. That was never
made clear to me. For example, does the star have
planets?"

"It's too small and faint for us to establish that, at
the distance from which we observed. Ah, I am
surprised, sir. Were you so little interested that you
didn't ask questions?"

"Why should he, when he was vetoing our mission?" Dorcas interjected. It brought her to their
notice. Tregennis started to rise. "No, please stay
seated." He looked so fragile. "No offense intended,
Landholder Markham. I'm afraid I expressed myself
tactlessly, but it seemed obvious. After all, you were—
are a busy man with countless claims on your
attention."

"I understand, Mme. Saxtorph," the Wunderlander
said stiffly. "You are correct. Feeling as I did, I took
care to suppress my curiosity."

Tregennis shook his head in a bemused fashion.
He doubtless wasn't very familiar with the twists and
turns the human mind can take. Dorcas recalled that
he had never been married, except to his science—
though he did seem to regard Laurinda as a surrogate daughter.

The computerman sat down. "In fact," she said
conciliatingly, "I still wonder why you felt you could
be spared from your post for as long as we may be
gone. You could have sent somebody else."

"Trustworthy persons are hard to find," Markham
stated, "especially in the younger generation."

"I've gathered you don't approve of postwar developments on your planet." Dorcas glanced at Tregennis.

"That's apropos the reason I hoped you would be here, Professor. I'm reading *The House on Crowsnest*—"

"What do you mean?" Markham interrupted. "Crowsnest is an area on top of Mount Lookitthat."

Dorcas curbed exasperation. Maybe he couldn't help being arrogant. "I understand it's considered the greatest novel ever written on Plateau," she said.

Tregennis nodded. "Many think so. I confess the language in it gets too strong for my taste."

"Well, the author is a Colonist, telling how things were before and during the revolution," Dorcas said in Markham's direction. "Oppression does not make people nice. The wonder is that Crew rule was overthrown almost bloodlessly."

"If you please," Tregennis responded, "we of the Crew families were not monsters. Many of us realized reform was overdue and worked for it. I sympathized myself, you know, although I did not take an active role. I do believe Nairn exaggerates the degree and extent of brutality under the old order."

"That's one thing I wanted to ask you about. His book's full of people, places, events, practices that must be familiar to you but that nobody on any other planet ever heard of. Laurinda herself couldn't tell me what some passages refer to."

Tregennis smiled. "She has only been on Plateau as a student, and was born into a democracy. Why should she concern herself about old, unhappy, far-off things? Not that she is narrow, she comes from a cultured home, but she is young and has a whole universe opening before her."

Dorcas nodded. "A lucky generation, hers."

"Yes, indeed. Landholder Markham, I must disagree with views you have expressed. Taken as a whole, on every world the young are rising marvel-ously well to their opportunities—better, I fear, than their elders would have done."

"It makes a huge difference, being free," Dorcas said.

Markham sat bolt upright. "Free to do what?" he snapped. "To be vulgar, slovenly, ignorant, self-centered, materialistic, *common*? I have seen the degradation go on, year by year. You have stayed safe in your ivory tower, Professor. You, Mme. Saxtorph, operate in situations where a measure of discipline, sometimes old-fashioned self-sacrifice, is a condition of survival. But I have gotten out into the muck and tried to stem the tide of it."

"I heard you'd run for your new parliament, and I know you don't care for the popular modern styles," Dorcas answered dryly. She shrugged. "I often don't myself. But why should people not have what they want, if they can come by it honestly? Nobody forces you to join them. It seems you'd force them to do what pleases you. Well, that might not be what pleases me!"

Markham swallowed. His ears lay back. "I suspect our likes are not extremely dissimilar. You are a person of quality, a natural leader." Abruptly his voice quivered. He must be waging battle to keep his feelings under control. "In a healthy society, the superior person is recognized for what he or she is, and lesser ones are happy to be guided, because they realize that not only they but generations to come will benefit. The leader is not interested in power or glory for their own sake. At most, they are means to an end, the end to which he gives his life, the organic evolution of the society toward its destiny, the full flowering of its soul. But we are replacing living *Gemeinschaft* with mechanical *Gesellschaft*. The cyborg civilization! It goes as crazy as a cyborg individual. The leading classes also lose their sense of responsibility. Those members who do not become openly corrupt turn into reckless megalomaniacs."

Dorcas paled, which was her body's way of showing anger. "I've seen that kind of thinking described in history books," she said. "I thought better of you, sir. For your information, my grandfather was a cyborg after an accident. Belters always believed it was as criminal to send convicts into the organ banks as any crime of theirs could be. He was the sanest man I've known. Nor have I noticed leaders of free folk doing much that is half as stupid or evil as what the master classes used to order. I'll make my own mistakes, thank you."

"You certainly will. You already have. I must speak plainly. Your husband's insistence on this expedition, against every dictate of sound judgment, merely because it suits him to go, is a perfect example of a leader who has ceased to be a shepherd. Or perhaps you yourself are, since you have aided and abetted him. *You* could have remembered how full of terrible unknowns space is. Belters are born to that understanding. He is a flatlander."

Dorcas whitened entirely. Her crest bristled. She stood up, fists on hips, to loom over Markham and say word by word: "That will do. We have endured your presence, that you pushed on us, in hopes you would prove to be housebroken. We have now listened to your ridiculous rantings because we believe in free speech where you do not, and in hopes you would soon finish. Instead, you have delivered an intolerable racist insult. You will go to your cabin and remain there for twenty-four hours. Bread and water will be brought to you."

Markham gaped. "What? Are you mad?"

"Furious, yes. As for sanity, I refrain from expressing an opinion about who may lack it." Dorcas consulted her watch. "You can walk to your cabin in about five minutes. Therefore, do not be seen outside it, except for visits to the head, until 1737 hours tomorrow. Go."

He half rose himself, sank back down, and exclaimed, "This is impossible! Professor Tregennis, I call you to witness."

"Yes," Dorcas said. "Please witness that he has received a direct order from me, who am second in command of the ship. Shall we call Captain Saxtorph to confirm it? You can be led off in irons, Markham. Better you obey. Go."

The commissioner clambered to his feet. He breathed hard. The others could smell his sweat. "Very well," he said tonelessly. "Of course I will file a complaint when we return. Meanwhile we shall minimize further conversation. Good day." He jerked a bow and marched off.

After a time in which only the multitudinous low murmurings of the vessel had utterance, Tregennis breathed, "Dear me. Was that not a . . . slightly excessive reaction?"

Dorcas sat down again. Her iciness was dissolving in calm. "Maybe. Bob would think so, though naturally he'd have backed me up. He's more good-natured than I am. I do not tolerate such language about him. This hasn't been the only incident."

"There is a certain prejudice against the Earth-born among the space-born. I understand it is quite widespread."

"It is, and it's not altogether without foundation—in a number of cases." Dorcas laughed. "I shared it, at the time Bob and I met. It caused some monumental quarrels the first couple of years, years when we could already have been married. I finally got rid of it and took to judging individuals on their merits."

"Forgive me, but are you not a little intolerant of those who have not had your enlightening experience?"

"Doubtless. However, between you and me, I welcomed the chance to show Markham who's boss here. I worried that if we have an emergency he could get insubordinate. That would be an invitation to disaster."

"He is a strange man," Tregennis mused. "His behavior, his talk, his past career, everything seems such a welter of contradictions. Or am I being naive?"

"Not really, unless I am, too. Oh, people aren't self-consistent like the laws of mechanics—even quantum mechanics. But I do think we lack some key fact about Landholder Markham, and will never understand him till we have it." Dorcas made a gesture of dismissal. "Enough. Now may I do what I originally intended and quiz you about Plateau?"

7

While *Rover* was in hyperspace, all five of her gang stood mass detector watch, six hours a day for four days, fifth day off. It was unpopular duty, but they would have enjoyed still less letting the ship fly blind, risking an entry into a gravity well deep enough to throw her to whatever fate awaited vessels which did not steer clear. The daydream was becoming commonplace among their kind, that someday somebody would gain sufficient understanding of the psionics involved that the whole operation could be automated.

It wasn't torture, of course, once you had schooled yourself never to look into the Less Than Void which filled the single port necessarily left unshuttered. You learned how to keep an eye on the indicator globe while you exercised, read, watched a show, practiced a handicraft. On the infrequent occasions when it registered something, matters did get interesting.

"And I've decided I don't mind it in the least," said Juan Yoshii after Kamehameha Ryan had relieved him.

"Really?" asked Laurinda Brozik. She had met him below the flight deck by agreement.

He offered her his arm, a studied, awkward gesture not used in his native society. She smiled and took it. He was a young Sol-Belter. Unlike Dorcas Saxtorph, or most folk of his nation, he eschewed spectacular garb. Small, slim, with olive-skinned, almost girlish features, he did wear his hair in the crest, but it was cut short.

"I have just heard complaints about the monotony," Laurinda said.

"Monotony, or peacefulness?" he countered in his diffident fashion. "I chafed, too. Then gradually I realized what an opportunity this is to be alone and think. Or compose."

"You don't sound like a rockjack," she said needlessly. It was what had originally attracted her to him.

He chuckled. "How are rockjacks supposed to sound? We have the rough, tough image, yes. Pilot the boat, find the ore, wrench it out, bring it home, and damn the meteoroids. Or the sun-flare or the fusion generator failure or anything else. But we are simply persons making a living. Quite a few of us look forward to a day when we can use different talents."

"What else would you like to do?"

His smile was stiff. He stared before him. "Prepare yourself to laugh."

"Oh, no." Her tone made naught of the eight centimeters by which she topped him. "How could I laugh at a man who handles the forces that I only measure?"

He flushed and had no answer. They walked on. The ship hummed around them. Bulkheads were brightly painted, pictures were hung on them and often changed, here and there were pots whose flowers Carita Fenger maintained, but nonetheless this was a barren environment. The two had a date in his cabin, where he would provide tea while they screened d'Auvergne's Fifth Chromophony. An appreciation of her work was one thing among others that they discovered they had in common.

"What is your hope?" Laurinda asked at last, low.

He gulped. "To be a poet."

"Why, how . . . how remarkable."

"Not that there's a living in it," he said hastily. "I'll need a groundside position. But I will anyway when I get too old for this berth—and am still fairly young by most standards." He drew breath. "In the centuries of spaceflight, how much true poetry has been written? Plenty of verse, but how much that makes your hair rise and you think yes, this is the real truth? It's as if we've been too busy to find the words for what we've been busy with. I want to try. I am trying, but know quite well I won't have a chance of succeeding with a single line till I've worked at it for another ten years or more."

"You're too modest, Juan. Genius flowers early oftener than not. I would like to see what you have done."

"No, I, I don't think it's that good. Maybe my

efforts never will be. Not even equal to—well, actually minor stuff, but it does have the spirit—"

"Such as what?"

"Oh, ancient pieces, mostly, pre-space.

" *'To follow knowledge like a sinking star,*

"Beyond the utmost bound of human thought.' "
Yoshii cackled a laugh. "I'm really getting bookish, am I not? An easy trap to fall into. Spacemen have a lot of free time in between crises."

"You've put yours to good use," she said earnestly. "Is that poem you quoted from in the ship's database? I'd like to read it."

"I don't know, but I can recite it verbatim."

"That would be much better. Romantic—" Laurinda broke off. She turned her glance away.

He sensed her confusion and blurted in his own, "Please don't misunderstand me. I know—your customs, your mores—I mean to respect them. Completely."

She achieved a smile, though she could not yet look back his way. "Why, I'm not afraid of you." Unspoken: You're not unbearably frustrated. It's obvious that Carita is your mistress as well as Kam's. "You are a gentleman." And what we have coming to life between us is still small and frail, but already very sweet.

8

Rover re-entered normal space ten astronomical units from the destination star. That was unnecessarily distant for a mass less than a fourth of Sol's, but the Saxtorphs were more cautious than Markham admitted. Besides, the scientists wanted to begin with a long sweep as baseline for their preliminary observations, and it was their party now.

As soon as precise velocity figures were available, Dorcas computed the vectors. The star was hurtling at well over a thousand kilometers per second with respect to galactic center. That meant the ship needed considerable delta v to get down to interplanetary speeds and into the equatorial plane where any attendant bodies were likeliest to be. That boost phase must also serve those initial requirements of the astronomers. Course and thrust could be adjusted as data came in and plans for the future were developed.

The star's motion meant, too, that it was escaping the galaxy, bound for the gulfs beyond. Presumably an encounter with one or more larger bodies had cast it from the region where it formed. A question the expedition hoped to get answered, however incompletely, was where that might have happened—and when.

Except for Dorcas, who worked with Tregennis to process the data that Laurinda mostly gathered, the crew had little to do but housekeeping. Occasionally someone was asked to lend a hand with some task of the research.

Going off watch, Carita Fenger stopped by the saloon. A large viewscreen there kept the image of the sun at the cross-haired center. Else nobody could have identified it. It was waxing as the ship drove inward but thus far remained a dim dull-red point, outshone by stars light-years away. The undertone of power through the ship was like a whisper of that which surged within, around, among them, nuclear fires, rage of radiation, millennial turmoil of matter, births and funeral pyres and ashes and rebirths, the universe forever in travail. Like most spacefarers, Carita could lose herself, hour upon hour, in the contemplation of it.

She halted. Markham sat alone, looking. His face was haggard.

"Well, hi," she said tentatively.

Markham gave her a glance. "How do you do, Pilot Fenger." The words came flat.

She plumped herself down in the chair beside him. "Quite a sight, eh?"

He nodded, his gaze back on the screen.

"A trite thing to say," she persisted. "But I suspect Juan's wrong. He hopes to find words grand enough. I suspect it can't be done."

"I was not aware Pilot Yoshii had such interests," said Markham without unbending.

"Nah, you wouldn't be. You've been about as outgoing as a black hole. What's between you and Dorcas? You seem to be off speaking terms with her."

"If you please, I am not in the mood for gossip." Markham started to rise, to leave.

Carita took hold of his arm. It was a gentle grip, but he could easier have broken free of a salvage grapple. "Wait a minute," she said. "I've been halfway on the alert for a chance to talk with you. Who does any more, except 'Pass the salt' at mess, that sort of thing? How lonesome you must be."

He refrained from ineffectual resistance, continued to stare before him, and clipped, "Thank you for your concern, but I manage. Kindly let go."

"Look," she said, "we're supposed to be shipmates. It's a hell of an exciting adventure—Christ, we're the first, the very first, in all this weird wonder— but it's cold out, too, and doesn't care an atom's worth about human beings. I keep thinking how awful it must be, cut off from any friendship the way you are. Not that you've exactly encouraged us, but we could try harder."

Now he did regard her. "Are you inviting me to your bed?" he asked in the same tone as before.

Slightly taken aback, she recovered, smiled, and replied, "No, I wasn't, but if it'll make you feel better we can have a go at it."

"Or make you feel better? I am not too isolated to have noticed that lately Pilot Yoshii has ceased visiting your cabin. Is Quartermaster Ryan insufficient?"

Carita's face went sulfur black. She dragged her fingers from him. "My mistake," she said. "The rest were right about you. Okay, you can take off."

"With pleasure." He stalked out.

She mumbled an oath, drew forth a cigar, lit and blew fumes that ran the ventilators and air renewers up to capacity. Calm returned after a while. She laughed ruefully. Ryan had told her more than once that she was too soft-hearted; and he was a man prone to fits of improvident generosity.

She was about to go when Saxtorph's voice boomed from the intercom: "Attention, please. Got an announcement here that I'm sure will interest everybody.

"We'll hold a conference in a few days, when more information is in. Then you can ask whatever questions you want. Meanwhile, I repeat my order, do not pester the science team. They're working around the clock and don't need distractions.

"However, Arthur Tregennis has given me a quick rundown on what's been learned so far, to pass on to you. Here it is, in my layman's language. Don't blame him for any garbling.

"They have a full analysis of the sun's composition, along with other characteristics. That wasn't too easy. For one thing, it's so cool that its peak emission frequency is in the radio band. Because the absorption and re-emission of the interstellar medium in between isn't properly known, we *had* to come here to get decent readings.

"They bear out what the prof and Laurinda thought. This sun isn't just metal-poor, it's metal-impoverished. — No trace of any element heavier than iron, and little of that. Yes, you've all heard as how it must be very old, and has only stayed on the main sequence this long because it's such a feeble dwarf. But now they have a better idea of just how long 'this' has been.

"Estimated age, fifteen billion years. Our star is damn near as old as the universe.

"It probably got slung out of its parent galaxy early on. In that many years you can cover a lot of kilometers. We're lucky that we—meaning the human species—are alive while it's in our neighborhood.

"And . . . in the teeth of expectations, it's got planets. Already the instruments are finding signs of oddities in them, no two alike, nothing we could have foreseen. Well, we'll be taking a close look. Stand by. Over."

Carita sprang to her feet and cheered.

9

Once when they were young bucks, chance-met, beachcombing together in the Islands, Kam Ryan and Bob Saxtorph acquired a beat-up rowboat, cat-rigged it after a fashion, stowed some food and plenty of beer aboard, and set forth on a shakedown cruise across Kaulakahi Channel. Short runs off Waimea had gone reasonably well, but they wanted to be sure of the seaworthiness before making it a lure for girls. They figured they could reach Niihau in 12 or 15 hours, land if possible, rest up in any case, and come back. They didn't have the price of an outboard, but in a pinch they could row.

To avoid coping with well-intentioned busybodies, they started after dark. By that time sufficient beer had gone down that they forgot about tuning in a weather report before leaving their tent—at the verge of kona season.

It was a beautiful night, half a moon aloft and so many stars they could imagine they were in space. Wind lulled, seas whooshed, rigging creaked, the boat rocked forward and presently a couple of dolphins appeared, playing alongside for hours, a marvel that made even Kam sit silent in wonder. Then toward dawn, the goal a vague darkness ahead, clouds boiled out of the west, wind sharpened and shrilled, suddenly rain slanted like a flight of spears and through murk the mariners heard waves rumble against rocks.

It wasn't much of a storm, really, but ample to deal with *Wahine*. Seams opened, letting in water to join that which dashed over the gunwales. Sail first reefed, soon struck, stays nonetheless gave way and the mast went. It would have capsized the hull had Bob not managed to heave it free. Thereafter he had the oars, keeping bow on to the waves, while Kam bailed. A couple of years older, and no weakling, the Hawaiian couldn't have rowed that long at a stretch. Eventually he did his share and a bit at the rudder, when somehow he worked the craft through a gap between two reefs which roared murder at them. They hit coral a while later, but close enough to shore that they could swim, never sure who saved the life of who in the surf. Collapsing behind a bush, they slept the weather out.

Afterward they limped off till they found a road and hitched a ride. They'd been blown back to Kauai.

Side by side, they stood on the carpet before a Coast Guard officer and endured what they must.

Next day in their tent, Kam said, unwontedly solemn—the vast solemnity of youth—"Bob, listen. You've been my *hoa* since we met, you became my *hoaloha*, but what we've been through, what you did, makes you a *hoapili*."

"Aw, wasn't more'n I had to, and you did just as much," mumbled the other, embarrassed. "If you mean what I suppose you do, okay, I'll call you *kammerat*, and let's get on with whatever we're going to do."

"How about this? I've got folks on the Big Island. A tiny little settlement tucked away where nobody ever comes. Beautiful country, mountains and woods. People still live in the old kanaka style. How'd you like that?"

"Um-m, how old a style?"

Kam was relieved at being enabled to laugh. "You won't eat long pig! Everybody knows English, though they use Hawaiian for choice, and never fear, you can watch the Chimp Show. But it's a great, relaxed, cheerful life—you've got to experience the girls to believe—the families don't talk about it much when they go outside, or invite *haolena* in, because tourists would ruin it—but you'll be welcome, I guarantee you. How about it?"

The month that followed lived up to his promises, and then some.

Recollections of it flew unbidden across the years as Ryan worked in the galley. Everybody else was in the gym, where chairs and projection equipment had been brought, for the briefing the astronomers would give. *Rover* boosted on automatic; her instruments showed nothing ahead that she couldn't handle by herself for the next million kilometers. The quartermaster could have joined the group, but he wanted to make a victory feast ready. Before long, they'd be too busy to appreciate his art.

He did have a screen above the counter, monitoring the assembly.

Tregennis and Laurinda stood facing their audience. The Plateaunian said, with joy alive beneath the dry words:

"It is a matter of semantics whether we call this a first- or a second-generation system. Hydrogen and helium are overwhelmingly abundant, in proportions consistent with condensation shortly after the Big Bang—about which, not so incidentally, we may learn something more than hitherto. However, oxygen, nitrogen, carbon, silicon, and neon are present in significant quantities; magnesium and iron are not insignificant; other elements early in the periodic table are detectable. There has naturally been a concentration of heavier atoms in the planets, especially the inner ones, as gases selectively escaped. They are not mere balls of water ice.

"It seems clear, therefore, that this system formed out of a cloud which had been enriched by mass loss from older stars in their red giant phase. A few supernovae may have contributed, too, but any elements heavier than iron which they may have supplied are so scant that we will only find them by mass spectrography of samples from the solid bodies. They may well be nonexistent. Those older stars must have come into being as soon after the Beginning as was physically possible, in a proto-galaxy not too far then from the matter which was to become ours, but now surely quite distant from us."

"As we dared hope," said the Crashlander. Tears glimmered in her eyes like dew on rose petals.

"Oh, good for you!" called Yoshii.

"A relic—hell, finding God's fingerprints," Carita said, and clapped a hand to her mouth. Ryan grinned. Nobody else noticed.

"How many planets?" asked Saxtorph.

"Five," Tregennis replied.

"Hm. Isn't that kind of few, even for a dwarf? Are you sure?"

"Yes. We would have found anything of a size much less than what you would call a planet's."

"Especially since the Bode function is small, as you'd expect," Dorcas added. Having worked with the astronomers, she scarcely needed this session. "The planets huddle close in. We haven't found an Oort cloud either. No comets at all, we think."

"Outer bodies may well have been lost in the collision that sent this star into exile," Laurinda said. "And in fifteen billion years, any comets that were left got . . . used up."

"There probably was a sixth planet until some unknown date in the past," Tregennis stated. "We have indications of asteroids extremely close to the sun. Gravitational radiation—no, it must chiefly have been friction with the interstellar medium that caused a parent body to spiral in until it passed the Roche limit and was disrupted."

"Hey, wait," Saxtorph said. "Dorcas talks of a Bode function. That implies the surviving planets are about where theory says they ought to be. How'd they avoid orbital decay?"

Tregennis smiled. "That's a good question."

Saxtorph laughed. "Shucks, you sound like I was back in the Academy."

"Well, at this stage any answers are hypothetical, but consider. In the course of its long journey, quite probably through more galaxies than ours, the system must sometimes have crossed nebular regions where matter was comparatively dense. Gravitation would draw the gas and dust in, make it thickest close to the sun, until the sun swallowed it altogether. As a matter of fact, the planetary orbits have very small eccentricities—friction has a circularizing effect—and their distances from the primary conform only roughly to the theoretical distribution." Tregennis paused. "A further anomaly we cannot explain, though it may be related. We have found—marginally; we think we have found—molecules of water and OH radicals among the asteroids, almost like a ring around the sun." He spread his hands. "Well, I won't live to see every riddle we may come upon solved."

He had fought to get here, Ryan remembered.

"Let's hear about those planets," Carita said impatiently. Her job would include any landings. "Uh, have you got names for them? One, Two, Three might cause mixups when we're in a hurry."

"I've suggested using Latin ordinals," Laurinda answered. She sounded almost apologetic.

"Prima, Secunda, Tertia, Quarta, Quinta," Dorcas supplied. "Top-flight idea. I hope it becomes the standard for explorers." Laurinda flushed.

"I have agreed," Tregennis said. "The philologists can bestow official names later, or whoever is to be in charge of such things. Let us give you a précis of what we have learned to date."

He consulted a notator in his hand. "Prima," he recited. "Mean orbital radius, approximately 0.4 A.U. Diameter, approximately 16,000 kilometers. Since it has no satellite, the mass is still uncertain, but irradiation is such that it cannot be icy. We presume the material is largely silicate, which—allowing for self-compression—gives a mass on the order of Earth's. No signs of air.

"Secunda, orbiting at 0.7 A.U., resembles Prima,

but is slightly larger and does have a thin atmosphere, comparable to Mars'. It has a moon as well. Remarkably, the moon has a higher albedo than expected, a yellowish hue. The period tells us the mass, of course, which reinforces our guess about Prima.

"Tertia is almost exactly one A.U. out. It is a superterrestrial, mass of five Earths, as confirmed by four moons, also yellowish. A somewhat denser atmosphere than Secunda's; we have confirmed the presence of nitrogen and traces of oxygen."

"What?" broke from Saxtorph. "You mean it might have life?"

Laurinda shivered a bit. "The water is forever frozen," she told him. "Carbon dioxide must often freeze. We don't know how there can be any measurable amount of free oxygen. But there is."

Tregennis cleared his throat. "Quarta," he said. "A gas giant at 1.5 A.U., mass 230 Earths, as established by ten moons detected thus far. Surprisingly, no rings. Hydrogen and helium, presumably surrounding a vast ice shell which covers a silicate core with some iron. It seems to radiate weakly in the radio frequencies, indicating a magnetic field, though the radio background of the sun is such that at this distance we can't be sure. We plan a flyby on our way in. Quarta will be basic to understanding the dynamics of the system. It is its equivalent of Jupiter."

"Otherwise we have only detected radio from Secunda," Laurinda related, "but it is unmistakable, cannot be of stellar origin. It is really curious—intermittent, seemingly modulated, unless that is an artifact of our skimpy data." She smiled. "How lovely if intelligent beings are transmitting."

Markham stirred. He had put his chair behind the row of the rest. "Are you serious?" he nearly shouted.

Surprised looks went his way. "Oh, no," Laurinda said. "Just a daydream. We'll find out what is actually causing it when we get there."

"Well, Quinta remains," Tregennis continued, "in several respects, the most amazing object of all. Mass 103 Earths—seven moons found—at 2.8 A.U. It does have a well-developed ring system. Hydrogen-helium atmosphere, but with clear spectra of methane, ammonia, and . . . water vapor. Water in huge quantities. Turbulence, and a measured temperature far above expectations. Something peculiar has happened.

"Are there any immediate questions? If not, Laurinda and Dorcas have prepared graphics—charts, diagrams, tables, pictures—which we would like to show. Please feel free to inquire, or to propose ideas. Don't be bashful. You are all intelligent people with a good understanding of basic science. Any of you may get an insight which we specialists have missed."

Markham rose. "Excuse me," he said.

"Huh?" asked Saxtorph, amiably enough. "You want to go now when this is really getting interesting?"

"I do not expect I can make a contribution." Markham hesitated. "I am a little indisposed. Best I lie down for a while. Do not worry. I will soon be well. Carry on." He sketched a bow and departed.

"What do you know, he is human," Carita said.

"We ought to be kinder to him than we have been, poor man," Laurinda murmured.

"He hasn't given us much of a chance, has he?" replied Yoshii.

"Stow that," Saxtorph ordered. "No backbiting."

"Yes," added Dorcas, "let's proceed with the libretto."

Eagerness made Tregennis tremble as he obliged. In his galley, Ryan frowned. Something didn't feel quite right. While he followed the session he continued slicing the mahimahi he had brought frozen from Earth, but his mind was no longer entirely on either.

Time passed. It became clear that the Quarta approach was going to be an intellectual orgy, the more so because Quinta happened to be near inferior conjunction and thus a lot of information about that planet would be arriving, too. Ryan wiped hands on apron, left his preparations, and stumped up toward the flight deck.

He met Markham coming back. They halted and regarded each other. The companionway thrummed around them. "Hello, there," the quartermaster said slowly. "I thought you were in your cabin."

Markham stiffened. "I am on my way, if it is any of your business."

"Long way 'round."

"It . . . occurred to me to check certain stations. This is an old ship, refitted. Frankly, Captain Saxtorph relies too much on his machinery."

"What sort of thing did you want to check on?"

"Who are you to ask?" Markham flung. "You are the quartermaster."

"And you are the passenger." Ryan's bulk blocked the stairs. "I wouldn't be in this crew if I didn't have a pretty fair idea of how all the equipment works. I'm responsible for maintaining a lot of it."

"I have commanded spacecraft."

"Then you know each system keeps its own record." Ryan's smile approximated a leer, or a snarl. "Save the skipper a bunch of data retrievals. Where were you and what were you doing?"

Markham stood silent while the ship drove onward. At length: "I should, I shall report directly to the captain. But to avoid rumors, I tell you first. Listen well and do not distort what I say if you are able not to. I beamed a radio signal on a standard band at Secunda. It is against the possibility—the very remote possibility, Mlle. Brozik assured us—that sentient beings are present. Natives, Outsiders, who knows? In the interest of peaceful contact, we must provide evidence that we did not try to sneak in on them. Not that it is likely they exist, but—this is the sort of contigency I am here for. Saxtorph and I can dispute it later if he wishes. I have presented him with a *fait accompli*. Now let me by."

Ryan stood aside. Markham passed downward. Ryan stared after him till he was gone from sight, then went back to his galley.

10

Quarta fell astern as *Rover* moved on sunward. In the boat called *Fido*, Juan Yoshii swung around the giant planet and accelerated to overtake his ship. Vectors programmed, he could relax, look out the ports, seek to sort the jumbled marvels in his mind. Most had gone directly from instruments to the astronomers; he was carrying back certain observations taken farside. A couple of times there had been opportunity for Laurinda Brozik to tell him briefly about the latest interpretation, but he had been too busy on his flit to think much beyond the piloting.

Stars thronged, the Milky Way torrented, a sky little different from the skies he remembered. Less than 30 light-years' travel—a mite's leap in the galaxy. Clearly alien was the sun ahead. Tiny but perceptible, its ember of a disc was slow to dazzle his eyes, yet already cast sufficient light for him to see things by.

An outer moon drifted across vision. This was his

last close passage, and instruments worked greedily. Clicks and whirrs awoke beneath the susurrus of air through the hull. Yoshii pointed his personal camera; photography was an enthusiasm of his. The globe glimmered wan red under its sun. It was mainly ice, and smooth; any cracks and craters had slumped in the course of gigayears. The surface was lighter than it might have been and mottled with yellow spots. Ore deposits? The same material that tinted most airless bodies here? Tregennis was puzzled. You got dark spots in Solar-type systems. They were due to photolysis of frozen methane. Of course, this sun was so feeble. . . . .

It nonetheless illuminated the planet aft. Quarta's hue was pale rose, overlaid with silvery streaks that were ice clouds: crystals of carbon dioxide, ammonia, in the upper levels methane. No twists, no vortices, no sign of any Jovian storminess marred the serenity. Though the disc was visibly flattened, it rotated slowly, taking more than 40 hours. Tidal forces through eons had worn down even the spin of this huge mass. They had likewise dispersed whatever rings it once had, and surely drawn away moons. The core possessed a magnetic field, slight, noticeable only because it extended so far into space that it snatched radio waves out of incoming cosmic radiation—remanent magnetism, locked into iron as that core froze. For gravitational energy release had long since reached its end point; and long, long before then, K-40 and whatever other few radionuclei were once on hand had guttered away beyond measurement. The ice sheath went upward in tranquil allotropic layers to a virtually featureless surface and an enormous, quietly circulating atmosphere of starlike composition. Quarta had reached Nirvana.

It fell ever farther behind. *Fido* closed in on *Rover*.

The ship swelled until she might have been a planet herself. Instructions swept back and forth, electronic, occasionally verbal. A boat bay opened its canopy. Yoshii maneuvered through and docked. The canopy closed, shutting off heaven. Air hissed back in from the recovery tanks. A bulb flashed green. Yoshii unharnessed, operated the lock, crawled forth, and walked under the steady weight granted him by the ship's polarizer, into her starboard reception room.

Laurinda waited.

Yoshii stopped. She was alone. White hair tumbled past delicate features to brush the dress, new to him, that hugged her slenderness. She reached out. Her eyes glowed. "W-welcome back, Juan," she whispered.

"Why, uh, thanks, thank you. You're the . . . committee?"

She smiled, dropped her glance, became briefly the color of the world he had rounded. "Kam met Carita. As for you, Dorcas—Mate Saxtorph suggested—"

He took her hands. They felt reed-thin and silk-soft. "How nice of her. And the rest. I've data discs for you."

"They'll keep. We have more work than we can handle. Observations of Quinta were, have been incredibly fruitful." Ardor pulsed in her voice. The outermost planet was a safe subject. "We think we can guess its nature, but of course there's no end of details we don't understand, and we could be entirely wrong—"

"Good for you," he said, delighted by her delight. "I missed out on that, of course." Transmissions to him, including hers, had dealt with the Quartan system exclusively; any bit of information about it might perhaps save his life. "Tell me."

"Oh, it's violent, multi-colored, with spots like Jupiter's—one bigger than the Red—and—the surface is liquid water. It's Arctic-like; we imagine continent-sized ice floes clashing together."

"But warmer than Quarta! Why?"

"We suppose a large satellite crashed, a fraction of a million years ago. Debris formed the rings. The main mass released enough heat to melt the upper part of the planetary shell, and, and we'll need years, science will, to learn what else has happened."

He stood for an instant in awe, less of the event than of the time-scale. That moon must have been close to start with, but still it had taken the casual orbital erosion of . . . almost a universe's lifespan so far—how many passages through nebulae, galaxies, the near-ultimate vacuum of intergalactic space?—to bring it down. *What is man, that thou art mindful of him—?*

What is man, that he should waste the little span which is his?

"That's wonderful," he said, "but—we—"

Impulsively, he embraced her. Astoundingly, she responded.

Between laughter and tears she said in his ear, "Come, let's go, Kam's spread a feast for the two of us in my cabin."

Set beside that, the cosmos was trivial.

Saxtorph's voice crackled from the intercom: "Now hear this. Now hear this. We've just received a message from what claims to be a kzin warship. They're demanding we make rendezvous with them. Keep calm but think hard. We'll meet in the gym in an hour, 1530, and consider this together."

11

Standing with back to bulkhead, the captain let silence stretch, beneath the pulsebeat and whispers of the ship, while he scanned the faces of those seated before him. Dorcas, her Athene countenance frozen into expressionlessness; Kam Ryan's full lips quirked a bit upward, defiantly cheerful; Carita Fenger a-scowl; Juan Yoshii and Laurinda Brozik unable to keep from glancing at each other, hand gripping hand; Arthur Tregennis, who seemed almost as concerned about the girl; Ulf Markham, well apart from the rest, masked in haughtiness—Ulf *Reichstein* Markham, if you please. . . . The air renewal cycle was at its daily point of ozone injection. That tang smelled like fear.

Which must not be let out of its cage. Saxtorph cleared his throat.

"Okay, let's get straight to business," he said. "You must've noticed a quiver in the interior g-field and change in engine sound. You're right, we altered acceleration. *Rover* will meet the foreign vessel, with velocities matched, in about 35 hours. It could be sooner, but Dorcas told them we weren't sure our hull could take that much stress. What we wanted, naturally, was as much time beforehand as possible."

"Why don't we cut and run?" Carita asked.

Saxtorph shrugged. "Whether or not we can outrun them, we for sure can't escape the stuff they can throw, now that they've locked onto us. If they really are kzinti navy, they'll never let us get out where we can go hyperspatial. They may be lying, but Dorcas and I don't propose to take the chance."

"I presume evasion tactics are unfeasible," said Tregennis in his most academic voice.

"Correct. We could stop the engine, switch off the

generator, and orbit free, with batteries supplying the life support systems, but they'd have no trouble computing our path. As soon as they came halfway close, they'd catch us with a radar sweep.

"From what data we have on them, I believe they were searching for some time before they acquired us, probably with amplified optics. That's assuming they were in orbit around Secunda when they first learned of our arrival. The assumption is consistent with what would be a reasonable search curve for them and with the fact that there are modulated radio bursts out of that planet—transmissions to and from their base."

Nobody before had seen Yoshii snarl. "And how did they learn about us?" he demanded.

Looks went to Markham. He gave them back. "Yes, undoubtedly through me," he said. Strength rang in the words. "You all know I took it upon myself to beam a signal at Secunda—in my capacity as this expedition's officer of the government. The result has surprised me, too, but I acknowledge no need to apologize. If we, approaching a kzin base unbeknownst, had suddenly become manifest to their detectors, they would most likely have blown us out of existence."

Ryan nodded. "Without stopping to ask questions," he supplied. "Yeah, that'd be kzin style. If they are. How're you so sure?"

"I think we can take it for granted," Dorcas said. "Who else would have reason to call themselves kzinti?"

"Who else would want to?" Carita growled.

"Save the cuss words for later," Saxtorph counselled. "We're in too much of a pickle for luxuries. I might add that although the vocal transmission was through a translator, the phrasing, the responses to us, everything was pure kzin. They are here—on the far side of human space from their own. You realize what this means, don't you, folks? The kzinti have gotten the hyperdrive."

That conclusion had indeed become clear to everyone, but Laurinda asked, "How could they?" as if in pain.

Yoshii grimaced. "Once you know something can be done, you're halfway to doing it yourself," he told her.

"I know," she answered. "But I had the, the impression they aren't quite as clever at engineering as humans, even if they did invent the gravity polarizer. And, and wouldn't we have known?"

"Collecting intelligence in kzin space isn't exactly easy," Saxtorph explained. "Anyhow, they may have done the R and D on some planet we aren't aware of. I'll grant you, I'm surprised myself that they've been this quick. Well, they were." His grin was lopsided. "Once I heard about an epitaph on an old New England tombstone. 'I expected this, but not so soon.'"

"Why have they established themselves here?" Tregennis wondered. "As you observed, it is a long journey for them, especially if they went around human space in order to avoid any chance that their possession of the hyperdrive would be discovered. True, this system is uniquely interesting, but I didn't think kzin civilization gave scientific research as high a value as ours does."

"That's a good question," Saxtorph said.

His gallows humor drew a chuckle from none but Ryan. Dorcas uttered the thought in every mind: "They won't let us go home to tell about them if they can help it."

"Which is why we are being nice and meeting

them as they request," Saxtorph added. "It gives them an alternative to putting a nuke on our track."

Markham folded his arms and stated, "I hope you people have the wit to be glad, at last, that I came along. They will understand that I am authorized to negotiate with them. They will likewise understand that my disappearance would in due course cause a second expedition to come, with armed escort, as the loss of an entirely private group might not."

"Could be," Saxtorph said. "However, I can think of several ways to fake a natural disaster for us."

"Such as?"

"Well, for instance, giving us a lethal dose of radiation, then sending the corpses back with the ship gimmicked to seem this was an accident. The kzin pilot could return on an accompanying vessel after ours left hyperspace."

"What would the log show?"

"What the 'last survivor' was tortured into entering."

"Nonsense. You have been watching too many spy dramas."

"I disagree. Besides, that was just one of the notions that occurred to Dorcas and me. The kzinti might be more inventive yet."

"We have decided not to rely exclusively on their sweet nature," the mate declared. "Listen carefully.

"We can launch the boats without them detecting it, if we act soon. They'll float free while *Rover* proceeds to rendezvous. When she's a suitable distance off, nobody looking for any action in this volume of space, they'll scramble."

Carita smacked fist in palm. "Hey, terrific!" she cried.

Markham sounded appalled: "Have you gone crazy? How will you survive, let alone return, in two little interplanetary flitters?"

"They're more than that," Saxtorph reminded. "They're rugged and maneuverable and full to the scuppers with delta v. In either of 'em I'd undertake to outrace or dodge a tracking missile, and make it tough or impossible to hold a laser beam on her long enough to do much damage. Air and water recycler are in full working order and rations for one man-year are stowed aboard."

"I, I ate some," Yoshii stammered. "Carita must have, too."

"I've already replaced it," Ryan informed them.

"Good thinking!" Saxtorph exclaimed. "Did you expect this tactic?"

"Oh, general principles. Take care of your belly and your belly will take care of you."

"Stop that schoolboy chatter," Markham snapped. "What in the cosmos can you hope to do but antagonize the kzinti?"

"How do you tell an antagonized kzin from an unantagonized one?" Saxtorph retorted. "I am dead serious. Nobody has to follow me who doesn't want to."

"I certainly do not. Someone has to stay and . . . try to repair the harm your lunacy will have done."

"I figured you would. But I supposed you, of all people, would have a better hold on kzin psychology than you're showing. You ought to know they don't resent an opponent giving them a proper fight. Fighting's their nature. Whoever surrenders becomes no more than a captured animal in their eyes. Dorcas and I aim to put some high cards in your hand before you sit down at their poker table. A spacecraft on the loose is a weapon. The drive, or the sheer kinetic energy, can wreck things quite as thoroughly as the average nuke. Come worst to worst, we might smash a boat into their base at several thousand k.p.h. The other boat might take out their ship and leave them stranded; I've a hunch they've kept just a single hyperdrive vessel, as scarce as those must still be among them. Yah, going out like that would be a sight better than going into the stewpot. Kzinti like long pig."

Yoshii brightened. He and Laurinda exchanged a wonder-smitten look. Carita whooped. Tregennis smiled faintly. Ryan went oddly, abruptly thoughtful.

Markham gnawed his lip a moment, then straightened in his chair and rapped, "Very well. I do not approve, and I ask the crew to refrain from this foolishness of yours, but I cannot stop you. Therefore I must factor your action into my calculations. What terms shall I try to get for us?"

"Freedom to leave, of course," Dorcas responded. "Let *Rover* retreat to hyperspacing distance and wait, while the kzinti withdraw too far to intercept our boats. We can verify that on instruments before we come near. We'll convey any message they want, or even a delegate."

"There could be a delegation on board, waiting," Ryan warned.

Tregennis stirred. "I will remain behind," he said.

Tears sprang into Laurinda's eyes. "Oh, no!" she pleaded.

He smiled again, at her. "I am too old to go blatting around space like that. I would merely be a burden, and quite likely die on your hands. Not only will I be more comfortable here, I will be an extra witness to the bona fides of the kzinti. Landholder Markham alone could not keep track of everything they might stealthily do."

"It will show them there are two reasonable human beings in this outfit," the Wunderlander said.

"That might be marginally helpful to me. Anyone else?"

"Speaking," Ryan answered.

"Huh?" broke from Saxtorph. "Hey, Kam, no. Whatever for?"

"For this," the quartermaster said calmly. "Haven't you thought of it yourself? The boats will be on the move, or holed up someplace unknown to the kzinti. They can only be reached by broadcast. Planar broadcast, maybe, but still the signal's bound to be down in the milliwatts or microwatts when it reaches your receivers—with the sun's radio background to buck. Nothing but voice transmission will carry worth diddly. Given a little time to record how the humans talk who were left behind, the kzinti can write a computer program to fake it. 'Sure, come on back, fellows, all is forgiven and they've left a case of champagne for us to celebrate with.' How're you going to know that's for real?"

Dorcas frowned. "We did consider it," she told him. "We'll use a secret password."

"Which a telepath of theirs can fish right out of a human skull, maybe given a spot of torture to unsettle the brain first. Nope, I know a trick worth two of that. How well do you remember your Hawaiian, Bob? You picked up a fair amount while we were in the village." Ryan laughed. "That worked on the girls like butter on a toboggan slope."

Saxtorph was a long while silent before he answered: "I think, if I practiced for a few days, I think . . . enough of it . . . would come back to me."

Ryan nodded. "The kzinti have programs for the important human languages in their translators, but I doubt Hawaiian is included. *Or* Danish."

Yoshii swallowed. "You'd certify everything is kosher?" he mumbled. "But what if—well—"

"If the kzinti aren't stupid, they won't try threatening or torturing me into feeding you a lie," Ryan responded. "How'd they savvy what I was saying? I assure you, it wouldn't be complimentary to them."

"A telepath would know."

Ryan shrugged. "He'd know I was not going to be their Judas goat, no matter what they did. Therefore they won't do it."

Saxtorph's right hand half reached out. "Kam, old son—" he croaked. The hand dropped.

Dorcas rose and confronted the rest, side by side with her husband. "I'm sorry, but time is rationed for us and you must decide at once," she said. "If you think you'd better stay, then do. We won't consider you a coward or anything. You may be right. We can't be sure at this stage. All we are certain of is that we don't have time for debate. Who's going?"

Hands went up, Carita's, Yoshii's, and after an instant Laurinda's.

"Okay," Dorcas continued. "Now we're not about to put our bets on a single number. The boats will go separate ways. Which ways, we'll decide by tight beam once we're alone in space. You understand, Kam, Arthur, Landholder Markham. What you don't know, a telepath or a torturer can't get out of you. Bob and I have already considered the distribution. Carita and Juan will take *Fido*. We thought Kam would ride with them, but evidently not. Laurinda, you'll be with Bob and me in *Shep*."

"Wait a minute!" Yoshii protested. The girl brought fingertips to open mouth.

"Sorry, my dears," Dorcas said. "It's a matter of practicality, as nearly as we could estimate on short notice. Not that we imagine you two would play Romeo and Juliet to the neglect of your duties. However, Juan and Carita are our professional pilots,

rockjacks, planetside prospectors. Together they make
our strongest possible team. They can pull stunts
Bob and I never could. We need that potential, don't
we? Bob and I are no slouches, but we do our best
work in tandem. To supply some of what we lack as
compared to Juan and Carita, Laurinda has knowledge, including knowledge of how to use instruments we plan to pack along. Don't forget, more is
involved than us. The whole human race needs to
know what the kzinti are up to. We must maximize
our chances of getting the news home. Agreed?"

Yoshii clenched his free hand into a fist, stared at
it, raised his head, and answered, "Aye. And you can
take better care of her."

The Crashlander flushed. "I'm no piece of porce-
lain!" Immediately contrite, she stroked the Belter's
cheek while she asked unevenly, "How soon do we
leave?"

Dorcas smiled and made a gesture of blessing.
"Let's say an hour. We'll need that much to stow
gear. You two can have most of it to yourselves."

12

The kzin warship was comparatively small, Prowling Hunter class, but not the less terrifying a sight.
Weapon pods, boat bays, sensor booms, control domes
studded a spheroid whose red hue, in the light of
this sun, became like that of clotted blood. Out of it
and across the kilometers between darted small fierce
gleams that swelled into space-combat armor enclos-
ing creatures larger than men. They numbered a
dozen, and each bore at least two firearms.

Obedient to orders, Ryan operated the main personnel airlock and cycled four of them through. The

first grabbed him and slammed him against the bulkhead so hard that it rang. Stunned, he would have slumped to the deck were it not for the bruising grip on his shoulders. The next two crouched with weapons ready. The last one took over the controls and admitted the remaining eight.

At once, ten went off in pairs to ransack the ship. It was incredible how fast they carried the mass of metal upon them. Their footfalls cast booming echoes down the passageways.

Markham and Tregennis, waiting in the saloon, were frisked and put under guard. Presently Ryan was brought to them. "My maiden aunt has better manners than they do," he muttered, and lurched toward the bar. The kzin used his rifle butt to push him into a chair and gestured for silence. Time passed.

Within an hour, which felt longer to the humans, the boarding party was satisfied that there were no traps. Somebody radioed a report from the airlock; the rest shed their armor and stood at ease outside the saloon. Its air grew full of their wild odor.

A new huge and ruddy-gold form entered. The guard saluted, sweeping claws before his face. Markham jumped up. "For God's sake, stand," he whispered. "That's the captain."

Tregennis and, painfully, Ryan rose. The kzin's gaze flickered over them and came back to dwell on Markham, recognizing leadership. The Wunderlander opened his mouth. Noises as of a tiger fight poured forth.

Did the captain register surprise that a man knew his language? He heard it out and spat a reply. Markham tried to continue. The captain interrupted, and Markham went mute. The captain told him something.

Markham turned to his companions. "He forbids

me to mangle the Hero's Tongue any more," he related wryly. "He grants my request for a private talk—in the communications shack, where our translator is, since I explained that we do have one and it includes the right program. Meanwhile you may talk with each other and move freely about this cabin. If you must relieve yourselves, you may use the sink behind the bar."

"How gracious of him," Ryan snorted.

Markham raised brows. "Consider yourselves fortunate. He is being indulgent. Don't risk provoking him. High-ranking kzinti are even more sensitive about their honor than the average, and he has earned a partial name, Hraou-Captain."

"We will be careful," Tregennis promised. "I am sure you will do your best for us."

The commander went majestically out. Markham trailed. Ryan gusted a sigh, sought the bar, tapped a liter of beer, and drained it in a few gulps. The guard watched enviously but then also left. Discipline had prevented him from shoving the human aside and helping himself. He and a couple of his fellows remained in the passage. They conversed a bit, rumbling and hissing.

"We'll be here a while," Ryan sighed. "Care for a round of gin?"

"It would be unwise of us to drink," Tregennis cautioned. "Best you be content with that mugful you had."

"I mean gin rummy."

"What is that, if not a, ah, cocktail?"

"A card game. They don't play it on Plateau? I can teach you."

"No, thank you. Perhaps I am too narrow in my interests, but cards bore me." Tregennis brightened. "However, do you play chess?"

Ryan threw up his hands. "You expect me to concentrate on woodpushing *now?* Hell, let's screen a show. Something light and trashy, with plenty of girls in it. Or would you rather seize the chance to at last read *War and Peace?*"

Tregennis smiled. "Believe it or not, Kamehameha, I have my memories. By all means, girls."

The comedy was not quite finished when a kzin appeared and jerked an unmistakable gesture. The men followed him. He didn't bother with a companion or with ever glancing rearward. At the flight deck he proceeded to Saxtorph's operations cabin, waved them through, and closed the door on them.

Markham sat behind the desk. He was very pale and reeked of the sweat that stained his tunic, but his visage was set in hard lines. Hraou-Captain loomed beside him, too big to use a human's chair, doubtless tired of being cramped in the comshack and maybe choosing to increase his dominance by sheer height. Another kzin squatted in a far corner of the room, a wretched-looking specimen, fur dull and unkempt, shoulders slumped, eyes turned downward.

"Attention," rasped Markham. "I wish I did not have to tell you this—I hoped to avoid it—but the commander says I must. He . . . feels deception is pointless and . . . besmirches his honor. His superior on Secunda agrees; we have been in radio contact."

The newcomers braced themselves.

Nonetheless it was staggering to hear: "For the past five years I have been an agent of the kzinti. Later I will justify myself to you, if your minds are not totally closed. It is not hatred for my species that drove me to this, but love and concern for it, hatred for the decadence that is destroying us. Later, I say. We dare not waste Hraou-Captain's time with arguments."

Regarding the faces before him, Markham made his tone dry. "The kzinti never trusted me with specific information, but after I began sending them information about hyperdrive technology, they gave me a general directive. I was to use my position as commissioner to forestall, whenever possible, any exploration beyond the space containing the human-occupied worlds. That naturally gave me an inkling of the reason—to prevent disclosure of their activities—and it became clear to me that some of the most important must be in regions distant from kzin space. When hope was lost of keeping you from this expedition, I decided my duty was to join it and stand by in case of need. Not that I anticipated the need, understand. The star looked so useless. But when you did get those radio indications, I knew better than you what they could mean, and was glad I had provided against the contingency, and beamed a notice of our arrival."

"Your parents were brothers," Ryan said.

Markham laid back his ears. "Spare the abuse. Remember, by forewarning the kzinti I saved your lives. If you had simply blundered into detector range—"

"They may be impulsive," Tregennis said, "but they are not idiotic. I do not accept your assertion that they would reflexively have annihilated us."

Markham trembled. "Silence. Bear in mind that I am all that stands between you and—It has been a long time since the kzinti in this project tasted fresh meat."

"What are they doing?" Ryan asked.

"Constructing a naval base. They chose the system precisely because it seemed insignificant—the dimmest star in the whole region, devoid of heavy elements and impoverished in the light—though it does happen to have a ready source of iron and certain other crucial materials, together with a strategic location. They never expected humans to seek it out. They underestimated the curiosity of our species. They are . . . cats, not monkeys."

"Uh-huh. Not noisy, sloppy, free-swinging monkeys like you despise. Kzinti respect rank. Once they've overrun us, they'll put the niggers back in their proper place. From here they can grab off Beta Hydri, drive a salient way into our space—How many more prongs will there be to the attack? When is the next war scheduled for?"

"Silence!" Markham shouted. "Hold your mouth! One word from me, and—"

"And what? You need us, Art and me, you need us, else we wouldn't be having this interview. Kill us, and your boss just gets a few meals."

"Killing can be in due course. I imagine he would enjoy your testicles for tomorrow's breakfast."

Ryan rocked on his feet. Tregennis' lips squeezed together till they were white.

Markham's voice softened. "I am warning, not threatening," he said in a rush. "I'll save you if I can, unharmed, but if you don't help me I can promise nothing."

He leaned forward. "Listen, will you? Obviously you can't be released to spread the news—not yet— but some years of detention are better than death." He could not quite hold back the sneer. "In *your* minds, I suppose. You're lucky, lucky that I was aboard. Once my status has been verified, the high commandant can let me bring home a convincing tale of disaster. Else he would probably have had to kill us and make our bodies stage props, as Saxtorph suggested. I think he will spare you if I ask; it will cost him little, and kzinti reward faithful service.

They also keep their promises. But you must earn your lives."

"The boats," Tregennis whispered.

Ryan ndded. "You've got a telepath on hand, I see," he said flat-voiced. "He could make sure that my call in Hawaiian tells how everything is hearts and flowers. Except if he reads my mind, he'll see that I ain't gonna do it, no matter what. Or, okay, maybe they can break me, but Bob will hear that in his old pal's voice."

"I've explained this to Hraou-Captain," Markham said, cooler now. "It is necessary to neutralize those boats, but they don't pose any urgent threat, so we will start with methods less time-consuming than . . . interrogation and persuasion. Later, though, when we are on Secunda—that's where we are going—later your cooperation in working up a plausible disaster for me to return with, that is what will buy you your lives. If you refuse, you'll die for nothing, because we can always devise some deception which will keep humans away from here. You'll die for nothing."

"What the hell can we do about the boats? We don't know where they've gone."

Markham's manner became entirely impersonal. "I have explained this to Hraou-Captain. I went on to explain that their actions will not be random. What Captain Saxtorph decides—has decided to do is a multivariable function of the logic of the situation and of his personality. You and he are good friends, Ryan. You can make shrewd guesses as to his behavior. They won't be certain, of course, but they will eliminate some possibilities and assign rough probabilities to others. Your input may have some value, too, Professor. And even mine—in the course of establishing that I have been telling the truth.

"Sit down on the deck. This will not be pleasant, you know."

Hraou-Captain, who had stood like a pillar, turned his enormous body and growled a command. The telepath raised his head. Eyes glazed by the drug that called forth his total abilities came to a focus.

In their different ways, the three humans readied for what was about to happen. They'd have sundering headaches for hours afterward, too.

13

Small though it was, at its distance from Prima the sun showed more than half again the disc which Sol presents to Earth. Blotches of darkness pocked its sullen red. Corona shimmered around the limb, not quite drowned out of naked-eye vision.

Yoshii ignored it. His attention was on the planet which *Fido* circled in high orbit. Radar, spectroscope, optical amplifier, and a compact array of other instruments fed data to a computer which spun forth interpretations on screen and printout. Click and whirr passed low through the rustling ventilation, the sometimes uneven human breath within the control cabin. Body warmth and a hint of sweat tinged the air.

Yoshii's gaze kept drifting from the equipment, out a port of the globe itself. "Unbelievable," he murmured.

Airless, it stood sharp-edged athwart the stars, but the illuminated side was nearly a blank, even at first and last quarter when shadows were long. Then a few traces of hill and dale might appear, like timeworn Chinese brush strokes. Otherwise there was yellowish-white smoothness, with ill-defined areas of faint gray, brown, or blue. The whole world could almost have been a latex ball, crudely made for a child of the giants.

"What now?" Carita asked. She floated, harnessed in her seat, her back to him. They had turned off the gravity polarizer and were weightless, to eliminate that source of detectability. Her attention was clamped to the long-range radar with which she swept the sky, to and fro as the boat swung around.

"Oh, everything," said the Belter.

"Any ideas? You've had more chance to think, these past hours, than I have."

"Well, a few things *look* obvious, but I wouldn't make book on their being what they seem."

"Why don't you give me a rundown?" proposed the Jinxian. "Never mind if you repeat what I've already heard. We should try putting things in context."

Yoshii plunged into talk. It was an escape of sorts from their troubles, from not knowing what the fate of *Shep* and those aboard her might be.

"The planet's about the mass of Earth but only about half as dense. Must be largely silicate, some aluminum, not enough iron to form a core. Whatever atmosphere and hydrosphere it once outgassed, it lost—weak gravity, and temperatures around 400 K at the hottest part of the day. That day equals 131 of Earth's; two-thirds rotational lock, like Mercury. No more gas comes out, because vulcanism, tectonics, all geology ended long ago. Unless you want to count meteoroid erosion wearing down the surface; and I'd guess hardly any objects are left that might fall on these planets.

"Then what is that stuff mantling the surface? The computer can't figure it out. Shadows of what relief there is indicate it's thin, a few centimeters deep, with local variations. Reflection spectra suggest carbon compounds but that's not certain. It just lies there, you see, doesn't do anything. Try analyzing a lump of some solid plastic across a distance. Is that what we have here, a natural polymer? I wish I knew more organic chemistry."

"Can't help you, Juan," Carita said. "All I remember from my class in it, aside from the stinks in the lab, is that the human sex hormones are much the same, except that the female is ketonic and the male is alcoholic."

"We'll have time to look and think further, of course." Yoshii sighed. "Time and time and time. I never stopped to imagine how what fugitives mostly do is sit. Hiding, huddling, while—" He broke off and struggled for self-command.

"And we don't dare let down our guard long enough to take a little recreation," Carita grumbled.

Yoshii reddened. "Uh, if we could, I—well—"

She chuckled and said ruefully, "I know. The fair Laurinda. Don't worry, your virtue will be safe with me till you realize it can't make any possible diff— Hold!" she roared.

He tensed where he floated. "What?"

"Quiet. No, secure things and get harnessed."

For humming minutes she studied the screen and meters before her. Yoshii readied himself. Seated at her side he could see the grimness grow. Pale hair waved around sable skin when at last she nodded. "Yes," she said, "somebody's bound this way. From the direction of the sun. About ten million klicks off. He barely registered at first, but it's getting stronger by the minute. He's boosting *fast*. We'd tear our hull apart if we tried to match him, supposing we had that kind of power. Definitely making for Prima."

"What . . . is it?"

"What but a kzin ship with a monster engine? I'm afraid they've caught on to our strategy." Carita's tone grew wintry. "I'd rather not hear just how they did."

"G-guesswork?" Yoshii faltered.

"Maybe. I don't know kzin psych. How close to us can they make themselves think?" She turned her head to clamp her vision on him. "Well, maybe the skipper's plan failed and it's actually drawn the bandits to us. Or maybe it's the one thing that can save us."

(Saxtorph's words drawled through memory: "We don't know how much search capability the kzin have, but a naval vessel means auxiliaries, plus whatever civilian craft they can press into service. A boat out in the middle of the far yonder, drifting free, would be near-as-damn impossible to find. But as soon as she accelerates back toward where her crew might do something real, she screams the announcement to any alert, properly organized watchers— optical track, neutrino emission, the whole works till she's in effective radar range. After that she's sold to the licorice man, as they say in Denmark. On the other hand, if she can get down onto a planetary surface, she can probably make herself almost as invisible as out in the deep. A worldful of topography, which the kzinti cannot have had time or personnel to map in anything but the sketchiest way. So how about one of ours goes to Prima, the other to Tertia, and lies low in orbit? Immediately when we get wind of trouble, we drop down into the best hidey-hole the planet has got, and wait things out."

(It had been the most reasonable idea that was broached.)

"You've been doing our latest studies," Carita went on. "Found any prospective burrows? The kzinti may or may not have acquired us by now. Maybe not. That vessel may not be as well equipped to scan as this prospector, and she's probably a good deal bigger. But they're closing in fast, I tell you."

Yoshii made a shushing gesture, swiveled his seat, and evoked pictures, profiles, data tabulations. Shortly he nodded. "I think we have a pretty respectable chance." Pointing: "See here. Prima isn't all an unbroken plain. This range, its small valleys—and on the night side, too."

Carita whistled. "Hey, boy, we live right!"

"I'll set up for a detailed scan and drop into low orbit to make it. We should find some cleft we can back straight down into. The kzinti would have to arc immediately above and be on the lookout for that exact spot to see us." Yoshii said nothing about what a feat of piloting he had in mind. He was a Belter. She had almost comparable experience, together with Jinxian reflexes.

14

"Yah, I do think our best bet is to land and snuggle in." Saxtorph's look ranged through the port and across the planet, following an onward sweep of daylight as *Shep* orbited around to the side of the sun.

That disc was less than half the size of Sol's at Earth, its coal-glow light little more than one onehundredth. Nevertheless Tertia shone so brightly as to dazzle surrounding stars out of sight. Edges softened by atmosphere, it was bestrewn with glaciers, long streaks and broad plains and frozen seas bluishly aglimmer from pole to pole. Bared rock reached darkling on mountainsides or reared in tablelands. Five Terrestrial masses had been convulsed enough as they settled toward equilibrium that the last of the heights they thrust upward had not worn away entirely during the post-tectonic eons.

The glaciers were water, with some frozen carbon dioxide overlying them in the antarctic zone where winter now reigned. The air, about twice as dense as Earth's, was almost entirely nitrogen, the oxygen in it insufficient to sustain fire or life. It was utterly clear save where slow winds raised swirls of glitter, dust storms whose dust was fine ice.

A small moon, inmost of four, hove in view. It sheened reddish-yellow, like amber. The largest, Luna-size, was visible, too, patched with the same hue, ashen where highlands were uncovered. It had no craters; spalling and cosmic sand had long since done away with them.

"But, but on the surface we'll see only half the sky at best," Laurinda ventured. "And atmospherics will . . . hinder the seeing."

Saxtorph nodded. "True. Ordinarily I'd opt for staying in space in hopes of early warning. That does have its own drawbacks, though. A kzin search vessel could likelier than not detect us the moment we commenced boost. Since we might not be able to skedaddle flat-out from them, we'd probably drop planetside. That's the whole idea of being where we are, remember? If we did it right, the ratcats wouldn't know where we'd squatted, but they'd know we were someplace yonder for sure, and that would be a bigger help to them than they deserve."

"Treacherous terrain for landing," Dorcas warned.

Saxtorph nodded again. "Indeed. Which means we'll be smart to take our time while we've still got it, come down cautiously and settle in thoroughly. As for knowing when a spacecraft is in the neighborhood, at a minimum there's our neutrino detector.

It's not what you'd call precise, but it will pick up an operating fusion generator within a couple million klicks, clear through the body of the planet."

He paused before adding, "I realize this isn't quite what we intended when we said goodbye. But we didn't know what Tertia is like. Doctrine exists to be modified as circumstances dictate. I'd guess the sensible thing for Juan and Carita to do is quite different."

Laurinda's fingers twisted together. She turned her face from the other two.

"I vote with you," Dorcas declared. They had been considering tactics for hours, while they gained knowledge of the world they had reached. "What are the specs of a landing site? Safe ground; concealment from anything except an unlikely observation from directly overhead, unless we can avoid that too; but we don't want to be in a radio shadow, because we hope for—we expect—a broadcast message in the fairly near future."

"Don't forget defensibility," Saxtorph reminded.

"What?" asked Laurinda, startled. "How can we possibly—"

The man grinned. "I didn't tell you, honey, because it's not a thing to blab about, but Dorcas and I always travel with a few weapons. I took them along packed among my personal effects. Managed to slip Carita a rifle and some ammo when nobody else was looking. That leaves us with another rifle, a Pournelle rapid-fire automatic, choice of solid or explosive shells; a .38-caliber machine pistol with detachable stock; and a 9-mm. mulekiller."

"Plus a certain amount of blasting sticks," Dorcas informed him.

Saxtorph goggled. "Huh?" He guffawed. "That's my nice little wifey. The standard mining equipment aboard includes knives, geologists' hammers, crowbars, and such, useful for mayhem." He sobered. "Not that we want a fight. God, no! But if we're able to give a good account of ourselves—it might make a difference."

"A single small warhead will make a much bigger difference, unless we have dispersal and concealment capability," Dorcas observed. "All right, let's take a close look at what topographical data we've collected."

The choice was wide, but decision was quick. *Shep* dropped out of orbit and made for a point about 30 degrees north latitude. It was at midafternoon, which was a factor. Lengthening shadows would bring out details, while daylight would remain—in a rotation period of 40 hours, 37-plus minutes—for preliminary exploration of the vicinity.

A mesa loomed stark, thinly powdered with ice crystals, above a glacier that had flowed under its own weight, down from the heights, until a jumble of hills beneath had brought it to a halt. As it descended, the glacier had gouged a deep, almost sheer-walled coulee through slopes and steeps. The bottom was talus, under a dusting of sand, but solid; with gravity a third higher than on Earth, and epochs of time, shards and particles had settled into gridlock.

Or so the humans reasoned. The last few minutes of maneuver were very intent, very quiet except for an occasional low word of business. Saxtorph, manning the console, was prepared to cram on emergency boost at the first quiver of awryness. But Dorcas talked him down and *Shep* grounded firmly. For a while, nobody spoke or moved. Then husband and wife unharnessed and kissed. After a moment, Laurinda made it a threeway embrace.

Saxtorph peered out. The canyon walls laid gloom over stone. "You ladies unlimber this and stow that while I go take a gander," he said. "Yes, dear, I won't be gone long and I will be careful."

His added weight dragged at him, but not too badly. It wasn't more than physiology could take, even a Belter's or a Crashlander's, and distributed over the whole body. The women would get used to it, sort of, and in fact it ought to be valuable, continuous exercise in the cramped quarters of the boat. The spacesuit did feel pretty heavy.

He cycled through and stood for a few minutes learning to see the landscape. Every cue was alien, subtly or utterly, light, shadow, shapes. The cobbles underfoot were smooth as those on a beach. They and the rubble along the sides and the cliffs above were tawny-gray, sparked with bits of what might be mica but was likelier something strange—diamond dust? Several crags survived, eroded to laciness. The lower end of the gorge, not far off, was blocked by a wall of glacier. Above reached purple sky. An ice-devil whirled on the heights. Wind whittered.

Saxtorph decided his party had better plant an antenna and relay inconspicuously up there. Any messages ought to be on a number of simultaneous bands, at least one of which could blanket a Tertian hemisphere, but the signal would be tenuous and these depths might screen it out altogether. He walked carefully from the arrowhead of the boat to the right-hand side and started downslope, looking for safe routes to the top. Lateral ravines appeared to offer them.

Abruptly he halted. What the flapping hellfire?

He stooped and stared. Could it be—? No, some freak of nature. He wasn't qualified to identify a fossil.

He went on. By the time he had tentatively found the path he wanted, he was so near the glacier that he continued. It lifted high, not grimy like its counterparts on terrestroid planets but clear, polished glassy-smooth, a cold and mysterious blue. Whatever mineral grains once lay on it had sunken to the bottom, and—

And—

Saxtorph stood moveless. The time was long before he breathed, "Oh. My. God."

From within the ice, the top half of a skull stared at him. It could only be that, unhuman though it was. And other bones were scattered behind, and shaped stones, and pieces of what was most surely earthenware—

Chill possessed him from within. How old were those remnants?

Big Tertia must in its youth have had a still denser atmosphere than now, greenhouse effect, heat from a contracting interior, and . . . those molecules that are the kernel from which life grows, perhaps evolved not here but in interstellar space, organics which the wan sun did not destroy as they drifted inward. . . . Life arose. It liberated oxygen. It gave birth to beings that made tools and dreams. But meanwhile the planetary core congealed and chilled, the oceans began to freeze, plants died, nothing replaced the oxygen that surface rocks bound fast. . . . Without copper, tin, gold, iron, any metal they could know for what it was, the dwellers had never gone beyond their late stone age, never had a chance to develop the science that might have saved them or at least have let them understand what was happening. . . .

Saxtorph shuddered. He turned and hastened back to the boat.

15

Unsure what kind of surface awaited them, Carita and Yoshii descended on the polarizer and made a feather-soft landing. They were poised to spring instantly back upward. All they felt was a slight resilience, more on their instruments than in their bones. It damped out and *Fido* rested quiet.

"Elastic?" Yoshii wondered. "Or viscous, or what?"

"Never mind, we'll investigate later, right now we're down safe," Carita replied. She wiped her brow. "Hoo, but I need a stiff drink and a hot shower!"

Yoshii leered at her. "In the opposite order, please." She cuffed him lightly. The horseplay turned into mutual unharnessing and a hug.

"Hey-y," she purred, "you really do want to celebrate, don't you? Later, we'll share that shower."

His arms dropped. She released him in her turn and he made a stumbling backward step. "I, I'm sorry, I didn't intend—Well, we should take a good look outside, shouldn't we?"

The Jinxian was briefly silent before she smiled wryly and shrugged. "Okay. I'll forgive you this time if you'll fix dinner. Your yakitori tacos are always consoling. You're right, anyway."

They turned off the fluoros and peered forth. As their eyes adapted, they saw well enough through airlessness, by the thronging stars and the cold rush of the Milky Way. Bowl-shaped, the dell in which they were parked curved some 50 meters wide to heights twice as far above the bottom. *Fido* sat close to one side; direct sunlight would only touch her for a small part of the day, weeks hence. Every edge and lump was rounded off by the covering of the planet. In this illumination it appeared pale gray.

"What *is* the stuff?" Carita muttered.

"I've hit on an idea," Yoshii said. "I do not warrant that it is right. It may not even make sense."

Her teeth flashed white in the darkness. "The universe is not under obligation to make sense. Speak your piece." She switched cabin illumination back on. Radiance made the ports blank.

"I think it must be organic—carbon-based," Yoshii said. "It doesn't remotely match any mineral I've ever seen or heard of or imagined, whereas it does resemble any number of plastics."

"Hm, yeah, I had the same thought, but discarded it. Where would the chemistry come from? Life can't have started in the short time Prima hung onto its atmosphere, can it? Whatever carbon, hydrogen, oxygen, nitrogen are left must be locked up in solid-state materials. At most we might find hydrates or something."

"This could have come from space."

"What?" She gaped at him. "If that's a joke, it's too deep for me."

"There is matter in space, in the nebulae and even in the emptiest stretches between. It includes organic compounds, some of them fairly complex."

"Not quite concentrated enough for soup."

"Sure, the densest nebula is still a pretty hard vacuum by Terrestrial standards. However, this system has had time to pass through many. Between them, too—yes, between galaxies—gravity has found atoms and molecules to draw in. During any single year, hardly a measurable amount. But it's been fifteen *billion* years, Carita."

"Um'h," she uttered, almost as if punched in the stomach.

"The sun doesn't give off any ultraviolet to speak of," Yoshii pursued. "Its wind is puny. Carbon-based molecules land intact. The sun does maintain a day-

time temperature at which they can react with each
other. I daresay cosmic radiation energizes the chemistry, too. Fine grains of sand and dust—crumbled off
rocks, together with meteoroid powder—provide col-
loidal surfaces where the stuff can cluster till there's
a fairly high concentration and complicated exchanges
become possible. Unsaturated bonds grab the free
atoms of carbon, hydrogen, oxygen, anything included
in the downdrift except noble gases, and incorporate
them. Maybe, here and there, some such growing
patch 'learns' how to take stuff from surface rocks.
It's a slow, slow process—or set of processes—but
it's had time. Eventually patches meet as they ex-
pand. What happens then depends on just what their
compositions happen to be. I'd expect some weird
interactions while they join. Those could be going on
yet. That would explain why we saw differently colored areas. But it's only the terminal reactions."

Yoshii's words had come faster and faster. He was
developing his idea as he described it. Excitement
turned into awe and he whispered, "A polymer. A
single multiplex molecule, the size of this planet."

Carita was mute for a whole minute before she
murmured, "Whew! But why isn't the same stuff on
every airless body? . . . No wait. Stupid of me to ask.
This is the only one where conditions have been
right."

Yoshii nodded. "I suspect that what yellows the
rest is a carbon compound, too, but something formed
in space. You get some fairly complicated ones there,
you know. If that particular one can't react with the
organics I was talking about—too cold—then they
are a minor part of the downdrift compared to it. We
haven't noticed the same thing in other planetary
systems because they are all too young, and maybe

because none of them have made repeated passages through nebulae."

"You missed your calling," Carita said tenderly. "Should've been a scientist. Is it too late? We can go out, take samples, put 'em through our analyzers. When we get home, you can write a paper that'll have scholarships piled around you up to your bellybutton. Though I hope you'll keep on with the poetry. I like what you—"

A quiver went through the boat. "What the Finagle!" she exclaimed.

"A quake?" Yoshii asked.

"The prof's told us these planets are as far beyond quakes as a mummy is beyond hopscotch," Carita snapped.

Another tremor made slight noises throughout the hull. Yoshii reached for the searchlight switch. Carita caught his arm. "Hold that," she said. "The kzinti— No, unless they beef up that already wild boost they are under, they won't arrive for a couple more hours." Nevertheless he refrained.

The pair studied their instrument panel. "We've been tilted a bit," Yoshii pointed out. "Should we reset the landing jacks?"

"Let's wait and see," Carita said. "I'd guess the rock beneath has settled under our weight, or one layer has slid over another, or something like that. If it's reached a new equilibrium, we don't want to upset it by shifting mass around. No sense in moving yet, when we can't tell what the ground is like anywhere else."

"Right. I'm afraid, though, we can't relax as we had hoped."

"How much relaxing could we do anyway, with kzinti sniffing after us?"

"And Laurinda—" Yoshii whispered. Harshly: "Do

you want to take the controls, stand by to jump out
of here, in case? I'll snug things down and, yes,
throw a meal together."

Lightfoot under the low gravity, he descended aft
to the engine compartment. Delicate work needed
doing. The idling fusion generator must be shut down
entirely, lest its neutrino smoke betray the boat—not
that the kzinti could home in on it, but they would
know with certainty the humans were on Prima, and
in which quadrant. Batteries, isotopic and crystalline
as well as chemical, held energy for weeks of life
support and ordinary operations. Yet it had to be
possible to restart the generator instantly, full power
within a second, should there be a sudden need to
scramble. That meant disconnecting the safety inter-
locks. Yoshii fetched tools and got busy. The task was
demanding, but not too much for his spirit to wing
elsewhere in space, elsewhen in time—the Belt, Plateau, We Made It, *Rover's* folk on triumphal progress after their return. . . .

Carita's voice came over the intercom. "This is
dull duty. I think I will turn on the searchlight while
it's still safe to do so. Might get a clue to what caused
those jolts."

"Good idea," he agreed absent-mindedly, and
continued his task.

The metal around him throbbed. Small objects
rattled on the deck.

"Juan!" Carita shouted. "The, the material—it's
rippling, crawling—" The hull rocked. "I'm getting
us out of here!"

"Yes, do," he called back, and grabbed for the
nearest handhold.

Within its radiation shield, the generator hummed.
Needles sprang across dials, displays onto screens.
Yoshii felt the upward thrust of the deck against his

feet. It was slight. Carita was a careful pilot, applying barely sufficient boost to rise off the ground before she committed to a leap.

The boat screamed. Things tilted. Yoshii clung. Loose things hailed around him. A couple of them drew blood. The boat canted over, toppled, struck lengthwise, tolled so that he was half deafened.

Stillness crashed down, except for a shrill whistle that he knew too well. Air was escaping from one or more rents nearby. He hauled himself erect and out of his daze. The emergency valve had already shut, sealing off this section. He had to get through the lock built into it before the pressure differential made operation fatally slow.

Somehow he passed forth, and on along the companionway that was now a corridor, toward the control cabin. Lights were still shining, ventilators still whirring, and few articles lay strewn around. This was a good, sturdy craft, kept shipshape. How had she failed?

Carita met him in the entrance. "Hey, you sure got battered, didn't you? I was secured. Here, let me help you." She practically carried him to his chair, which she had adjusted for the new orientation. Meanwhile she talked on: "The trouble's with the landing gear, I think. Is that damn stuff a glue? No, how could it be? Take over. I'm going to suit up and go out for a look."

"Don't," he protested. "You might get stuck there, too."

"I'll be careful. Keep watch. If I don't make it back—" She stooped, brushed lips across his, and hurried aft.

His ears rang and pained him, his head ached, he was becoming conscious of bruises, but his eyes worked. The searchlight made clear the motion in the mantle. It was slight in amplitude, as thin as the layer was, and slow, but intricate, like wave patterns spreading from countless centers to form an ever-changing moiré. Those nodes were darker than the ripple-shadows and seemed to pass the darknesses on from one to the next, so that a shifting stipple went outward from the boat, across the dell floor and, as he watched, up the side. The hull rocked a little, off and on, in irregular wise.

"Do you read me?" he heard after a while. "I'm in the Number Two lock, outer valve open, looking over the lip."

"I read you," he answered unevenly. At least the radio system remained intact. "What do you see?"

"The same turbulence in the . . . stuff. Nothing clear aft, where the main damage is. The searchbeam doesn't diffuse, and—I'm off to inspect."

"Better not. If you lost your footing and fell down into—"

She barked scorn. "If you think I could, then I'm for sure the right person for this job." He clenched his fists but must needs admit that induction boots gave plenty of grip on the metal for a rockjack—a rockjill, she often called herself. "I'm crawling out. . . . Standing. . . . On my way." The hull pitched. "Hey! That damn near threw me." Starkly: "I think *Fido* just settled more at the after end."

"But into what?" he cried. "Solid rock?"

"No, I guess not. I do know what we *are* deep down into. . . . Okay, proceeding. Landing gear in sight now, spraddled against the sky. It's dark, I can't see much except stars. Let me unlimber my flashlight. . . . A-a-ah!" she nearly screamed.

He half rose in his seat. "What happened? Carita, dear, are you there?"

"Yes. A nasty shock, that sight. Listen, the Num-

ber Three leg is off the ground. The bottom end
sticks up—ragged, holes in it—like a badly corroded
thing that got so weak it tore apart when it came
under stress. . . . But Juan, this is melded steel and
titanium alloy. What could've eaten it?"

"We can guess," Yoshii said between his teeth.
"Come back."

"No, I need to see the rest. Don't worry, I'll creep
down the curve like a cat burglar. . . . I'm at the
socket of Number Two. I'm shining my light along
it. Yes. Nothing left of the foot. Seems to be sort
of—absorbed into the ground. Number One—more
yet is missing, and, yes, that's the unit which pulled
partly loose from its mounting and made the hole in
the engine compartment. I can see the skin ripped
and buckled—"

The boat swayed. Her nose twisted about and
lifted a few degrees as her tail sank. Groans went
through the hull.

"I'm okay, mate. Well anchored. But holy Finagle!
The stuff is going wild underneath. Has it come to a
boil?"

Yoshii could not see that where he was, but he did
spy the quickening and thickening of the wave fronts
farther off. Understanding blasted him. "Douse your
flash!" he yelled. "Get back inside!" He grabbed for
the searchlight switch as for the throat of a foeman.

"Hey, what is this?" Carita called.

"Douse your flash, I said. Can't you see, bright
light is what causes the trouble? Find your way by
the stars." He clutched his shoulders and shivered in
the dark. The boat shivered with him, diminuendo.

"I read you," Carita said faintly.

Yoshii darkened the cabin as well. "Let's meet in
my stateroom," he proposed. The sarcastically named
cubbyhole did not give on the outside. He groped till

he found it. When again he dared grant himself vision, he bent above the locker where a bottle was, shook his head, straightened, and stood looking at a photograph of Laurinda on the bulkhead.

Carita entered. Her coverall was wet and pungent. Sweat glistened on the dark face. "Haven't you poured me a drink?" she asked hoarsely.

"I decided that would be unwise."

"Maybe for you, sonny boy. Not for me." The Jinxian helped herself, tossed off two mouthfuls, and sighed. "That's better. Thank you very much."

Yoshii gestured at his bunk. It was roughly horizontal, that being how the polarizer field was ordinarily set in flight. They sat down on it, side by side. Her bravado dwindled. "So you know what's happened to us?" she murmured.

"I have a guess," Yoshii replied with care. "It depends on my idea of the supermolecule being correct."

"Say on."

"Well, you see, it grew. Or rather, I think, different ones grew till they met and linked up. There must have been all possible combinations, permutations of radicals and bases and—every kind of chemical unit. Cosmic radiation drives that kind of change. So does quantum mechanics, random effects; that was probably dominant in intergalactic space. So the chemistry . . . mutated. Whatever structure was better at assimilating fresh material would be favored. It would grow at the expense of the rest."

Carita whistled. "Natural selection, evolution? You mean the stuff's alive?"

"No, not like you and me or bacteria or even viruses. But it would develop components which could grab onto new atoms, and other components that are catalytic, and—and I think ways of passing an atom on from ring to ring until it's gone as far as there are receptors for it. That would leave room for taking up more at the near end. Because I think finally the molecule evolved beyond the point of depending on whatever fell its way from the skies. I think it began extracting matter from the planet, whenever it spread to where there was a suitable substance. Breaking down carbonates and silicates and—and incorporating metallic atoms too. Clathrate formation would promote growth, as well as chemical combination. But of course metal is ultra-scarce here, so the molecule became highly efficient at stealing it."

"At eating things." Carita stared before her. "That's close enough to life for me."

"The normal environment is low-energy," Yoshii said. "Things must go faster during the day. Not that there is much action then, either; nothing much to act on, any more. But we set down on our metal landing gear, and pumped out light-frequency quanta."

"And it . . . woke."

Yoshii grimaced but stayed clear of semantic argument. "It must be strongly bound to the underlying rock. It was quick to knit the feet of our landing jacks into that structure."

"And gnaw its way upward, till I—"

He caught her hand. "You couldn't have known. I didn't."

The deck swayed underfoot. The liquor sloshed in Carita's glass. "But we're blacked out now," she protested, as if to the devourer.

"We're radiating infrared," Yoshii answered. "The boat's warmer on the outside than her surroundings. Energy supply. The chemistry goes on, though slower. We can't stop it, not unless we want to freeze to death."

"How long have we got?" she whispered.

He bit his lip. "I don't know. If we last till sunrise we'll dissolve entirely soon after, like spooks in an ancient folk tale."

"That's more than a month away."

"I'd estimate that well before then, the hull will be eaten open. No more air."

"Our suits recycle. We can jury-rig other things to keep us alive."

"But the hull will weaken and collapse. Do you want to be tossed down into . . . that?" Yoshii sat straight. Resolution stiffened his tone. "I'm afraid we have no choice except to throw ourselves on the mercy of the kzinti. They must have arrived."

Carita ripped forth a string of oaths and obscenities, knocked back her drink, and rose. "*Shep* is still on the loose," she said.

Yoshii winced. "Man the control cabin. I'm going to suit up and get back into the engine compartment."

"What for?"

"Isn't it obvious? The energy boxes are stored there."

"Oh. Yes. You're thinking we'll have to take orbit under our own power and let the kzinti pick us up? I'm not keen on that."

"Nor I. But I don't imagine they'll be keen on landing here."

He rejoined her an hour later. By starlight she saw how he trembled. "I was too late," dragged from him. "Maybe if I hadn't had to operate the airlock hydraulics manually—What I found was a seething mass of—of—The entire locker where the boxes were is gone."

"That fast?" she wondered, stunned, though they had been in communication until he passed through into the after section. And then, slowly: "Well, the capacitors in those boxes are—were fully charged. Energy concentrated like the stuff's never known before. Too bad so much didn't poison it. Instead, it got a kick in the chemistry making it able to eat everything in three gulps. We're lucky the life-support batteries weren't there, too."

"Let's hope the kzinti want us enough to come down for us."

Shielding a flashlight with a clipboard, they activated the radio, standard-band broadcast. Yoshii spoke. "SOS. SOS. Two humans aboard a boat, marooned," he said dully. "We are sinking into a—solvent—the macromolecule—You doubtless know about it. Rescue requested.

"We can't lift by ourselves. The drive units in our spacesuits have only partial charge, insufficient to reach orbital speed in this field. We can't recharge. That equipment is gone. So are all the reserve energy boxes. We can flit a goodly distance around the planet or rise to a goodly height, but we can't escape.

"Please take us off. Please inform. We will keep our receiver open on this band, and continue transmission so you can locate us."

Having recorded his words, he set them to repeat directly on the carrier wave and leaned back. "Not the most eloquent speech ever made," he admitted. "But they won't care."

She took his hand. Heaven stood gleamful above them. Time passed. Occasionally the vessel moved a bit.

A spaceship flew low, from horizon to horizon. They had only the barest glimpse. Perhaps cameras took note of theirs.

Carita choked. "Alien."

"Kzin," Yoshii said. "Got to be."

"But I never heard of anything like—"

"Nor I. What did you see?"

"Big. Sphere with fins or flanges or—whatever they are—all around. Mirror-bright. Doesn't look like she's intended for planetfall."

Yoshii nodded. "Me too. I wanted to make sure of my impression, as fast as she went by. Just the same, I think we have a while to wait." He stood up. "Suppose I go fix us some sandwiches and also bring that bottle. We may as well take it easy. We've played our hand out."

"But won't they—Oh, yes, I see. That's no patrol craft. She was called off her regular service to come check Prima. We being found, she'll call Secunda for further orders, and relay our message to a translator there."

"About a five-minute transmission lag either way, at the present positions. A longer chain-of-command lag, I'll bet. Leave the intercom on for me, please, but just for the sake of my curiosity. You can talk to them as well as I can."

"There isn't a lot to say," Carita agreed.

Yoshii was in the galley when he heard the computer-generated voice: "Werlith-Commandant addressing you directly. Identify yourselves."

"Carita Fenger, Juan Yoshii, of the ship *Rover*, stuck on Prima—on Planet One. Your crew has seen us. I suppose they realize our plight. We're being . . . swallowed. Please take us off. If your vessel here can't do it, please dispatch one that can. Over."

Silence hummed and rustled. Yoshii kept busy.

He was returning when the voice struck again: "We lost two boats with a total of eight heroes aboard before we established the nature of the peril. I will not waste time explaining it to you. Most certainly I will not hazard another craft and more lives. On the basis of observations made by the crew of *Sun Defier*, if you keep energy output minimal you have approximately five hundred hours left to spend as you see fit."

A click signalled the cutoff.

Werlith-Commandant had been quite kindly by his lights, Yoshii acknowledged.

He entered the control cabin. "I'm sorry, Carita," he said.

She rose and went to meet him. Starlight guided her through shadows and glinted off her hair and a few tears. "I'm sorry too, Juan," she gulped. "Now let's both of us stop apologizing. The thing has happened, that's all. Look, we can try a broadcast that maybe they'll pick up in *Shep*, so they'll know. They won't dare reply, I suppose, but it's nice to think they might know. First let's eat, though, and have a couple of drinks, and talk, and, and go to bed. The same bed."

He lowered his tray to the chart shelf. "I'm exhausted," he mumbled.

She threw her arms around him and drew his head down to her opulent bosom. "So'm I, chum. And if you want to spend the rest of what time we've got being faithful, okay. But let's stay together. It's cold out there. Even in a narrow bunk, let's be together while we can."

16

The sun in the screen showed about half the Sol-disc at Earth. Its light equaled more than 10,000 full Lunas, red rather than off-white but still ample to make Secunda shine. The planetary crescent was mostly yellowish-brown, little softened by a tenuous atmosphere of methane with traces of carbon dioxide and ammonia. A polar cap brightened its wintered northern hemisphere, a shrunken one the southern. The latter was all water ice, the former enlarged by carbon dioxide and ammonia that had frozen out. These two gases did it everywhere at night, most times, evaporating again by day in summer and the tropics, so that sunrises and sunsets were apt to be violent. Along the terminator glittered a storm of fine silicate dust mingled with ice crystals.

The surface bore scant relief, but the slow rotation, 57 hours, was bringing into view a gigantic crater and a number of lesser neighbors. Probably a moon had crashed within the past billion years; the scars remained, though any orbiting fragments had dissipated. A sister moon survived, three-fourths Lunar diameter, dark yellowish like so many bodies in this system.

Thus did Tregennis interpret what he and Ryan saw as they sat in *Rover*'s saloon watching the approach. Data taken from afar, before the capture, helped him fill in details. Talking about them was an anodyne for both men.

Markham entered. Silence rushed through like a wind.

"I have an announcement," he said after a moment.

Neither prisoner stirred.

"We are debarking in half an hour," he went on. "I have arranged for your clothing and hygienic equipment to be brought along. Including your medication, Professor."

"Thank you," Tregennis said flatly.

"Why shouldn't he?" Ryan sneered. "Keep the animals alive till the master race can think of a need for them. I wonder if he'll share in the feast."

Markham's stiffness became rigidity. "Have a care," he warned. "I have been very patient with you."

During the 50-odd hours of 3-g flight—during which Hraou-Captain allowed the polarizer to lighten weight—he had received no word from either, nor eye contact. To be sure, he had been cultivating the acquaintance of such kzinti among the prize crew as deigned to talk with him. "Don't provoke me."

"All right," Ryan answered. Unable to resist: "Not but what I couldn't put up with a lot of provocation myself, if I were getting paid what they must be paying you."

Markham's cheekbones reddened. "For your information, I have never had one mark of recompense, nor ever been promised any. Not one."

Tregennis regarded him in mild amazement. "Then why have you turned traitor?" he asked.

"I have not. On the contrary—" Markham stood for several seconds before he plunged. "See here, if you will listen, if you will treat me like a human being, you can learn some things you will be well advised to know."

Ryan scowled at his beer glass, shrugged, nodded, and grumbled, "Might as well."

"Can you talk freely?" Tregennis inquired.

Markham sat down. "I have not been forbidden to. Of course, what I have been told so far is quite limited. However, certain kzinti, including Hraou-Captain, have been reasonably forthcoming. They have been bored by their uneventful duty, are intrigued by me, and see no immediate threat to security."

"I can understand that," said Tregennis dryly.

Markham leaned forward. His assurance had shrunk enough to notice. He tugged his half-beard. His tone became earnest:

"Remember, for a dozen Earth-years I fought the kzinti. I was raised to it. They had driven my mother

into exile. The motto of the House of Reichstein was
'*Ehre*—' well, in English, 'Honor Through Service.'
She changed it to 'No Surrender.' Most people had
long since given up, you know. They accepted the
kzin order of things. Many had been born into it, or
had only dim childhood memories of anything before. Revolt would have brought massacre. Aristocrats who stayed on Wunderland—the majority—saw
no alternative to cooperating with the occupation
forces, at least to the extent of preserving order
among humans and keeping industries in operation.
They were apt to look on us who fought as dangerous
extremists. It was a seductive belief. As the years
wore on, with no end in sight, more and more members of the resistance despaired. Through the aristocrats at home they negotiated terms permitting them
to come back and pick up the pieces of their lives.
My mother was among those who had the greatness
of spirit to refuse the temptation. 'No Surrender.' "

Ryan still glowered, but Tregennis said with a
dawn of sympathy, "Then the hyperdrive armada
arrived and she was vindicated. Were you not glad?"

"Of course," Markham said. "We jubilated, my
comrades and I, after we were through weeping for
the joy and glory of it. That was a short-lived happiness. We had work to do. At first it was clean. The
fighting had caused destruction. The navy from Sol
could spare few units; it must go on to subdue the
kzinti elsewhere. On the men of the resistance fell
the tasks of rescue and relief.

"Then as we returned to our homes on Wunderland—
I and many others for the first time in our lives—we
found that the world for whose liberation we had
fought, the world of our vision and hope, was gone,
long gone. Everywhere was turmoil. Mobs stormed
manor after manor of the 'collaborationist' aristocrats,

lynched, raped, looted, burned—as if those same proles had not groveled before the kzinti and kept war production going for them! Lunatic political factions rioted against each other or did actual armed combat. Chaos brought breakdown, want, misery, death.

"My mother took a lead in calling for a restoration of law. We did it, we soldiers from space. What we did was often harsh, but necessary. A caretaker government was established. We thought that we could finally get on with our private lives—though I, for one, busied myself in the effort to build up Centaurian defense forces, so that never again could my people be overrun.

"In the years that my back was turned, they, my people, were betrayed." Markham choked on his bitterness.

"Do you mean the new constitution, the democratic movement in general?" Tregennis prompted.

Markham recovered and nodded. "No one denied that reform, reorganization was desirable. I will concede, if only because our time to talk now is limited, most of the reformers meant well. They did not foresee the consequences of what they enacted. I admit I did not myself. But I was busy, often away for long periods of time. My mother, on our estates, saw what was happening, and piece by piece made it clear to me."

"Your estates. You kept them, then. I gather most noble families kept a substantial part of their former holdings; and Wunderland's House of Patricians is the upper chamber of its parliament. Surely you don't think you have come under a . . . mobocracy."

"But I do! At least, that is the way it is tending. That is the way it will go, to completion, to destruction, if it is not stopped. A political Gresham's Law prevails; the bad drives out the good. Look at me, for example. I have one vote, by hereditary right, in the Patricians, and it is limited to federal matters. To take a meaningful role in restoring a proper society— through enactment of proper laws—a role which it is my hereditary duty to take—I must begin by being elected a consul of my state, Braefell. That would give me a voice in choosing who goes to the House of Delegates— No matter details. I went into politics."

"Holding your well-bred nose," Ryan murmured.

Markham flushed again. "I am for the people. The honest, decent, hard-working, sensible common people, who know in their hearts that society is tradition and order and reverence, not a series of cheap bargains between selfish interests. One still finds them in the countryside. It is in the cities that the maggots are, the mobs, the criminals, the parasites, the . . . politicians."

For the first time, Ryan smiled a little. "Can't say I admire the political process either. But I will say the cure is not to domesticate the lower class. How about letting everybody see to his own business, with a few cops and courts to keep things from getting too hairy?"

"I heard that argument often enough. It is stupid. It assumes the obvious falsehood that an individual can function in isolation like an atom. Oh, I did my share of toadying. I shook the clammy hands and said the clammy words, but it was hypocritical ritual, a sugar coating over the cynicism and corruption—"

"In short, you lost."

"I learned better than to try."

Ryan started to respond but checked himself. Markham smiled like a death's head. "Thereupon I decided to call back the kzinti, is that what you wish to say?" he gibed. Seriously: "No, it was not that simple at all. I had had dealings with them throughout my war career, negotiations, exchanges, interrogation and care of prisoners, the sort of relationships one always has with an opponent. They came to fascinate me and I learned everything about them that I could. The more I knew, the more effective a freedom fighter I would be, not so?

"After the . . . liberation, my knowledge and my reputation caused me to have still more to do with them. There were mutual repatriations to arrange. There were kzinti who had good cause to stay behind. Some had been born in the Centaurian System; the second and later fleets carried females. Others came to join such kinfolk, or on their own, as fugitives, because their society too was in upheaval and many of them actually admired us, now that we had fought successfully. Remember, most of those newcomers arrived on human hyperdrive ships. This was official policy, in the hope of earning goodwill, of learning more about kzinti in general, and of—frankly—having possible hostages. Even so, they were often subject to cruel discrimination or outright persecution. What could I do but intervene in their behalf? They, or their brothers, had been brave and honorable enemies. It was time to become friends."

"That was certainly a worthy feeling," Tregennis admitted.

Markham made a chopping gesture. "Meanwhile I not only grew more and more aware of the rot in Wunderland, I discovered how much I had been lied to. The kzinti were never monsters, as propaganda had claimed. They were relentless at first and strict afterward, yes. They imposed their will. But it was a dynamic will serving a splendid vision. They were not wantonly cruel, nor extortionate, nor even pettily thievish. Humans who obeyed kzin law enjoyed its protection, its order, and its justice. Their lives went on peacefully, industriously, with old folkways respected—by the commoners *and* the kzinti. Most hardly ever saw a kzin. The Great Houses of Wunderland were the intermediaries, and woe betide the human lord who abused the people in his care. Oh, no matter his rank, he must defer to the lowliest kzin. But he received due honor for what he was, and could look forward to his sons rising higher, his grandsons to actual partnership."

"In the conquest of the galaxy," Ryan said.

"Well, the kzinti have their faults, but they are not like the Slavers that archeologists have found traces of, from a billion years ago or however long it was. Men who fought the kzinti and men who served them were more fully *men* than ever before or since. My mother first said this to me, years afterward, my mother whose word had been 'No Surrender.'"

Markham glanced at his watch. "We must leave soon," he reminded. "I didn't mean to go on at such length. I don't expect you to agree with me. I do urge you to think, think hard, and meanwhile cooperate."

Regardless, Tregennis asked in his disarming fashion, "Did you actually decide to work for a kzin restoration? Isn't that the sort of radicalism you oppose?"

"My decision did not come overnight either," Markham replied, "nor do I want kzin rule again over my people. It would be better than what they have now, but manliness of their own is better still. Earth is the real enemy, rich fat Earth, its bankers and hucksters and political panderers, its vulgarity and whorishness that poison our young everywhere—on your world, too, Professor. A strong planet Kzin will challenge humans to strengthen themselves. Those who do not purge out the corruption will die. The rest, clean, will make a new peace, a brotherhood, and go on to take possession of the universe."

"Together with the kzinti," Ryan said.

Markham nodded. "And perhaps other worthy races. We shall see."

"I don't imagine anybody ever promised you this."

"Not in so many words. You are shrewd, Quartermaster. But shrewdness is not enough. There is such a thing as intuition, the sense of destiny."

Markham waved a hand. "Not that I had a religious experience. I began by entrusting harmless, perfectly sincere messages to kzinti going home, messages for their authorities. 'Please suggest how our two species can reach mutual understanding. What can I do to help bring a détente?' Things like that. A few kzinti do still travel in and out, you know, on human ships, by prearrangement. They generally come to consult or debate about what matters of mutual concern our species have these days, diplomatic, commercial, safety-related. Some do other things, clandestinely. We haven't cut off the traffic on that account. It is slight—and, after all, the exchange helps us plant our spies in their space.

"The responses I got were encouraging. They led to personal meetings, even occasionally to coded hyperwave communications; we have a few relays in kzin space, you know, by agreement. The first requests I got were legitimate by anyone's measure. The kzinti asked for specific information, no state secrets, merely data they could not readily obtain. I felt that by aiding them toward a better knowledge of us I was doing my race a valuable service. But of course I could not reveal it."

"No, you had your own little foreign policy," Ryan scoffed. "And one thing led to another, also inside your head, till you were sending stuff on the theory and practice of hyperdrive which gave them a ten- or twenty-year leg up on their R and D."

Markham's tone was patient. "They would inevitably have gotten it. Only by taking part in events can we hope to exercise any influence."

Again he consulted his watch. "We had better go," he said. "They will bring us to their base. You will be meeting the commandant. Perhaps what I have told will be of help to you."

"How about *Rover*?" Ryan inquired. "I hope you've explained to them she isn't meant for planetfall."

"That was not necessary," Markham said, irritated. "They know space architecture as well as we do—possibly better than you do, Quartermaster. We will go down in a boat from the warship. They will put our ship on the moon."

"What? Why not just in parking orbit?"

"I'll explain later. We must report now for debarkation. Have no fears. The kzinti won't willingly damage *Rover*. If they can—if we think of some way to prevent future human expeditions here that does not involve returning her—we'll keep her. The hyperdrive makes her precious. Otherwise *Kzarr-Siu—Vengeful Slasher*, the warship—is the only vessel currently in this system which has been so outfitted. They'll put *Rover* on the moon for safety's sake. Secunda orbits have become too crowded. The moon's gravity is low enough that it won't harm a freightship like this. Now come."

Markham rose and strode forth. Ryan and Tregennis followed. The Hawaiian nudged the Plateaunian and made little circling motions with his forefinger near his temple. Unwontedly bleak of countenance, the astronomer nodded, then whispered, "Be careful. I have read history. All too often, his kind is successful."

17

Kzinti did not use their gravity polarizers to maintain a constant, comfortable weight within spacecraft—unless accelerations got too high even for them to tolerate. The boat left with a roar of power. Humans sagged in their seats. Tregennis whitened. The thin flesh seemed to pull back over the bones of his face, the beaky nose stood out like a crag and blood trickled from it. "Hey, easy, boy," Ryan gasped. "Do you want to lose this man . . . already?"

Markham spoke to Hraou-Captain, who made a contemptuous noise but then yowled at the pilot. Weightlessness came as an abrupt benediction. For a minute silence prevailed, except for the heavy breathing of the Wunderlander and the Hawaiian, the rattling in and out of the old Plateaunian's.

Harnessed beside Tregennis, Ryan examined him as well as he could before muttering, "I guess he'll be all right in a while, if that snotbrain will take a little care." Raising his eyes, he looked past the other, out the port. "What's that?"

Close by, a kilometer or two, a small spacecraft—the size and lines indicated a ground-to-orbit shuttle—was docked at a framework which had been assembled around a curiously spheroidal dark mass, a couple of hundred meters in diameter. The framework secured and supported machinery which was carrying out operations under the direction of suited kzinti who flitted about with drive units on their backs. Stars peered through the lattice. In the distance passed a glimpse of *Rover*, moon-bound, and the warship.

The boat glided by. A new approach curve computed, the pilot applied thrust, this time about a single g's worth. Hraou-Captain registered impatience at the added waiting aboard. Markham did not venture to address him again. It must have taken courage to do so at all, when he wasn't supposed to defile the language with his mouth.

Instead the Wunderlander said to Ryan, on a note of awe, "That is doubtless one of their iron sources. Recently arrived, I would guess, and cooled down enough for work to commence on it. From what I have heard, a body that size will quickly be reduced."

Ryan stared at him, forgetting hostility in surprise. "Iron? I thought there was hardly any in this system. What it has ought to be at the center of the planets. Don't the kzinti import their metals for construction?"

Markham shook his head. "No, that would be quite impractical. They have few hyperdrive ships as yet—I told you *Vengeful Slasher* alone is so outfitted here, at present. Once the transports had brought personnel and the basic equipment, they went back for duty closer to home. Currently a warship calls about twice a year to bring fresh workers and needful items. It relieves the one on guard, which carries back kzinti being rotated. A reason for choosing this sun was precisely that humans won't suspect anything important can ever be done at it." He hesitated. "Except pure science. The kzinti did overlook that."

"Well, where do they get their metals? Oh, the lightest ones, aluminum, uh, beryllium, magnesium, . . . manganese?—I suppose those exist in ordinary ores. But I don't imagine those ores are anything but scarce and low-grade. And iron—"

"The asteroid belt. The planet that came too close to the sun. Disruption exposed its core. The metal content is low compared to what it would be in a later-generation world, but when you have a whole planet, you get an abundance. They have had to bring in certain elements from outside, nickel, cobalt, copper, et cetera, but mostly to make alloys. Small quantities suffice."

Tregennis had evidently not fainted. His eyelids fluttered open. "Hold," he whispered. "Those asteroids . . . orbit within . . . less than half a million kilometers . . . of the sun surface." He panted feebly before adding, "It may be a . . . very late type M . . . but nevertheless, the effective temperature—" His voice trailed off.

The awe returned to Markham's. "They have built a special tug."

"What sort?" Ryan asked.

"In principle, like the kind we know. Having found a desirable body, it lays hold with a grapnel field. I think this vessel uses a gravity polarizer system rather than electromagnetics. The kzinti originated that technology, remember. The tug draws the object into the desired orbit and releases it to go to its destination. The tug is immensely powerful. It can handle not simply large rocks like what you saw, but whole asteroids of reasonable size. As they near Secunda— tangential paths, of course—it works them into planetary orbit. That's why local space is too crowded for the kzinti to leave *Rover* in it unmanned. Besides ferrous masses on hand, two or three new ones are usually en route, and not all the tailings of worked-out old ones get swept away."

"But the heat near the sun," Ryan objected. "The crew would roast alive. I don't see how they can trust robotics alone. If nothing else, let the circuits get too hot and—"

"The tug has a live crew," Markham said. "It's built double-hulled and mirror-bright, with plenty of radiating surfaces. But mainly it's ship size, not boat size, because it loads up with water ice before each mission. There is plenty of that around the big plan-

ets, you know, chilled well below minus a hundred
degrees. Heated, melted, evaporated, vented, it main-
tains an endurable interior until it has been spent."

"I thought we . . . found traces of water and OH
. . . in a ring around the sun," Tregennis breathed.
"Could it actually be—?"

"I don't know how much ice the project has con-
sumed to date," Markham said, "but you must agree
it is grandly conceived. That is a crew of heroes.
They suffer, they dare death each time, but their will
prevails."

Ryan rubbed his chin. "I suppose otherwise the
only spacecraft are shuttles. And the warcraft and
her boats."

"They are building more." Markham sounded
proud. "And weapons and support machinery. This
will be an industrial as well as a naval base."

"For the next war—" Tregennis seemed close to
tears. Ryan patted his hand. Silence took over.

The boat entered atmosphere, which whined as
she decelerated around the globe. A dawn storm,
grit and ice, obscured the base, but the humans
made out that it was in the great crater, presumably
because the moonfall had brought down valuable
ores and caused more to spurt up from beneath.
Interconnected buildings made a web across several
kilometers, with a black central spider. Doubtless
much lay underground. An enterprise like this was
large-scale or it was worthless. True, it had to start
small, precariously—the first camp, the assembling
of life support systems and food production facilities
and a hospital for victims of disasters such as were
inevitable when you drove hard ahead with your
work on a strange world—but demonic energy had
joined the exponential-increase powers of automated
machines to bring forth this city of warriors.

No, Ryan thought, a city of workers in the service of future warriors. Thus far few professional fighters would be present except the crew of *Vengeful Slasher*. They weren't needed . . . yet. The warship was on hand against unlikely contingencies. Well, in this case kzin paranoia had paid off.

The pilot made an instrument landing into a cradle. Ryan spied more such units, three of them holding shuttles. The field on which they stood, though paved, must often be treacherous because of drifted dust. Secunda had no unfrozen water to cleanse its air; and the air was a chill wisp. Most of the universe is barren. Hawaii seemed infinitely far away.

A gang tube snaked from a ziggurat-like terminal building. Airlocks linked. An armed kzin entered and saluted. Hraou-Captain gestured at the humans and snarled an imperative before he went out. Markham unharnessed. "I am to follow him," he said. "You go with this guard. Quarters are prepared. Behave yourselves and . . . I will do my best for you."

Ryan rose. Two-thirds Earth weight felt good. He collected his and Tregennis' bags in his right hand and gave the astronomer his left arm for support. Kzinti throughout a cavernous main room stared as the captives appeared. They didn't goggle like humans, they watched like cats. Several naked tails switched to and fro. An effort had been made to brighten the surroundings, a huge mural of some hero in hand-to-hand combat with a monster; the blood jetted glaring bright.

The guard led his charges down corridors which pulsed with the sounds of construction. At last he opened a door, waved them through, and closed it behind them. They heard a lock click shut.

The room held a bed and a disposal unit, meant

for kzinti but usable by humans; the bed was ample
for two, and by dint of balancing and clinging you
could take care of sanitation. "I better help you till
you feel better, Prof," Ryan offered. "Meanwhile,
why don't you lie down? I'll unpack." The bags and
floor must furnish storage space. Kzinti seldom went
in for clothes or for carrying personal possessions
around.

They did hate sensory deprivation, still more than
humans do. There was no screen, but a port showed
the spacefield. The terminator storm was dying out
as the sun rose higher, and the view cleared fast.
Under a pale red sky, the naval complex came to an
end some distance off. Tawny sand reached onward,
strewn with boulders. In places, wind had swept
clear the fused crater floor. It wasn't like lava, more
like dark glass. Huge though the bowl was, Secunda—
much less dense than Earth, but significantly larger—
had a wide enough horizon that the nearer wall
jutted above it in the west, a murky palisade.

Tregennis took Ryan's advice and stretched himself out. The quartermaster smiled and came to remove
his shoes for him. "Might as well be comfortable,"
Ryan said, "or as nearly as we can without beer."

"And without knowledge of our fates," the Plateaunian said low. "Worse, the fates of our friends."

"At least they are out of Markham's filthy hands."

"Kamehameha, please. Watch yourself. We shall
have to deal with him. And he—I think he too is
feeling shocked and lonely. He didn't expect this
either. His orders were merely to hamper exploration beyond the limits of human space. He wants to
spare us. Give him the chance."

"Ha! I'd rather give a shark that kind of chance.
It's less murderous."

"Oh, now, really."

Ryan thumped fist on wall. "Who do you suppose put that kzin up to attacking Bob Saxtorph back in Tiamat? It has to have been Markham, when his earlier efforts failed. Nothing else makes sense. And this, mind you, this was when he had no particular reason to believe our expedition mattered as far as the kzinti were concerned. They hadn't trusted him with any real information. But he went ahead anyway and tried to get a man killed to stop us. That shows you what value he puts on human life."

"Well, maybe . . . maybe he is deranged," Tregennis sighed. "Would you bring me a tablet, please? I see a water tap and bowl over there."

"Sure. Heart, huh? Take it easy. You shouldn't've come along, you know."

Tregennis smiled. "Medical science has kept me functional far longer than I deserve.

" *'But fill me with the old familiar Juice,*
" *'Methinks I might recover by-and-by!' "*

Ryan lifted the white head and brought the bowl, from which a kzin would have lapped, carefully close to the lips. "You've got more heart than a lot of young bucks I could name," he said.

Time crept past.

The door opened. "Hey, food?" Ryan asked.

Markham confronted them, an armed kzin at his back. He was again pallid and stiff of countenance. "Come," he said harshly.

Rested, Tregennis walked steady-footed beside Ryan. They went through a maze of featureless passages with shut doors, coldly lighted, throbbing or buzzing. When they encountered other kzinti they felt the carnivore stares follow them.

After a long while they stopped at a larger door. This part of the warren looked like officer country, though Ryan couldn't be sure when practically everything he saw was altogether foreign to him. The guard let them in and followed.

The chamber beyond was windowless, its sole ornamentation a screen on which a computer projected colored patterns. Kzin-type seats, desk, and electronics suggested an office, but big and mostly empty. In one corner a plastic tub had been placed, about three meters square. Within stood some apparatus, and a warrior beside, and the drug-dazed telepath huddled at his feet.

The prisoners' attention went to Hraou-Captain and another—lean and grizzled by comparison—seated at the desk. "Show respect," Markham directed. "You meet Werlith-Commandant."

Tregennis bowed, Ryan slopped a soft salute.

The head honcho spat and rumbled. Markham turned to the men. "Listen," he said. "I have been in . . . conference, and am instructed to tell you . . . *Fido* has been found."

Tregennis made a tiny noise of pain. Ryan hunched his shoulders and said, "That's what they told you."

"It is true," Markham insisted. "The boat went to Prima. The interrogation aboard *Rover* led to a suspicion that the escapers might try that maneuver. *Ya-Nar-Ksshinn*—call it *Sun Defier*, the asteroid tug, was prospecting. The commandant ordered it to Prima, since it could get there very fast. By then *Fido* was trapped on the surface. Fenger and Yoshii broadcast a call for help, so *Sun Defier* located them. Just lately, *Fido* has made a new broadcast which the kzinti picked up. You will listen to the recording."

Werlith-Commandant condescended to touch a control. From the desk communicator, wavery through a seething of radio interference, Juan Yoshii's voice came forth.

"Hello, Bob, Dorcas, Lau-laurinda—Kam, Arthur,

. . . Ulf, if you hear—hello from Carita and me. We'll set this to repeat on different bands, hoping you'll happen to tune it in somewhere along the line. It's likely goodbye."

"No," said Carita's voice, "it's 'good luck.' To you. Godspeed."

"Right," Yoshii agreed. "Before we let you know what the situation is, we want to beg you, don't ever blame yourselves. There was absolutely no way to foresee it. And the universe is full of much worse farms we could have bought.

"However—" Unemotionally, now and then aided by his companion, he described things as they were. "We'll hang on till the end, of course," he finished. "Soon we'll see what we can rig to keep us alive. After the hull collapses altogether, we'll flit off in search of bare rock to sit on, if any exists. Do not, repeat do not risk yourselves in some crazy rescue attempt. Maybe you could figure out a safe way to do it if you had the time and no kzinti on your necks. Or maybe you could talk them into doing it. But neither one is in the cards, eh? You concentrate on getting the word home."

"We mean that," Carita said.

"Laurinda, I love you," Yoshii said fast. "Farewell, fare always well, darling. What really hurts is knowing you may not make it back. But if you do, you have your life before you. Be happy."

"We aren't glum." Carita barked a laugh. "I might wish Juan weren't quite so noble, Laurinda, dear. But it's no big thing either way, is it? Not any more. Good luck to all of you."

The recording ended. Tregennis gazed beyond the room—at this new miracle of nature? Ryan stood swallowing tears, his fists knotted.

"You see what Saxtorph's recklessness has caused," Markham said.

"No!" Ryan shouted. "The kzinti could lift them off! But they—tell his excellency yonder they're afraid to!"

"I will not. You must be out of your mind. Besides, *Sun Defier* cannot land on a planet, and carries no auxiliary."

"A shuttle—No. But a boat from the warship."

"Why? What have Yoshii and Fenger done to merit saving, at hazard to the kzinti for whom they only want to make trouble? Let them be an object lesson, gentlemen. If you have any care whatsoever for the rest of your party, help us retrieve them before it is too late."

"I don't know where they are. Not on P-prima, for sure."

"They must be found."

"Well, send that damned tug."

Markham shook his head. "It has better uses. It was about ready to return anyway. It will take Secunda orbit and wait for an asteroid that is due in shortly." He spoke like a man using irrelevancies to stave off the moment when he must utter his real meaning.

"Okay, the warship."

"It too has other duties. I've told them about Saxtorph's babbling of kamikaze tactics. Hraou-Captain must keep his vessel prepared to blow that boat out of the sky if it comes near—until Saxtorph's gang is under arrest, or dead. He will detach his auxiliaries to search."

"Let him," Ryan jeered. "Bob's got this whole system to skulk around in."

"Tertia is the first place to try."

"Go ahead. That old fox is good at finding burrows."

Werlith-Commandant growled. Markham grew paler yet, bowed, turned on Ryan and said in a rush: "Don't waste more time. The master wants to resolve this business as soon as possible. He wants Saxtorph and company preferably alive, dead will do, but disposed of, so we can get on with the business of explaining away at Wunderland what happened to *Rover*. You will cooperate."

Sweat studded Ryan's face. "I will?"

"Yes. You shall accompany the search party. Broadcast your message in Hawaiian. Persuade them to give themselves up."

Ryan relieved himself of several obscenities.

"Be reasonable," Markham almost pleaded. "Think what has happened with *Fido*. The rest can only die in worse ways, unless you bring them to their senses."

Ryan shifted his feet wide apart, thrust his head forward, and spat, "No surrender."

Markham took a backward step. "What?"

"Your mother's motto, ratcat-lover. Have you forgotten? How proud of you she's going to be when she hears."

Markham closed his eyes. His lips moved. He looked forth again and said in a string of whipcracks: "You will obey. Werlith-Commandant orders it. Look yonder. Do you see what is in the corner? He expected stubbornness."

Ryan and Tregennis peered. They recognized frame and straps, pincers and electrodes; certain items were less identifiable. The telepath slumped at the feet of the torturer.

"Hastily improvised," Markham said, "but the database has a full account of human physiology, and I made some suggestions as well. The subject will not die under interrogation as often happened in the past."

Ryan's chest heaved. "If that thing can read my mind, he knows—"

Markham sighed. "We had better get to work." He glanced at the kzin officers. They both made a gesture. The guard sprang to seize Ryan from behind. The Hawaiian yelled and struggled, but that grip was unbreakable by a human.

The torturer advanced. He laid hands on Tregennis.

"Watch, Ryan," Markham said raggedly. "Let us know when you have had enough."

The torturer half dragged, half marched Tregennis across the room, held him against the wall, and, claws out on the free hand, ripped the clothes from his scrawniness.

"That's your idea, Markham!" Ryan bellowed. "You unspeakable—"

"Hold fast, Kamehameha," Tregennis called in his thin voice. "Don't yield."

"Art, oh, Art—"

The kzin secured the man to the frame. He picked up the electrodes and applied them. Tregennis screamed. Yet he modulated it: "Pain has a saturation point, Kamehameha. Hold fast!"

The business proceeded.

"You win, you Judas, okay, you win," Ryan wept.

Tregennis could no longer make words, merely noises.

Markham inquired of the officers before he told Ryan, "This will continue a few minutes more, to drive the lesson home. Given proper care and precautions, he should still be alive to accompany the search party." Markham breathed hard. "To make sure of your cooperation, do you hear? This is your fault!" he shrieked.

18

"No," Saxtorph had said. "I think we'd better stay put for the time being."

Dorcas had looked at him across the shoulder of Laurinda, whom she held close, Laurinda who had just heard her man say farewell. The cramped command section was full of the girl's struggles not to cry. "If they thought to check Prima immediately, they will be at Tertia before long," the captain's wife had stated.

Saxtorph had nodded. "Yah, sure. But they'll have a lot more trouble finding us where we are than if we were in space, even free-falling with a cold generator. We could only boost a short ways, you see, else they'd acquire our drive-spoor if they've gotten anywhere near. They'd have a fairly small volume for their radars to sweep."

"But to sit passive! What use?"

"I didn't mean that. Thought you knew me better. Got an idea I suspect you can improve on."

Laurinda had lifted her head and sobbed, "Couldn't we . . . m-make terms? If we surrender to them . . . they rescue Juan and, and Carita?"

" 'Fraid not, honey," Saxtorph had rumbled. Anguish plowed furrows down his face. "Once we call 'em, they'll have a fix on us, and what's left to dicker with? Either we give in real nice or they lob a shell. They'd doubtless like to have us for purposes of faking a story, but we aren't essential—they hold three as is—and they've written *Fido*'s people off. I'm sorry."

Laurinda had freed herself from the mate's embrace, stood straight, swallowed hard. "You must be right," she had said in a voice taking on an edge.

"What can we do? Thank you, Dorcas, dear, but I, I'm ready now . . . for whatever you need."

"Good lass." The older woman had squeezed her hand before asking the captain: "If we don't want to be found, shouldn't we fetch back the relay from above?"

Saxtorph had considered. The same sensitivity which had received, reconstructed, and given to the boat a radio whisper from across more than two hundred million kilometers, could betray his folk. After a moment: "No, leave it. A small object, after all, which we've camouflaged pretty well, and its emission blends into the sun's radio background. If the kzinti get close enough to detect it, they'll be onto us anyway."

"You don't imagine we can hide here forever."

"Certainly not. They can locate us in two, three weeks at most if they work hard. However, meanwhile they won't know for sure we are on Tertia. They'll spread themselves thin looking elsewhere, too, or they'll worry. Never give the enemy a free ride."

"But you say you have something better in mind than simply distracting them for a while."

"Well, I have a sort of a notion. It's loony as it stands, but maybe you can help me refine it. At best, we'll probably get ourselves killed, but plain to see, Markham's effort to cut a deal has not worked out, and—we can hope for some revenge."

Laurinda's albino eyes had flared.

—"*Aloha, hoapilina.*—"

Crouched over the communicator, Saxtorph heard the Hawaiian through. English followed, the dragging tone of a broken man:

"Well, that was to show you this is honest, Bob, if you're listening. The kzinti don't have a telepath along, because they know they don't need the poor creature. They do require me to go on in a language their translator can handle. Anyway, I don't suppose you remember much Polynesian.

"We're orbiting Tertia in a boat from the Prowling Hunter warship. 'We' are her crew, plus a couple of marines, plus Arthur Tregennis and myself. Markham stayed on Secunda. He's a kzin agent. Maybe you've gotten the message from *Fido*. I'm afraid the game's played out, Bob. I tried to resist, but they tortured not me—poor Art. I soon couldn't take it. He's alive, sort of. They give you three hours to call them. That's in case you've scrammed to the far ends of the system and may not be tuned in right now. You'll've noticed this is a powerful planar 'cast. They think they're being generous. If they haven't heard in three hours, they'll torture Art some more. Please don't let that happen!" Ryan howled through the wail that Laurinda tried to stifle. "Please call back!"

Saxtorph waited a while, but there was nothing further, only the hiss of the red sun. He took his finger from the transmission key, which he had not pressed, and twisted about to look at his companions. Light streaming wanly through the westside port found Dorcas' features frozen. Laurinda's writhed; her mouth was stretched out of shape.

"So," he said. "Three hours. Dark by then, as it happens."

"They hurt him," Laurinda gasped. "That good old man, they took him and hurt him."

Dorcas peeled lips back from teeth. "Shrewd," she said. "Markham in kzin pay? I'm not totally surprised. I don't know how it was arranged, but I'm not too surprised. He suggested this, I think. The kzinti probably don't understand us that well."

"We can't let them go on . . . with the professor," Laurinda shrilled. "We can't, no matter what."

"He's been like a second father to you, hasn't he?" Dorcas asked almost absently. Unspoken: But your young man is down on Prima, and the enemy will let him die there.

"No argument," Saxtorph said. "We won't. We've got a few choices, though. Kzinti aren't sadistic. Merciless, but not sadistic the way too many humans are. They don't torture for fun, or even spite. They won't if we surrender. Or if we die. No point in it then."

Dorcas grinned in a rather horrible fashion. "The chances are we'll die if we do surrender," she responded. "Not immediately, I suppose. Not till they need our corpses, or till they see no reason to keep us alive. Again, quite impersonal."

"I don't feel impersonal," Saxtorph grunted.

Laurinda lifted her hands. The fingers were crooked like talons. "We made other preparations against them. Let's do what we planned."

Dorcas nodded. "Aye."

"That makes it unanimous," Saxtorph said. "Go for broke. Now, look at the sun. Within three hours, nightfall. The kzinti could land in the dark, but if I were their captain I'd wait for morning. He won't be in such a hurry he'll care to take the extra risk. Meanwhile we sit cooped for 20-odd hours losing our nerve. Let's not. Let's begin right away."

Willingness blazed from the women.

Saxtorph hauled his bulk from the chair. "Okay, we are on a war footing and I am in command," he said. "First Dorcas and I suit up."

"Are you sure I can't join you?" Laurinda wellnigh beseeched.

Saxtorph shook his head. "Sorry. You aren't trained for that kind of thing. And the gravity weighs you down still worse than it does Dorcas, even if she is a Belter. Besides, we want you to free us from having to think about communications. You stay inboard and handle the hardest part." He chucked her under the chin. "If we fail, which we well may, you'll get your chance to die like a soldier." He stooped, kissed her hand, and went out.

Returning equipped, he said into the transmitter: "*Shep* here. Spaceboat *Shep* calling kzin vessel. Hello, Kam. Don't blame yourself. They've got us. We'll leave this message replaying in case you're on the far side, and so you can zero in on us. Because you will have to. Listen, Kam. Tell that gonococcus of a captain that we can't lift. We came down on talus that slid beneath us and damaged a landing jack. We'd hit the side of the canyon where we are—it's narrow—if we tried to take off before the hydraulics have been repaired; and Dorcas and I can't finish that job for another several Earth-days, the two of us with what tools we've got aboard. The ground immediately downslope of us is safe. Or, if your captain is worried about his fat ass, he can wait till we're ready to come meet him. Please inform us. Give Art our love; and take it yourself, Kam."

The kzin skipper would want a direct machine translation of those words. They were calculated not to lash him into fury—he couldn't be such a fool— but to pique his honor. Moreover, the top brass back on Secunda must be almighty impatient. Kzinti weren't much good at biding their time.

Before they closed their faceplates at the airlock, Saxtorph kissed his wife on the lips.

—Shadows welled in the coulee and its ravines as the sun sank toward rimrock. Interplay of light and dark was shifty behind the boat, where rubble now decked the floor. The humans had arranged that by radio detonation of two of the blasting sticks Dorcas smuggled along. It looked like more debris than it was, made the story of the accident plausible, and guaranteed that the kzinti would land in the short stretch between *Shep* and glacier.

Man and woman regarded each other. Their spacesuits were behung with armament. She had the rifle and snub-nosed automatic, he the machine pistol; both carried potentially lethal prospector's gear. Wind skirled. The heights glowed under a sky deepening from royal purple to black, where early stars quivered forth.

"Well," he said inanely into his throat mike, "we know our stations. Good hunting, kid."

"And to you, hotpants," she answered. "See you on the far side of the monobloc."

"Love you."

"Love you right back." She whirled and hastened off. Under the conditions expected, drive units would have been a bad mistake, and she was hampered by a weight she was never bred to. Nonetheless she moved with a hint of her wonted gracefulness. Both their suits were first-chop, never mind what the cost had added to the mortgage under which Saxtorph Ventures labored. Full air and water recycle, telescopic option, power joints even in the gloves, self-seal throughout. . . . She rated no less, he believed, and she'd tossed the same remark at him. Thus they had a broad range of capabilities.

He climbed to his chosen niche, on the side of the canyon opposite hers, and settled in. It was up a boulderful gulch, plenty of cover, with a clear view downward. The ice cliff glimmered. He hoped that what was going to happen wouldn't cause damage yonder. That would be a scientific atrocity.

But those beings had had their day. This was humankind's, unless it turned out to be kzinkind's. Or somebody else's? Who knew how many creatures of what sorts were prowling around the galaxy? Saxtorph hunkered into a different position. He missed his pipe. His heart slugged harder than it ought and he could smell himself in spite of the purifier. Better do a bit of meditation. Nervousness would worsen his chances.

His watch told him an hour had passed when the kzin boat arrived. The boat! Good. They might have kept her safe aloft and dispatched a squad on drive. But that would have been slow and tricky; as they descended, the members could have been picked off, assuming the humans had firearms—which a kzin would assume; they'd have had no backup.

The sun had trudged farther down, but *Shep*'s nose still sheened above the blue dusk in the canyon, and the oncoming craft flared metallic red. He knew her type from his war years. Kam, stout kanaka, had passed on more information than the kzinti probably realized. A boat belonging to a Prowling Hunter normally carried six—captain, pilot, engineer, computerman, two fire-control officers; they shared various other duties, and could swap the main ones in an emergency. They weren't trained for groundside combat, but of course any kzin was pretty fair at that. Kam had mentioned two marines who did have the training. Then there were the humans. No wonder the complement did not include a telepath. He'd have been considered superfluous anyway, worth much more at the base. This mission was simply to collar three fugitives.

Sonic thunders rolled, gave way to whirring, and the lean shape neared. It put down with a care that Saxtorph admired, came to rest, instantly swiveled a gun at the human boat 50 meters up the canyon. Saxtorph's pulse leaped. The enemy had landed exactly where he hoped. Not that he'd counted on that, or on anything else.

His earphones received bland translator English; he could imagine the snarl behind. "Are you prepared to yield?"

How steady Laurinda's response was. "We yield on condition that our comrades are alive, safe. Bring them to us." Quite a girl, Saxtorph thought. The kzinti wouldn't wonder about her; their females not being sapient, any active intelligence was, in their minds, male.

"Do you dare this insolence? Your landing gear does not seem damaged as you claimed. Lift, and we fire."

"We have no intention of lifting, supposing we could. Bring us our comrades, or come pry us out."

Saxtorph tautened. No telling how the kzin commander would react. Except that he'd not willingly blast *Shep* on the ground. Concussion, in this thick atmosphere, and radiation would endanger his own craft. He might decide to produce Art and Kam—

Hope died. Battle plans never quite work. The main airlock opened; a downramp extruded; two kzinti in armor and three in regular spacesuits, equipped with rifles and cutting torches, came forth. The smooth computer voice said, "You will admit this party. If you resist, you die."

Laurinda kept silence. The kzinti started toward her.

Saxtorph thumbed his detonator.

In a well-chosen set of places under a bluff above a slope on his side, the remaining sticks blew. Dust and flinders heaved aloft. An instant later he heard the grumble of explosion and breaking. Under one-point-three-five Earth gravities, rocks hurtled, slid, tumbled to the bottom and across it.

He couldn't foresee what would happen next, but had been sure it would be fancy. The kzinti were farther along than he preferred. They dodged leaping masses, escaped the landslide. But it crashed around their boat. She swayed, toppled, fell onto the pile of stone, which grew until it half buried her. The gun pointed helplessly at heaven. Dust swirled about before it settled.

Dorcas was already shooting. She was a crack marksman. A kzin threw up his arms and flopped, another, another. The rest scattered. They hadn't thought to bring drive units. If they had, she could have bagged them all as they rose. Saxtorph bounded out and downslope, over the boulders. His machine pistol had less range than her rifle. It chattered in his hands. He zigzagged, bent low, squandering ammo, while she kept the opposition prone.

Out of nowhere, a marine grabbed him by the ankle. He fell, rolled over, had the kzin on top of him. Fingers clamped on the wrist of the arm holding his weapon. The kzin fumbled after a pistol of his own. Saxtorph's free hand pulled a crowbar from its sling. He got it behind the kzin's back, under the aircycler tank, and pried. Vapor gushed forth. His foe choked, went bug-eyed, scrabbled, and slumped. Saxtorph crawled from beneath.

Dorcas covered his back, disposed of the last bandit, as he pounded toward the boat. The outer valve of the airlock gaped wide. Piece of luck, that, though he and she could have gotten through both with a certain amount of effort. He wedged a rock in place to make sure the survivors wouldn't shut it.

She made her way to him. He helped her scramble across the slide and over the curve of hull above, to the chamber. She spent her explosive rifle shells breaking down the inner valve. As it sagged, she let him by.

He stormed in. They had agreed to that, as part of what they had hammered out during hour after hour after hour of waiting. He had the more mass and muscle; and spraying bullets around in a confined space would likely kill their friends.

An emergency airseal curtain brushed him and closed again. Breathable atmosphere leaked past it, a white smoke, but slowly. The last kzinti attacked. They didn't want ricochets either. Two had claws out— one set dripped red—and the third carried a power drill, whirling to pierce his suit and the flesh behind.

Saxtorph went for him first. His geologist's hammer knocked the drill aside. From the left, his knife stabbed into the throat, and slashed. Clad as he was, what followed became butchery. He split a skull and opened a belly. Blood, brains, guts were everywhere. Two kzinti struggled and ululated in agony. Dorcas came into the tumult. Safely point-blank, her pistol administered mercy shots.

Saxtorph leaned against a bulkhead. He began to shake.

Dimly, he was aware of Kam Ryan stumbling forth. He opened his faceplate—oxygen inboard would stay adequate for maybe half an hour, though God, the stink of death!—and heard:

"I don't believe, I can't believe, but you did it, you're here, you've won, only first a ratcat, must've lost his temper, he ripped Art, Art's dead, well, he was hurting so, a release, I scuttled aft, but Art's dead, don't let Laurinda see, clean up first, please, I'll do it, we can take time to bury him, can't we, this is where his dreams were—" The man knelt, embraced Dorcas' legs regardless of the chill on them, and wept.

19

They left Tregennis at the foot of the glacier, making a cairn for him where the ancients were entombed. "That seems very right," Laurinda whispered. "I hope the scientists who come in the future will—give him a proper grave—but leave him here."

Saxtorph made no remark about the odds against any such expedition. It would scarcely happen unless his people got home to tell the tale.

The funeral was hasty. When they hadn't heard from their boat for a while, which would be a rather short while, the kzinti would send another, if not two or three. Humans had better be well out of the neighborhood before then.

Saxtorph boosted *Shep* inward from Tertia. "We can get some screening in the vicinity of the sun, especially if we've got it between us and Secunda," he explained. "Radiation out of that clinker is no particular hazard, except heat; we'll steer safely wide and not linger too long." Shedding unwanted heat was always a problem in space. The best array of thermistors gave only limited help.

"Also—" he began to add. "No, never mind. A vague notion. Something you mentioned, Kam. But let it wait till we've quizzed you dry."

That in turn waited upon simple, dazed sitting, followed by sleep, followed by gradual regaining of strength and alertness. You don't bounce straight back from tension, terror, rage, and grief.

The sun swelled in view. Its flares were small and dim compared to Sol's, but their flame-flickers became visible to the naked eye, around the roiled ember disc. After he heard what Ryan knew about the asteroid tug, Saxtorph whistled. "Christ!" he murmured. "Imagine swinging that close. Damn near half the sky a boiling red glow, and you hear the steam roar in its conduits and you fly in a haze of it, and nevertheless I'll bet the cabin is a furnace you can barely endure, and if the least thing goes wrong— Yah, kzinti have courage, you must give them that. Markham's right—what you quoted, Kam—they'd make great partners for humans. Though he doesn't understand that we'll have to civilize them first."

Excitement grew in him as he learned more and his thoughts developed. But it was with a grim countenance that he presided over the meeting he called.

"Two men, two women, an unarmed interplanetary boat, and the nearest help light-years off," he said. "After what we've done, the enemy must be scouring the system for us. I daresay the warship's staying on guard at Secunda, but if I know kzin psychology, all her auxiliaries are now out on the hunt, and won't quit till we're either captured or dead."

Dorcas nodded. "We dealt them what was worse than a hurt, a humiliation," she confirmed. "Honor calls for vengeance."

Laurinda clenched her fists. "It *does*," she hissed. Ryan glanced at her in surprise; he hadn't expected that from her.

"Well, they do have losses to mourn, like us," Dorcas said. "As fiery as they are by nature, they'll press the chase in hopes of dealing with us personally. However, they know our foodstocks are limited." Little had been taken from the naval lockers. It was unpalatable, and stowage space was almost filled already. "If we're still missing after some months, they can reckon us dead. Contrary to Bob, I suppose they'll return to base before then."

"Not necessarily," Ryan replied. "It gives them something to do. That's the question every military command has to answer, how to keep the troops busy between combat operations." For the first time since that hour on Secunda, he grinned. "The traditional human solutions have been either (a) a lot of drill or (b) a lot of paperwork; but you can't force much of either on kzinti."

"Back to business," Saxtorph snapped. "I've been trying to reason like, uh, Werlith-Commandant. What does he expect? I think he sees us choosing one of three courses. First, we might stay on the run, hoping against hope that there will be a human follow-up expedition and we can warn it in time. But he's got Markham to help him prevent that. Second, we might turn ourselves in, hoping against hope our lives will be spared. Third, we might attempt a suicide dash, hoping against hope we'll die doing him a little harm. The warship will be on the lookout for that, and in spite of certain brave words earlier, I honestly don't give us a tax collector's chance at Paradise of getting through the kind of barrage she can throw.

"Can anybody think of any more possibilities?"

"No," sighed Dorcas. "Of course, they aren't mutually exclusive. Forget surrender. But we can stay on the run till we're close to starvation and then try to strike a blow."

Laurinda's eyes closed. *Juan*, her lips formed.

"We can try a lot sooner," Saxtorph declared.

Breaths went sibilant in between teeth.

"What Kam's told us has given me an idea that I'll bet has not occurred to any kzin," the captain went on. "I'll grant you it's hairy-brained. It may very well get us killed. But it gives us the single possibility I see of getting killed while accomplishing something real. And we might, we just barely might do better than that. You see, it involves a way to sneak close to Secunda, undetected, unsuspected. After that, we'll decide what, if anything, we can do. I have a notion there as well, but first we need hard information. If things look impossible, we can probably flit off for outer space, the kzinti never the wiser." A certain vibrancy came into his voice. "But time crammed inside this hull is scarcely lifetime, is it? I'd rather go out fighting. A short life but a merry one."

His tone dropped. "Granted, the whole scheme depends on parameters being right. But if we're careful, we shouldn't lose much by investigating. At worst, we'll be disappointed."

"You do like to lay a long-winded foundation, Bob," Ryan said.

"And you like to mix metaphors, Kam," Dorcas responded.

Saxtorph laughed. Laurinda looked from face to face, bemused.

"Okay," Saxtorph said. "Our basic objective is to recapture *Rover*, agreed? Without her, we're nothing but a bunch of maroons, and the most we can do is take a few kzinti along when we die. With her—ah, no need to spell it out.

"She's on Secunda's moon, Kam heard. The kzinti know full well we'd like to get her back. I doubt they keep a live guard aboard against the remote contingency. They've trouble enough as is with personnel growing bored and quarrelsome. But they'll've planted detectors, which will sound a radio alarm if anybody comes near. Then the warship can land an armed party or, if necessary, throw a nuke. The warship also has the duty of protecting the planetside base. If I were in charge—and I'm pretty sure What's-his-screech-Captain thinks the same—I'd keep her in orbit about halfway between planet and moon. Wide field for radars, optics, every kind of gadget; quick access to either body. Kam heard as how that space is cluttered with industrial stuff and junk, but she'll follow a reasonably clear path and keep ready to dodge or deflect whatever may be on a collision course.

"Now. The kzinti mine the asteroid belt for metals, mainly iron. They do that by shifting the bodies into eccentric orbits osculating Secunda's, then wangling them into planetary orbit at the far end. Kam heard as how an asteroid is about due in, and the tug was taking station to meet it and nudge it into place. To my mind, 'asteroid' implies a fair-sized object, not just a rock.

"But the tug was prospecting, Kam heard, when she was ordered to Prima. Afterward she didn't go back to prospecting, because the time before she'd be needed at Secunda had gotten too short to make that worthwhile. However, since she was in fact called from the sun, my guess is that the asteroid's not in need of attention right away. In other words, the tug's waiting.

"Again, if I were in charge, I wouldn't keep a crew idle aboard. I'd just leave her in Secunda orbit till she's wanted. That needs to be a safe orbit, though, and inner space isn't for an empty vessel. So the tug's circling wide around the planet, or maybe the moon. Unless she sits on the moon, too."

"She isn't able to land anywhere," Ryan reminded. "Those cooling fins, if nothing else. I suppose the kzinti put *Rover* down, on the planet-facing side, the easier to keep an eye on her. She's a lure for us, after all."

Saxtorph nodded. "Thanks," he said. "Given that the asteroid was diverted from close-in solar orbit, and is approaching Secunda, we can make a pretty good estimate of where it is and what the vectors are. How 'bout it, Laurinda?

"The Kzinti are expecting the asteroid. Their instruments will register it. They'll say, 'Ah, yes,' and go on about their business, which includes hunting for us and never suppose that we've glided to it and are trailing along behind."

Dorcas let out a war-whoop.

20

The thing was still molten. That much mass would remain so for a long while in space, unless the kzinti had ways to speed its cooling. Doubtless they did. Instead of venting enormous quantities of water to maintain herself near the sun, the tug could spray them forth. "What a show!" Saxtorph had said. "Pity we'll miss it."

The asteroid glowed white, streaked with slag, like a lesser sun trundling between planets. Its diameter was ample to conceal *Shep.* Secunda gleamed ahead, a perceptible tawny disc. From time to time the humans had ventured to slip their boat past her shield for a quick instrumental peek. They knew approximately the rounds which *Vengeful Slasher* and *Sun Defier* paced. Soon the tug must come to make rendezvous and steer the iron into its destination path. Gigantic though her strength was, she could shift millions of tonnes, moving at kilometers per second, only slowly. Before this began, the raiders must raid.

Saxtorph made a final despairing effort: "Damn it to chaos, darling, I can't let you go. I can't."

"Hush," Dorcas said low, and laid her hand across his mouth. They floated weightless in semi-darkness, the bunk which they shared curtained off. Their shipmates had, unspokenly, gone forward from the cubbyhole where everyone slept by turns, to leave them alone.

"One of us has to go, one stay," she whispered redundantly, but into his ear. "Nobody else would have a prayer of conning the tug, and Kam and Laurinda could scarcely bring *Rover* home, which is the object of the game. So you and I have to divide the labor, and for this part I'm better qualified."

"Brains, not brawn, huh?" he growled half resentfully.

"Well, I did work on translation during the war. I can read kzin a little, which is what's going to count. Put down your machismo." She drew him close and fluttered eyelids against his. "As for brawn, fellow, you do have qualifications I lack, and this may be our last chance . . . for a spell."

"Oh, love—you, you—"

Thus their dispute was resolved. They had been through it more than once. Afterward there wasn't time to continue it. Dorcas had to prepare herself.

Spacesuited, loaded like a Christmas tree with equipment, she couldn't properly embrace her husband at the airlock. She settled for an awkward kiss and a wave at the others, then closed her faceplate and cycled through.

Outside, she streaked off, around the asteroid. Its warmth beat briefly at her. She left the lump behind and deployed her diriscope, got a fix on the planet ahead, compared the reading with the computed coordinates that gleamed on a databoard, worked the calculator strapped to her left wrist, made certain of what the displays on her drive unit meters said— right forearm—and set the thrust controls for maximum. Acceleration tugged. She was on her way.

It would be a long haul. You couldn't eat distance in a spacesuit at anything like the rate you could in a boat. Its motor lacked the capacity—not to speak of

the protections and cushionings possible within a
hull. In fact, a large part of her load was energy
boxes. To accomplish her mission in time, she must
needs drain them beyond rechargeability, discard
and replace them. That hurt; they could have been
ferried down to Prima for the saving of Carita and
Juan. Now too few would be left, back aboard *Shep*.
But under present conditions rescue would be mean-
ingless anyway.

She settled down for the hours. Her insignificant
size and radiation meant she would scarcely show on
kzin detectors. Occasionally she sipped from the
water tube or pushed a foodbar through the chowlock.
Her suit took care of additional needs. As for comfort, she had the stars, Milky Way, nebulae, sister
galaxies, glory upon glory.

Often she rechecked her bearings and adjusted
her vectors. Eventually, decelerating, she activated a
miniature radar such as asteroid miners employ and
got a lock on her objective. By then Secunda had
swollen larger in her eyes than Luna over Earth.
From her angle of view it was a scarred dun crescent
against a circle of darkness faintly rimmed with light
diffused through dusty air. The moon, where *Rover*
lay, was not visible to her.

Saxtorph's guess had been right. Well, it was an
informed guess. The warship orbited the planet at
about 100,000 klicks. The supertug circled beyond
the moon, twice as far out. She registered dark
and cool on what instruments Dorcas carried; nobody aboard. Terminating deceleration, the woman
approached.

What a sight! A vast, brilliant spheroid with flanges
like convulsed meridians; drive units projecting within
a shielding sheath; no ports, but receptors from which
visuals were transmitted inboard; recesses for instru-

ments; circular hatches which must cover steam vents; larger doors to receive crushed ice— How did you get in? Dorcas flitted in search. She could do it almost as smoothly as if she were flying a manwing through atmosphere.

There—an unmistakable airlock— She was prepared to cut her way in, but when she had identified the controls, the valves opened and shut for her. Who worries about burglars in space? To the kzinti, *Rover* was the bait that might draw humans.

The interior was dark. Diffusion of her flashbeam, as well as a gauge on her left knee, showed full pressure was maintained. Hers wasn't quite identical; she equalized before shoving back her faceplate. The air was cold and smelled musty. Pumps muttered.

Afloat in weightlessness, she began her exploration. She'd never been in a kzin ship before. But she had studied descriptions; and the laws of nature are the same everywhere, and man and kzin aren't terribly unlike—they can actually eat each other; and she could decipher most labels; so she could piecemeal trace things out, figure how they worked, even in a vessel as unusual as this.

She denied herself haste. If the crew arrived before she was done, she'd try ambushing them. There was no point in this job unless it was done right. As need arose she ate, rested, napped, adrift amidst machinery. Once she began to get a solid idea of the layout, she stripped it. Supplies, motors, black boxes, whatever she didn't think she would require, she unpacked, unbolted, torched loose, and carried outside. There the grapnel field, the same force that hauled on cosmic stones, low-power now, clasped them behind the hull.

Alone though she was, the ransacking didn't actually take long. She was efficient. A hundred hours sufficed for everything.

"Very well," she said at last; and she took a pill and accepted ten hours of REM sleep, dreams which had been deferred. Awake again, refreshed, she nourished herself sparingly, exercised, scribbled a cross in the air and murmured, "Into Your hands—" for unlike her husband, she believed the universe was more than an accident.

Next came the really tricky part. Of course Bob had wanted to handle it himself. Poor dear, he must be in absolute torment, knowing everything that could go wrong. She was luckier, Dorcas thought: too busy to be afraid.

Shep's flickering radar peeks had gotten fair-to-middling readings on an object that must be the kzin warship. Its orbit was only approximately known, and subject both to perturbation and deliberate change. Dorcas needed exact knowledge. She must operate indicators and computers of nonhuman workmanship so delicately that Hraou-Captain had no idea he was under surveillance. Thereafter she must guess what her best tactics might be, calculate the maneuvers, and follow through.

When the results were in: "Here goes," she said into the hollowness around. "For you, Arthur—" and thought briefly that if the astronomer could have roused in his grave on Tertia, he would have reproved her, in his gentle fashion, for being melodramatic.

Sun Defier plunged.

Unburdened by tonnes of water, she made nothing of ten g's, 20, 30, you name it. Her kzin crew must often have used the polarizer to keep from being crushed, as Dorcas did. "Hai-ai-ai!" she screamed, and rode her comet past the moon, amidst the stars, to battle.

She never knew whether the beings aboard the warship saw her coming. Things happened so fast. If the kzinti did become aware of what was bearing down on them, they had scant time to react. Their computers surely told them that *Sun Defier* was no threat, would pass close by but not collide. Some malfunction? The kzinti would not gladly annihilate their iron gatherer.

When the precalculated instant flashed onto a screen before her, Dorcas punched for a sidewise thrust as great as the hull could survive. It shuddered and groaned around her. An instant later, the program that she had written cut off the grapnel field.

Those masses she had painstakingly lugged outside —they now had interception vectors, and at a distance too small for evasion. *Sun Defier* passed within 50 kilometers while objects sleeted through *Vengeful Slasher*.

The warship burst. Armor peeled back, white-hot, from holes punched by monstrous velocity. Missiles floated out of shattered bays. Briefly, a frost-cloud betokened air rushing forth into vacuum. The wreck tumbled among fragments of itself. Starlight glinted off the ruins. Doubtless crew remained alive in this or that sealed compartment; but *Vengeful Slasher* wasn't going anywhere out of orbit, ever again.

Sun Defier swooped past Secunda. Dorcas commenced braking operations, for eventual rendezvous with her fellow humans.

21

The moon was a waste of rock, low hills, boulder-fields, empty plains, here and there a crater not quite eroded away. Darkling in this light, under Sol it would have been brighter than Luna, powdered with yellow which at the bottoms of slopes had collected to form streaks or blotches. The sun threw long shadows from the west.

Against them, *Rover* shone like a beacon. Saxtorph cheered. As expected, the kzinti had left her on the hemisphere that always faced Secunda. The location was, however, not central but close to the north pole and the western edge. He wondered why. He'd spotted many locations that looked as good or better, when you had to bring down undamaged a vessel not really meant to land on anything this size.

He couldn't afford the time to worry about it. By now the warboats had surely learned of the disaster to their mother ship and were headed back at top boost. Kzinti might or might not suspect what the cause had been of their supertug running amok, but they would know when *Rover* took off—in fact, would probably know when he reached the ship. Their shuttles, designed for strictly orbital work, were no threat. Their gunboats were. If *Rover* didn't get to hyperspacing distance before those overtook her, she and her crew would be *ganz kaput*.

Saxtorph passed low overhead, ascended, and played back the pictures his scanners had taken in passing. As large as she was, the ship had no landing jacks. She lay sidelong on her lateral docking grapples. That stressed her, but not too badly in a gravity less than Luna's. To compound the trickiness of descent, she had been placed just under a particularly high and steep hill. He could only set down on the opposite side. Beyond the narrow strip of flat ground on which she lay, a blotch extended several meters across the valley floor. Otherwise that floor was strewn with rocks and somewhat downward sloping toward the hill. Maybe the kzinti had chosen this site precisely because it was a bitch for him to settle on.

"I can do it, though," Saxtorph decided. He pointed at the screen. "See, a reasonably clear area about 500 meters off."

Laurinda nodded. With the boat falling free again, the white hair rippled around her delicate features.

Saxtorph applied retrothrust. For thrumming minutes he backed toward his goal. Sweat studded his face and darkened his tunic under the arms. *Smell like a billy goat, I do,* he thought fleetingly. *When we come home, I'm going to spend a week in a Japanese hot bath. Dorcas can bring me sushi. She prefers showers, cold—* He gave himself entirely back to his work.

Contact shivered. The deck tilted. Saxtorph adjusted the jacks to level *Shep.* When he cut the engine, silence fell like a thunderclap.

He drew a long breath, unharnessed, and rose. "I can suit up faster if you help me," he told the Crashlander.

"Of course," she replied. "Not that I have much experience."

Never mind modesty. It had been impossible to maintain without occasional failures, by four people crammed inside this little hull. Laurinda had blushed all over, charmingly, when she happened to emerge from the shower cubicle as Saxtorph and Ryan came by. The quartermaster had only a pair of shorts on, which didn't hide the gallant reflex. Yet nobody ever did or said anything improper, and the girl overcame her shyness. Now a part of Saxtorph enjoyed the touch of her spiderey fingers, but most of him stayed focused on the business at hand.

"Forgive me for repeating what you've heard a dozen times," he said. "You are new to this kind of situation, and could forget the necessity of abiding by orders. Your job is to bring this boat back to Dorcas and Kam. That's *it*. Nothing else whatsoever. When I tell you to, you throw the main switch, and the program we've put in the autopilot will take over. I'd've automated that bit also, except rigging it would've taken time we can ill afford, and anyway, we do want some flexibility, some judgment in the control loop." Sternly: "If anything goes wrong for me, or you think anything has, whether or not I've called in, you go. The three of you must have *Shep*. The tug's fast but clumsy, impossible to make planetfall with, and only barely provisioned. Your duty is to *Shep*. Understood?"

"Yes," she said mutedly, her gaze on the task she was doing. "Besides, we have to have the boat to rescue Juan and Carita."

A sigh wrenched from Saxtorph. "I told you—" After Dorcas' flight, too few energy boxes remained to lift either of them into orbit. *Shep* could hover on her drive at low altitude while they flitted up, but she wasn't built for planetary rescue work, the thrusters weren't heavily enough shielded externally, at such a boost their radiation would be lethal.

Neither meek nor defiant, Laurinda replied, "I know. But after we've taken *Rover* to the right distance, why can't she wait, ready to flee, till the boat comes back from Prima?"

"Because the boat never would."

"The kzinti can land safely."

"More or less safely. They don't like to, remember. Sure, I can tell you how they do it. Obvious. They put detachable footpads on their jacks. The stickum may or may not be able to grab hold of, say, fluorosilicone, but if it does, it'll take a while to eat its way through. When the boat's ready to leave, she sheds those footpads."

"Of course. I've been racking my brain to comprehend why we can't do the same for *Shep*."

The pain in her voice and in himself brought anger into his. "God damn it, we're spacers, not sorcerers! Groundsiders think a spacecraft is a hunk of metal you can cobble anything onto, like a car. She isn't. She's about as complex and interconnected as your body is. A few milligrams of blood clot or of the wrong chemical will bring your body to a permanent halt. A spacecraft's equally vulnerable. I am *not* going to tinker with ours, light-years from any proper workshop. I am not. That's final!"

Her face bent downward from his. He heard her breath quiver.

"I'm sorry, dear," he added, softly once more. "I'm sorrier than you believe, maybe sorrier than you can imagine. Those are my crewfolk down and doomed. Oh, if we had time to plan and experiment and carefully test, sure, I'd try it. What should the footpads be made of? What size? How closely machined? How detached—explosive bolts, maybe? We'd have to wire those and—Laurinda, we won't have the time. If I lift *Rover* off within the next hour or two, we can pick up Dorcas and Kam, boost, and fly dark. If we're lucky, the kzin warboats won't detect us. But our margin is razor thin. We don't have the days or weeks your idea needs. *Fido*'s people don't either; their own time has gotten short. I'm sorry, dear."

She looked up. He saw tears in the ruby eyes, down the snowy cheeks. But she spoke still more quietly than he, with the briefest of little smiles. "No harm in asking, was there? I understand. You've told me what I was trying to deny I knew. You are a good man, Robert."

"Aw," he mumbled, and reached to rumple her hair.

The suiting completed, he took her hands between his gloves for a moment, secured a toolpack between his shoulders where the drive unit usually was, and cycled out.

The land gloomed silent around him. Nearing the horizon, the red sun looked bigger than it was. So did the planet, low to the southeast, waxing close to half phase. He could make out a dust storm as a deeper-brown blot on the fulvous crescent. Away from either luminous body, stars were visible—and yonder brilliancy must be Quarta. How joyously they had sailed past it.

Saxtorph started for his ship, in long low-gravity bounds. He didn't want to fly. The kzinti might have planted a boobytrap, such as an automatic gun that would lock on, track, and fire if you didn't radio the password. Afoot, he was less of a target.

The ground lightened as he advanced, for the yellow dust lay thicker. No, he saw, it was not actually dust in the sense of small solid particles, but more like spatters or films of liquid. Evidently it didn't cling to things, like that horrible stuff on Prima. A ghostly rain from space, it would slip from higher to lower places; in the course of gigayears, even cosmic rays would give some slight stirring to help it along downhill. It might be fairly deep near the ship, where its surface was like a blot. He'd better approach with care. Maybe it would prove necessary to fetch a drive unit and flit across.

Saxtorph's feet went out from under him. He fell slowly, landed on his butt. With an oath he started to get up. His soles wouldn't grip. His hands skidded on slickness. He sprawled over onto his back. And he was gliding down the slope of the valley floor, gliding down toward the amber-colored blot.

He flailed, kicked up dust, but couldn't stop. The damned ground had no friction, none. He passed a boulder and managed to throw an arm around. For an instant he was checked, then it rolled and began to descend with him.

"Laurinda, I have a problem," he managed to say into his radio. "Sit tight. Watch close. If this turns out to be serious, obey your orders."

He reached the blot. It gave way. He sank into its depths.

He had hoped it was a layer of just a few centimeters, but it closed over his head and still he sank. A pit where the stuff had collected from the heights—maybe the kzinti, taking due care, had dumped some extra in, gathered across a wide area—yes, this was very likely their boobytrap, and if they had ghosts, Hraou-Captain's must be yowling laughter. Odd how that name came back to him as he tumbled.

Bottom. He lay in blindness, fighting to curb his breath and heartbeat. How far down? Three meters, four? Enough to bury him for the next several billion years, unless— "Hello, *Shep*. Laurinda, do you read me? Do you read me?"

His earphones hummed. The wavelength he was using should have expanded its front from the top of the pit, but the material around him must be screening it. Silence outside his suit was as thick as the blackness.

Let's see if he could climb out. The side wasn't vertical. The stuff resisted his movements less than water would. He felt arms and legs scrabble to no avail. He could feel irregularities in the stone but he could not get a purchase on any. Well, could he swim? He tried. No. He couldn't rise off the bottom. Too high a mean density compared to the medium; and it didn't allow him even as much traction as water, it yielded to every motion, he might as well have tried to swim in air.

If he'd brought his drive unit, maybe it could have lifted him out. He wasn't sure. It was for use in space. This fluid might clog it or ooze into circuitry that there had never been any reason to seal tight. Irrelevant anyway, when he'd left it behind.

"My boy," he said, "it looks like you've had the course."

That was a mistake. The sound seemed to flap around in the cage of his helmet. If he was trapped, he shouldn't dwell on it. That way lay screaming panic.

He forced himself to lie quiet and think. How long till Laurinda took off? By rights, she should have already. If he did escape the pit, he'd be alone on the moon. Naturally, he'd try to get at *Rover* in some different fashion, such as coming around on the hillside. But meanwhile Dorcas would return in *Shep*, doubtless with the other two. She was incapable of cutting and running, off into futility. Chances were, though, that by the time she got here a kzin auxiliary or two would have arrived. The odds against her would be long indeed.

So if Saxtorph found a way to return topside and repossess *Rover*—soon—he wouldn't likely find his wife at the asteroid. And he couldn't very well turn back and try to make contact, because of those warboats and because of his overriding obligation to carry the warning home. He'd have to conn the ship all by himself, leaving Dorcas behind for the kzinti.

The thought was strangling. Tears stung. That was a relief, in the nullity everywhere around. Something he could feel, and taste the salt of on his lips. Was the tomb blackness thickening? No, couldn't be. How long had he lain buried? He brought his timepiece to his faceplate, but the hell-stuff blocked off luminosity. The blood in his ears hammered against a wall of stillness. Had a whine begun to modulate the rasping of his breath? Was he going crazy? Sensory deprivation did bring on illusions, weirdnesses, but he wouldn't have expected it this soon.

He made himself remember—sunlight, stars, Dorcas, a sail above blue water, fellowship among men, Dorcas, the tang of a cold beer, Dorcas, their plans for children—they'd banked gametes against the day they'd be ready for domesticity but maybe a little too old and battered in the DNA for direct begetting to be advisable—

Contact ripped him out of his dreams. He reached wildly and felt his gloves close on a solid object. They slid along it, along humanlike lineaments, a spacesuit, no, couldn't be!

Laurinda slithered across him till she brought faceplate to faceplate. Through the black he recognized the voice that conduction carried: "Robert, thank God, I'd begun to be afraid I'd never find you, are you all right?"

"What the, the devil are you doing here?" he gasped.

Laughter crackled. "Fetching you. Yes, mutiny. Court-martial me later."

Soberness followed: "I have a cable around my waist, with the end free for you. Feel around till you find it. There's a lump at the end, a knot I made beforehand and covered with solder so the buckyballs can't get in and make it work loose. You can use that to make a hitch that will hold for yourself, can't you? Then I'll need your help. I have two geologist's hammers with me. Secured them by cords so they can't be lost. Wrapped tape around the handles in thick bands, to give a grip in spite of no friction. Used the pick ends to chip notches in the rock, and hauled myself along, But I'm exhausted now, and it's an uphill pull, even though gravity is weak. Take the hammers. Drag me along behind you. You have the strength."

"The strength—oh, my God, you talk about *my* strength?" he cried.

—The cable was actually heavy-gauge wire from the electrical parts locker, lengths of it spliced together till they reached. The far end was fastened around a great boulder beyond the treacherous part of the slope. Slipperiness had helped as well as hindered the ascent, but when he reached safety, Saxtorph allowed himself to collapse for a short spell.

He returned to Laurinda's earnest tones: "I can't tell you how sorry I am. I should have guessed. But it didn't occur to me—such quantities gathered together like this—I simply thought 'nebular dust,' without stopping to estimate what substance would become dominant over many billions of years—"

He sat straight to look at her. In the level red light, her face was palely rosy, her eyes afire. "Why, how could you have foreseen, lass?" he answered. "I'd hate to tell you how often something in space has taken me by surprise, and that was in familiar parts. You did realize what the problem was, and figured out a solution. We needn't worry about your breaking orders. If you'd failed, you'd have been insubordinate; but you succeeded, so by definition you showed initiative."

"Thank you." Eagerness blazed. "And listen, I've had another idea—"

He lifted a palm. "Whoa! Look, in a couple of

minutes we'd better hike back to *Shep*, you take your station again, I get a drive unit and fly across to *Rover*. But first will you please, please tell me what the mess was that I got myself into?"

"Buckyballs," she said. "Or, formally, buckminster-fullerene. I didn't think the pitful of it that you'd slid down into could be very deep or the bottom very large. Its walls would surely slope inward. It's really just a . . . pothole, though surely the formation process was different, possibly it's a small astrobleme—" She giggled. "My, the academic in me is really taking over, isn't it? Well, essentially, the material is frictionless. It will puddle in any hole, no matter how tiny, and it has just enough cohesion that a number of such puddles close together will form a film over the entire surface. But that film is only a few molecules thick, and you can't walk on it or anything. In this slight gravity, though—and the metal-poor rock is friable—I could strike the sharp end of a hammerhead in with a single blow to act as a kind of . . . piton, is that the word?"

"Okay. Splendid. Dorcas had better look to her standing as the most formidable woman in known space. Now tell me what the—the hell buckyballs are."

"They're produced in the vicinity of supernovae. Carbon atoms link together and form a faceted spherical molecule around a single metal atom. Sixty carbons around one lanthanum is common, galactically speaking, but there are other forms, too. And with the molecule closed in on itself the way it is, it acts in the aggregate like a fluid. In fact, it's virtually a perfect lubricant, and if we didn't have things easier to use you'd see synthetic buckyballs on sale everywhere." A vision rose in those ruby eyes. "It's thought

they may have a basic role in the origin of life on
planets—"

"Damn near did the opposite number today,"
Saxtorph said. "But you saved my ass, and the rest of
me as well. I don't suppose I can ever repay you."

She got to her knees before him and seized his
hands. "You can, Robert. You can fetch me back my
man."

22

Ponderously, *Rover* closed velocities with the iron
asteroid. She couldn't quite match, because it was
under boost, but thus far the acceleration was low.

Ominously aglow, the molten mass dwarfed the
spacecraft that toiled meters ahead of it; yet *Sun
Defier*, harnessed by her own forcefield, was a
plowhorse dragging it bit by bit from its former path;
and the dwarf sun was at work, and Secunda's gravity
was beginning to have a real effect. . . .

Arrived a little before the ship, the boat drifted at
some distance, a needle in a haystack of stars. Laurinda
was still aboard. The tug had no place to receive
Shep, nor had the girl the skill to cross safely by
herself in a spacesuit even though relative speeds
were small. The autopilot kept her accompanying the
others.

In *Rover*'s command center, Saxtorph asked the
image of Dorcas, more shakily than he had expected
to, "How are you? How's everything?"

She was haggard with weariness, but triumph rang:
"Kam's got our gear packed to transfer over to you,
and I—I've worked the bugs out of the program.
Compatibility with kzin hardware was a stumbling
block, but—well, it's been operating smoothly for the

past several hours, and I've no reason to doubt it will continue doing what it's supposed to."

He whistled. "Hey, quite a feat, lady! I really didn't think it would be possible, at least in the time available, when I put you up to trying it. What're you going to do next—square the circle, invent the perpetual motion machine, reform the tax laws, or what?"

Her voice grew steely. "I was motivated." She regarded his face in her own screen. "How are you? Laurinda said something about your running into danger on the moon. Were you hurt?"

"Only in my pride. She can tell you all about it later. Right now we're in a hurry." Saxtorph became intent. "Listen, there's been a change of plan. You and Kam both flit over to *Shep*. But don't you bring her in; lay her alongside. Kam can help Laurinda aboard *Rover* before he moves your stuff. I'd like you to join me in a job around *Shep*. Simple thing and shouldn't take but a couple hours, given the two of us working together. Though I'll bet even money you'll have a useful suggestion or three. Then you can line out for deep space."

She sat a moment silent, her expression bleakened, before she said, "You're taking the boat to Prima while the rest of us ferry *Rover* away."

"You catch on quick, sweetheart."

"To rescue Juan and Carita."

"What else? Laurinda's hatched a scheme I think could do the trick. Naturally, we'll agree in advance where you'll wait, and *Shep* will come join you there. If we don't dawdle, the odds are pretty good that the kzinti won't locate you first and force you to go hyperspatial."

"What about them locating you?"

"Why should they expect anybody to go to Prima?

They'll buzz around Secunda like angry hornets. They
may well be engaged for a while in evacuating survivors from the warship; I suspect the shuttles aren't
terribly efficient at that sort of thing. Afterward they'll
have to work out a search doctrine, when *Rover* can
have skitted in any old direction. And sometime along
about then, they should have their minds taken off
us. The kzinti will notice a nice big surprise bound
their way, about which it is then too late to do
anything whatsoever."

"But you— How plausible is this idea of yours?"

"Plausible enough. Look, don't sit like that. Get
cracking. I'll explain when we meet."

"I can take *Shep*. I'm as good a pilot as you are."

Saxtorph shook his head. "Sorry, no. One of us has
to be in charge of *Rover*, of course. I hereby pull
rank and appoint you. I am the captain."

23

The asteroid concealed the ship's initial boost from
any possible observers around Secunda. She applied
her mightiest vector to give southward motion, out
of the ecliptic plane; but the thrust had an extra
component, randomly chosen, to baffle hunter ana-
lysts who would fain reduce the volume of space
wherein she might reasonably be sought. That volume would grow fast, become literally astronomical,
as she flew free, generator cold, batteries maintaining life support on a minimum energy level. Having
thus cometed for a time, she could with fair safety
apply power again to bring herself to her destination.

Saxtorph let her make ample distance before he
accelerated *Shep*, also using the iron to conceal his
start. However, he ran at top drive the whole way. It

wasn't likely that a detector would pick his little craft up. As he told Dorcas, the kzinti wouldn't suppose a human would make for Prima. It hurt them less, losing friends, provided the friends died bravely; and few of them had mastered the art of putting oneself in the head of an enemy.

Mainly, though, Carita and Juan didn't have much time left them.

Ever circling, the planets had changed configuration since *Rover* arrived. The navigation system allowed for that, but could do nothing to shorten a run of 30-odd hours. Saxtorph tried to compose his soul in peace. He played a lot of solitaire after he found he was losing most of the computer games, and smoked a lot of pipes. Books and shows were poor distraction, but music helped him relax and enjoy his memories. Whatever happened next, he'd have had a better life than 90 percent of his species—99 percent if you counted in everybody who lived and died before humankind went spacefaring.

Prima swelled in his view, sallow and faceless. The recorded broadcast came through clear from the night side, over and over. Saxtorph got his fix. *Fido* wasn't too far from the lethal dawn. He established a three-hour orbit and put a curt message of his own on the player. It ended with "Acknowledge."

Time passed. Heaviness grew within him. Were they dead? He rounded dayside and came back across darkness.

The voice leaped at him: "Bob, is that you? Juan here. We'd abandoned hope, we were asleep. Standing by now. Bob, is that you? Juan here—"

Joy surged. "Who else but me?" Saxtorph said. "How're you doing, you two?"

"Hanging on. Living in our spacesuits this past—I

don't know how long. The boat's a rotted, crumbling shell. But we're hanging on."

"Good. Your drive units in working order?"

"Yes. But we haven't the lift to get onto a trajectory which you can match long enough for us to come aboard." Unspoken: It would be easy in atmosphere, or in free space, given a pilot like you. But what a vessel can do above an airless planet, at suborbital speed, without coming to grief, is sharply limited.

"That's all right," Saxtorph said, "as long as you can go outside, sit in a lock chamber or on top of the wreck, and keep watch, without danger of slipping off into the muck. You can? . . . Okay, prepare yourselves. I'll land in view of you and open the main personnel lock."

"Hadn't we better all find an area free of the material?"

"I'm not sure any exists big enough and flat enough for me. Anyhow, looking for one would take more time than we can afford. No, I'm coming straight down."

Carita cut in. She sounded wrung out. Saxtorph suspected her physical strength was what had preserved both. He imagined her manhandling pieces of metal and plastic, often wrenched from the weakened structure, to improvise braces, platforms, whatever would give some added hours of refuge. "Bob, is this wise?" she asked. "Do you know what you're getting into? The molecule might bind you fast immediately, even if you avoid shining light on it. The decay here is going quicker all the while. I think the molecule is . . . learning. Don't risk your life."

"Don't you give your captain orders," Saxtorph replied. "I'll be down in, m-m, about an hour. Then get to me as fast as you prudently can. Every minute we spend on the surface does add to the danger. But I've put bandits on the jacks."

"What?"

"Footpads," he laughed childishly. "Okay, no more conversation till we're back in space. I've got my reconnoitering to do."

Starlight was brilliant but didn't illuminate an unknown terrain very well. His landing field would be minute and hemmed in. For help he had optical amplifiers, radar, data-analysis programs which projected visuals as well as numbers. He had his skill. Fear shunted from his mind, he became one with the boat.

Location . . . identification . . . positioning; you don't float around in airlessness the way you can in atmosphere . . . site picked, much closer to *Fido* than he liked but he could manage . . . coordinates established . . . down, down, nurse her down to touchdown. . . .

It was as soft a landing as he had ever achieved. It needed to be.

For a pulsebeat he stared across the hollow at the other boat. She was a ghastly sight indeed, a half-hull pocked, ragged, riddled, the pale devourer well up the side of what was left. Good thing he was insured; though multi-billionaire Stefan Brozik would be grateful, and presumably human governments—

Saxtorph grinned at his own inanity and hastened to go operate the airlock. Or was it stupid to think about money at an hour like this? To hell with heroics. He and Dorcas had their living to make.

Descent with the outer valve already open would have given him an imbalance: slight, but he had plenty else to contend with. He cracked it now without stopping to evacuate the chamber. Time was more precious than a few cubic meters of air. A light flashed green. His crewfolk were in. He closed the valve at once. A measure of pressure equalization was required before he admitted them into the hull proper. He did so the instant it was possible. A wind gusted by. His ears popped. Juan and Carita stumbled through. Frost formed on their spacesuits.

He hand-signalled: Grab hold. We're boosting right away.

He could be gentle about that, as well as quick.

Or need he have hastened? Afterward he inspected things at length and found Laurinda's idea had worked as well as could have been hoped, or maybe a little better.

Buckyballs scooped from that sink on the moon. (An open container at the end of a line; he could throw it far in the low gravity.) Bags fashioned out of thick plastic, heat-sealed together, filled with buckyballs, placed around the bottom of each landing jack, superglued fast at the necks. That was all.

The molecule had only eaten through one of them while *Shep* stood on Prima. Perhaps the other jacks rested on sections where most of the chemical bonds were saturated, less readily catalyzed. It didn't matter, except scientifically, because after the single bag gave way, the wonderful stuff had done its job. A layer of it was beneath the metal, a heap of it around. The devourer could not quickly incorporate atoms so strongly interlinked. As it did, more flowed in to fill the gaps. *Shep* could have stayed for hours.

But she had no call to. Lifting, the tension abruptly off him, Saxtorph exploded into tuneless song. It wasn't a hymn or anthem, though it was traditional: "The Bastard King of England." Somehow it felt right.

24

Rover drove though hyperspace, homeward bound.

Man and wife sat together in their cabin, easing off. They were flesh, they would need days to get back the strength they had spent. The ship throbbed and whispered. A screen gave views of Hawaii, heights, greennesses, incredible colors on the sea. Beethoven's Fifth lilted in the background. He had a mug of beer, she a glass of white wine.

"Honeymoon cruise," she said with a wry smile. "Laurinda and Juan. Carita and Kam."

"You and me, for that matter," he replied drowsily.

"But when will we get any proper work done? The interior is a mess."

"Oh, we've time aplenty before we reach port. And if we aren't quite holystoned-perfect, who's going to care?"

"Yes, we'll be the sensation of the day." She grew somber. "How many will remember Arthur Tregennis?"

Saxtorph roused. "Our kind of people will. He was . . . a Moses. He brought us to a scientific Promised Land, and . . . I think there'll be more explorations into the far deeps from now on."

"Yes. Markham's out of the way." Dorcas sighed. "His poor family."

The tug, rushing off too fast for recovery after it released the asteroid to hurtle toward Secunda—if all went as planned, straight at the base— Horror, a scramble to flee, desperate courage, and then the apparition in heaven, the flaming trail, Thor's hammer smites, the cloud of destruction engulfs everything and rises on high and spreads to darken the planet, nothing remains but a doubled crater plated with iron. It was unlikely that any kzinti who escaped would still be alive when their next starship came.

At the end, did Markham cry for his mother?

"And of course humans will be alerted to the situation," Saxtorph observed superfluously.

It was, in fact, unlikely that there would be more kzin ships to the red sun. Nothing was left for them, and they would get no chance to rebuild. Earth would have sent an armed fleet for a look-around. Maybe it would come soon enough to save what beings were left.

Dorcas frowned. "What will they do about it?"

"Why, uh, rebuild our navies. Defense has been grossly neglected."

"Well, we can hope for that much. We're certainly doing a service, bringing in the news that the kzinti have the hyperdrive." Dorcas shook her head. "But everybody knew they would, sooner or later. And this whole episode, it's no *casus belli*. No law forbade them to establish themselves in an unclaimed system. We should be legally safe, ourselves—self-defense—but the peace groups will say the kzinti were only being defensive, after Earth's planet grab following the war, and in fact this crew provoked them into overreacting. There may be talk of reparations due the pathetic put-upon kzinti."

"Yah, you're probably right. I share your faith in the infinite capacity of our species for wishful thinking." Saxtorph shrugged. "But we also have a capacity for muddling through. And you and I, sweetheart, have some mighty good years ahead of us. Let's talk about what to do with them."

Her mood eased. She snuggled close. The ship fared onward.

CATHOUSE

Dean Ing

Sampling war's minor ironies: Locklear knew so little about the *Weasel* or wartime alarms, he thought the klaxon was hooting for planetfall. That is why, when the *Weasel* winked into normal space near that lurking kzin warship, little Locklear would soon be her only survivor. The second irony was that, while the Interworld Commission's last bulletin had announced sporadic new outbursts of kzin hostility, Locklear was the only civilian on the *Weasel* who had never thought of himself as a warrior and did not intend to become one.

Moments after the *Weasel*'s intercom announced completion of their jump, Locklear was steadying himself next to his berth, waiting for the ship's gravity-polarizer to kick in and swallowing hard because, like ancient French wines, he traveled poorly. He watched with envy as Herrera, the hairless, whipcord-muscled Belter in the other bunk, swung out with one foot planted on the deck and the other against the wall. "Like a cat," Locklear said admiringly.

"That's no compliment anymore, flatlander," Herrera said. "It looks like the goddam tabbies want a fourth war. You'd think they'd learn," he added with a grim headshake.

Locklear sighed. As a student of animal psychology in general, he'd known a few kzinti well enough to admire the way they learned. He also knew Herrera was on his way to enlist if, as seemed likely, the kzinti were spoiling for another war. And in that case, Locklear's career was about to be turned upside down. Instead of a scholarly life puzzling out the meanings of Grog forepaw gestures and kzin ear-twitches, he would probably be conscripted into some warren full of psych warfare pundits, for the duration. These days, an ethologist had to be part historian, too—Locklear remembered more than he liked about the three previous man-kzin wars.

And Herrera was ready to fight the kzinti already, and Locklear had called *him* a cat. Locklear opened his mouth to apologize but the klaxon drowned him out. Herrera slammed the door open, vaulted into the passageway reaching for handholds.

"What's the matter," Locklear shouted. "Where are you—?"

Herrera's answer, half-lost between the door-slam and the klaxon, sounded like "atta nation" to Locklear, who did not even know the drill for a deadheading passenger during battle stations. Locklear was still waiting for a familiar tug of gravity when that door sighed, the hermetic seal swelling as always during a battle alert, and he had time to wonder why Herrera was in such a hurry before the *Weasel* took her fatal hit amidships.

An energy beam does not always sound like a thunderclap from inside the stricken vessel. This one sent a faint crackling down the length of the *Weasel's* hull, like the rustle of pre-space parchment crushed in a man's hand. Sequestered alone in a two-man cabin near the ship's aft galley, Locklear saw his bunk leap toward him, the inertia of his own body wrenching his grip from his handhold near the door. He did not have time to consider the implications of a blow powerful enough to send a twelve-hundred-ton Privateer-class patrol ship tumbling like a pinwheel, nor the fact that the blow itself was the reaction from most of the *Weasel's* air exhausting to space in explosive decompression. And, because his cabin had no external viewport, he could not see the scatter of human bodies into the void. The last thing he saw was the underside of his bunk, and the metal brace that caught him above the left cheekbone. Then he knew only a mild curiosity: wondering why he heard something like the steady sound of a thin whistle underwater, and why that yellow flash in his head was followed by an infrared darkness crammed with pain.

It was the pain that brought him awake; that, and the sound of loud static. No, more like the zaps of an arc welder in the hands of a novice—or like a catfight. And then he turned a blurred mental page and *knew* it, the way a Rorschach blot suddenly becomes a face half-forgotten but always feared. So it did not surprise him, when he opened his eyes, to see two huge kzinti standing over him.

To a man like Herrera they would merely have been massive. To Locklear, a man of less than average height, they were enormous; nearly half again his height. The broadest kzin, with the notched right ear and the black horizontal fur-mark like a frown over his eyes, opened his mouth in what, to humans, might be a smile. But kzinti smiles showed dagger teeth and always meant immediate threat.

This one was saying something that sounded like, "Clash-rowll whuff, rurr fitz."

Locklear needed a few seconds to translate it, and by that time the second kzin was saying it in Interworld: "Grraf-Commander says, 'Speak when you are spoken to.' For myself, I would prefer that you remained silent. I have eaten no monkeymeat for too long."

While Locklear composed a reply, the big one—the Grraf-Commander, evidently—spoke again to his fellow. Something about whether the monkey knew his posture was deliberately obscene. Locklear, lying on his back on a padded table as big as a Belter's honeymoon bed, realized his arms and legs were flung wide. "I am not very fluent in the Hero's tongue," he said in passable kzin, struggling to a sitting position as he spoke.

As he did, some of that pain localized at his right collarbone. Locklear moved very slowly thereafter. Then, recognizing the dot-and-comma-rich labels that graced much of the equipment in that room, he decided not to ask where he was. He could be nowhere but an emergency surgical room for kzin warriors. That meant he was on a kzin ship.

A faint slitting of the smaller kzin's eyes might have meant determination, a grasping for patience, or—if Locklear recalled the texts, and if they were right, a small "if" followed by a very large one—a pause for relatively cold calculation. The smaller kzin said, in his own tongue, "If the monkey speaks the Hero's tongue, it is probably as a spy."

"My presence here was not my idea," Locklear pointed out, surprised to find his memory of the language returning so quickly. "I boarded the *Weasel* on command to leave a dangerous region, not to enter one. Ask the ship's quartermaster, or check her records."

The commander spat and sizzled again: "The crew are all carrion. As you will soon be, unless you tell us why, of all the monkeys on that ship, you were the only one so specially protected."

Locklear moaned. This huge kzin's partial name and his scars implied the kind of warrior whose valor and honor forbade lies to a captive. All dead but himself? Locklear shrugged before he thought, and the shrug sent a stab of agony across his upper chest. "Sonofabitch," he gasped in agony. The navigator kzin translated. The larger one grinned, the kind of grin that might fasten on his throat.

Locklear said in kzin, very fast, "Not you! I was cursing the pain."

"A telepath could verify your meanings very quickly," said the smaller kzin.

"An excellent idea," said Locklear. "He will verify that I am no spy, and not a combatant, but only an ethologist from Earth. A kzin acquaintance once told me it was important to know your forms of address. I do not wish to give offense."

"Call me Tzak-Navigator," said the smaller kzin abruptly, and grasped Locklear by the shoulder, talons sinking into the human flesh. Locklear moaned again, gritting his teeth. "You would attack? Good," the navigator went on, mistaking the grimace, maintaining his grip, the formidable kzin body trembling with intent.

"I cannot speak well with such pain," Locklear managed to grunt. "Not as well protected as you think."

"We found you well-protected and sealed alone in that ship," said the commander, motioning for the navigator to slacken his hold. "I warn you, we must rendezvous the *Raptor* with another Ripping-Fang class cruiser to pick up a full crew before we hit the Eridani worlds. I have no time to waste on such a scrawny monkey as you, which we have caught nearer our home worlds than to your own."

Locklear grasped his right elbow as support for that aching collarbone. "I was surveying life-forms on purely academic study—in peacetime, so far as I knew," he said. "The old patrol craft I leased didn't have a weapon on it."

"You lie," the navigator hissed. "We saw them."

"The *Weasel* was not my ship, Tzak-Navigator. Its commander brought me back under protest; said the Interworld Commission wanted noncombatants out of harm's way—and here I am in its cloaca."

"Then it was already well-known on that ship that we are at war. I feel better about killing it," said the commander. "Now, as to the ludicrous cargo it was carrying: what is your title and importance?"

"I am scholar Carroll Locklear. I was probably the least important man on the *Weasel*—except to myself. Since I have nothing to hide, bring a telepath."

"Now it gives orders," snarled the navigator.

"Please," Locklear said quickly.

"Better," the commander said.

"It knows," the navigator muttered. "That is why it issues such a challenge."

"Perhaps," the commander rumbled. To Locklear he said, "A skeleton crew of four rarely includes a telepath. That statement will either satisfy your challenge, or I can satisfy it in more—conventional ways." That grin again, feral, willing.

"I meant no challenge, Grraf-Commander. I only want to satisfy you of who I am, and who I'm not."

"We know *what* you are," said the navigator. "You are our prisoner, an important one, fleeing the Patriarchy rim in hopes that the monkeyship could get you to safety." He reached again for Locklear's shoulder.

"That is pure torture," Locklear said, wincing, and saw the navigator stiffen as the furry orange arm dropped. If only he had recalled the kzinti disdain for torture earlier! "I am told you are an honorable race. May I be treated properly as a captive?"

"By all means," the commander said, almost in a purr. "We eat captives."

Locklear, slyly: "Even important ones?"

"If it pleases me," the commander replied. "More likely you could turn your coat in the service of the Patriarchy. I say you could; I would not suggest such an obscenity. But that is probably the one chance your sort has for personal survival."

"My sort?"

The commander looked Locklear up and down, at the slender body, lightly muscled with only the deep chest to suggest stamina. "One of the most vulnerable specimens of monkeydom I have ever seen," he said.

That was the moment when Locklear decided he was at war. "Vulnerable, and important, and captive. Eat me," he said, wondering if that final phrase was as insulting in kzin as it was in Interworld. Evidently not . . .

"Gunner! Apprentice Engineer," the commander called suddenly, and Locklear heard two responses through the ship's intercom. "Lock this monkey in a wiper's quarters." He turned to his navigator. "Perhaps Fleet Commander Skrull-Rrit will want this one alive. We shall know in an eight-squared of duty watches." With that, the huge kzin commander strode out.

* * *

After his second sleep, Locklear found himself roughly hustled forward in the low-polarity ship's gravity of the *Raptor* by the nameless Apprentice Engineer. This smallest of the crew had been a kitten not long before and, at two-meter height, was still filling out. The transverse mustard-tinted band across his abdominal fur identified Apprentice Engineer down the full length of the hull passageway.

Locklear, his right arm in a sling of bandages, tried to remember all the mental notes he had made since being tossed into that cell. He kept his eyes downcast to avoid a challenging look—and because he did not want his cold fury to show. These orange-furred monstrosities had killed a ship and crew with every semblance of pride in the act. They treated a civilian captive at best like playground bullies treat an urchin, and at worst like food. It was all very well to study animal behavior as a detached ethologist. It was something else when the toughest warriors in the galaxy attached you to their food chain.

He slouched because that was as far from a military posture as a man could get—and Locklear's personal war could hardly be declared if he valued his own pelt. He would try to learn where hand weapons were kept, but would try to seem stupid. He would . . . he found the last vow impossible to keep with the Grraf-Commander's first question.

Wheeling in his command chair on the *Raptor*'s bridge, the commander faced the captive. "If you piloted your own monkeyship, then you have some menial skills." It was not a question; more like an accusation. "Can you learn to read meters if it will lengthen your pathetic life?"

Ah, there *was* a question! Locklear was on the point of lying, but it took a worried kzin to sing a worried song. If they needed him to read meters, he might learn much in a short time. Besides, they'd know bloody well if he lied on this matter. "I can try," he said. "What's the problem?"

"Tell him," spat Grraf-Commander, spinning about again to the holo screen.

Tzak-Navigator made a gesture of agreement, standing beside Locklear and gazing toward the vast humped shoulders of the fourth kzin. This nameless one was of truly gigantic size. He turned, growling, and Locklear noted the nose scar that seemed very appropriate for a flash-tempered gunner. Tzak-Navigator met his gaze and paused, with the characteristic tremor of a kzin who prided himself on physical control. "Ship's Gunner, you are relieved. Adequately done."

With the final phrase, Ship's Gunner relaxed his ear umbrellas and stalked off with a barely creditable salute. Tzak-Navigator pointed to the vacated seat, and Locklear took it. "He has got us lost," muttered the navigator.

"But you were the navigator," Locklear said.

"Watch your tongue!"

"I'm just trying to understand crew duties. I asked what the problem was, and Grraf-Commander said to tell me."

The tremor became more obvious, but Tzak-Navigator knew when he was boxed. "With a four-kzin crew, our titles and our duties tend to vary. When I accept duties of executive officer and communications officer as well, another member may prove his mettle at some simple tasks of astrogation."

"I would think Apprentice Engineer might be good at reading meters," Locklear said carefully.

"He has enough of them to read in the engine room. Besides, Ship's Gunner has superior time in grade; to pass him over would have been a deadly insult."

"Um. And I don't count?"

"Exactly. As a captive, you are a nonperson—even if you have skills that a gunner might lack."

"You said it was adequately done," Locklear pointed out.

"For a gunner," spat the navigator, and Locklear smiled. A kzin, too proud to lie, could still speak with mental reservations to an underling. The navigator went on: "We drew first blood with our chance sortie to the galactic West, but Ship's Gunner must verify gravitational blips as we pass in hyperdrive."

Locklear listened, and asked, and learned. What he learned initially was fast mental translation of octal numbers to decimal. What he learned eventually was that, counting on the gunner to verify likely blips of known star masses, Grraf-Commander had finally realized that they were monumentally lost, light-years from their intended rendezvous on the rim of known space. *And that rendezvous is on the way to the Eridani worlds,* Locklear thought. He said, as if to himself but in kzin, "Out Eridani way, I hear they're always on guard for you guys. You really expect to get out of this alive?"

"No," said the navigator easily. "Your life may be extended a little, but you will die with heroes. Soon."

"Sounds like a suicide run," Locklear said.

"We are volunteers," the navigator said with lofty arrogance, making no attempt to argue the point, and then continued his instructions.

Presently, studying the screen, Locklear said, "That gunner has us forty parsecs from anyplace. Jump into normal space long enough for an astrogation fix and you've got it."

"Do not abuse my patience, monkey. Our last

Fleet Command message on hyperwave forbade us to make unnecessary jumps."

After a moment, Locklear grinned. "And your commander doesn't want to have to tell Fleet Command you're lost."

"What was that thing you did with your face?"

"Uh,—just stretching the muscles," Locklear lied, and pointed at one of the meters. "There; um, that has a field strength of, oh hell, three eights and four, right?"

Tzak-Navigator did not have to tremble because his four-fingered hand was in motion as a blur, punching buttons. "Yes. I have a star mass and," the small screen stuttered its chicken-droppings in Kzinti, "here are the known candidates."

Locklear nodded. In this little-known region, some star masses, especially the larger ones, would have been recorded. With several fixes in hyperdrive, he could make a strong guess at their direction with respect to the galactic core. But by the time he had his second group of candidate stars, Locklear also had a scheme.

Locklear asked for his wristcomp, to help him translate octal numbers—his chief motive was less direct—and got it after Apprentice Engineer satisfied himself that it was no energy weapon. The engineer, a suspicious churl quick with his hands and clearly on the make for status, displayed disappointment at his own findings by throwing the instrument in Locklear's face. Locklear decided that the kzin lowest on the scrotum pole was most anxious to advance by any means available. And that, he decided, just might be common in all sentient behavior.

Two hours later by his wristcomp, when Locklear tried to speak to the commander without prior permission, the navigator backhanded him for his trouble and then explained the proper channels. "I will decide whether your message is worth Grraf-Commander's notice," he snarled.

Trying to stop his nosebleed, Locklear told him.

"A transparent ruse," the navigator accused, "to save your own hairless pelt."

"It would have that effect," Locklear agreed. "Maybe. But it would also let you locate your position."

The navigator looked him up and down. "Which will aid us in our mission against your own kind. You truly disgust me."

In answer, Locklear only shrugged. Tzak-Navigator wheeled and crossed to the commander's vicinity, stiff and proper, and spoke rapidly for a few moments. Presently, Grraf-Commander motioned for Locklear to approach.

Locklear decided that a military posture might help this time, and tried to hold his body straight despite his pains. The commander eyed him silently, then said, "You offer me a motive to justify jumping into normal space?"

"Yes, Grraf-Commander: to deposit an important captive in a lifeboat around some stellar body."

"And why in the name of the Patriarchy would I want to?"

"Because it is almost within the reach of plausibility that the occupants of this ship might not survive this mission," Locklear said with irony that went unnoticed. "But en route to your final glory, you can inform Fleet Command where you have placed a vitally important captive, to be retrieved later."

"You admit your status at last."

"I have a certain status," Locklear admitted. *It's damned low, and that's certain enough.* "And while you were doing that in normal space, a navigator might just happen to determine exactly where you are."

"You do not deceive me in your motive. If I did not locate that spot," Tzak-Navigator said, "no Patriarchy ship could find you—and you would soon run out of food and air."

"And you would miss the Eridani mission," Locklear reminded him, "because we aren't getting any blips and you may be getting farther from your rendezvous with every breath."

"At the least, you are a traitor to monkeydom," the navigator said. "No kzin worthy of the name would assist an enemy mission."

Locklear favored him with a level gaze. "You've decided to waste all nine lives for glory. Count on me for help."

"Monkeys are clever where their pelts are concerned," rumbled the commander. "I do not intend to miss rendezvous, and this monkey must be placed in a safe cage. Have the crew provision a lifeboat but disable its drive, Tzak-Navigator. When we locate a stellar mass, I want all in readiness for the jump."

The navigator saluted and moved off the bridge. Locklear received permission to return to his console, moving slowly, trying to watch the commander's furry digits in preparation for a jump that might be required at any time. Locklear punched several notes into the wristcomp's memory; you could never tell when a scholar's notes might come in handy.

Locklear was chewing on kzin rations, reconstituted meat which met human teeth like a leather brick and tasted of last week's oysters, when the long-range meter began to register. It was not much of a blip but it got stronger fast, the vernier meter registering by the time Locklear called out. He watched the commander, alone while the rest of the crew were arranging that lifeboat, and used his wristcomp a few more times before Grraf-Commander's announcement.

Tzak-Navigator, eyeing his console moments after the jump and still light-minutes from that small stellar mass, was at first too intent on his astrogation to notice that there was no nearby solar blaze. But Locklear noticed, and felt a surge of panic.

"You will not perish in solar radiation, at least," said Grraf-Commander in evident pleasure. "You have found yourself a black dwarf, monkey!"

Locklear punched a query. He found no candidate stars to match this phenomenon. "Permission to speak, Tzak-Navigator?"

The navigator punched in a final instruction and, while his screen flickered, turned to the local viewscreen. "Wait until you have something worth saying," he ordered, and paused, staring at what that screen told him. Then, as if arguing with his screen, he complained, "But known space is not old enough for a completely burnt-out star."

"Nevertheless," the commander replied, waving toward the screens, "if not a black dwarf, a very, very brown one. Thank that lucky star, Tzak-Navigator; it might have been a neutron star."

"And a planet," the navigator exclaimed. "Impossible! Before its final collapse, this star would have converted any nearby planet into a gas shell. But there it lies!" He pointed to a luminous dot on the screen.

"That might make it easy to find again," Locklear said with something akin to faint hope. He knew, watching the navigator's split concentration between screens, that the kzin would soon know the *Raptor's* position. No chance beyond this brown dwarf now, an unheard-of anomaly, to escape this suicide ship.

The navigator ignored him. "Permission for proximal orbit," he requested.

"Denied," the commander said. "You know better than that. Close orbit around a dwarf could rip us asunder with angular acceleration. That dwarf may be only the size of a single dreadnaught, but its mass is enormous enough to bend distant starlight."

While Locklear considered what little he knew of collapsed star matter, a cupful of which would exceed the mass of the greatest warship in known space, the navigator consulted his astrogation screen again. "I have our position," he said at last. "We were on the way to the galactic rim, thanks to that untrained—well, at least he is a fine gunner. Grraf-Commander, I meant to ask permission for orbit around the planet. We can discard this offal in the lifeboat there."

"Granted," said the commander. Locklear took more notes as the two kzinti piloted their ship nearer. If lifeboats were piloted with the same systems as cruisers, and if he could study the ways in which that lifeboat drive could be energized, he might yet take a hand in his fate.

The maneuvers took so much time that Locklear feared the kzin would drop the whole idea, but, "Let it be recorded that I keep my bargains, even with monkeys," the commander grouched as the planet began to grow in the viewport.

"Tiny suns, orbiting the planet? Stranger and stranger," the navigator mused. "Grraf-Commander, this is—not natural."

"Exactly so. It is artificial," said the commander. Brightening, he added, "Perhaps a special project, though I do not know how we could move a full-sized planet into orbit around a dwarf. Tzak-Navigator, see if this tallies with anything the Patriarchy may have on file." No sound passed between them when the navigator looked up from his screen, but their shared glance did not improve the commander's mood. "No? Well, backup records in triplicate," he snapped. "Survey sensors to full gain."

Locklear took more notes, his heart pounding anew with every added strangeness of this singular discovery. The planet orbited several light-minutes from the dead star, with numerous satellites in synchronous orbits, blazing like tiny suns—or rather, like spotlights in imitation of tiny suns, for the radiation from those satellites blazed only downward, toward the planet's surface. Those satellites, according to the navigator, seemed to be moving a bit in complex patterns, not all of them in the same ways—and one of them dimmed even as they watched.

The commander brought the ship nearer, and now Tzak-Navigator gasped with a fresh astonishment. "Grraf-Commander, this planet is dotted with force-cylinder generators. Not complete shells, but open to space at orbital height. And the beam-spread of each satellite's light flux coincides with the edge of each force cylinder. No, not all of them; several of those circular areas are not bathed in any light at all. Fallow areas?"

"Or unfinished areas," the commander grunted. "Perhaps we have discovered a project in the making."

Locklear saw blazes of blue, white, red, and yellow impinging in vast circular patterns on the planet's surface. *Almost as if someone had placed small models of Sirius, Sol, Fomalhaut, and other suns out here,* he thought. He said nothing. If he or bited this bizarre mystery long enough, he might probe its secrets. If he orbited it too long, he would damned well die of starvation.

Then, "Homeworld," blurted the astonished navigator, as the ship continued its close pass around this planet that was at least half the mass of Earth.

Locklear saw it too, a circular region that seemed to be hundreds of kilometers in diameter, rich in colors that reminded him of a kzin's fur. The green expanse of a big lake, too, as well as dark masses that might have been mountain crags. And then he noticed that one of the nearby circular patterns seemed achingly familiar in its colors, and before he thought, he said it in Interworld: "Earth!"

The commander leaped to a mind-numbing conclusion the moment before Locklear did. "This can only be a galactic prison—or a zoo," he said in a choked voice. "The planet was evidently moved here, after the brown dwarf was discovered. There seems to be no atmosphere outside the force walls, and the planetary surface between those circular regions is almost as cold as interstellar deeps, according to the sensors. If it is a prison, each compound is well-isolated from the others. Nothing could live in the interstices."

Locklear knew that the commander had overlooked something that could live there very comfortably, but held his tongue awhile. Then, "Permission to speak," he said.

"Granted," said the commander. "What do you know of this—this thing?"

"Only this: whether it is a zoo or a prison, one of those compounds seems very Earthlike. If you left me there, I might find air and food to last me indefinitely."

"And other monkeys to help in Patriarch-knows-what," the navigator put in quickly. "No one is answering my all-band queries, and we do not know who runs this prison. The Patriarchy has no prison on record that is even faintly like this."

"If they are keeping Heroes in a kzinti compound," grated the commander, "this could be a planet-sized trap."

Tzak-Navigator: "But whose?"

Grraf-Commander, with arrogant satisfaction: "It will not matter whose it is, if they set a vermin-sized trap and catch an armed lifeboat. There is no shell over these circular walls, and if there were, I would try to blast through it. Re-enable the lifeboat's drive. Tzak-Navigator, as Executive Officer you will remain on alert in the *Raptor*. For the rest of us: sound planetfall!"

Caught between fright and amazement, Locklear could only hang on and wait, painfully buffeted during re-entry because the kzin-sized seat harness would not retract to fit his human frame. The lifeboat, the size of a flatlander's racing yacht, descended in a broad spiral, keeping well inside those invisible force-walls that might have damaged the craft on contact. At last the commander set his ship on a search pattern that spiraled inward while maintaining perhaps a kilometer's height above the yellow grassy plains, the kzin-colored steaming jungle, the placid lake, the dark mountain peaks of this tiny, synthesized piece of the kzin homeworld.

Presently, the craft settled near a promontory overlooking that lake and partially protected by the rise of a stone escarpment—the landfall of a good military mind, Locklear admitted to himself. "Apprentice Engineer: report on environmental conditions," the commander ordered. Turning to Locklear, he added, "If this is a zoo, the zookeepers have not yet learned to capture Heroes—nor any of our food animals, according to our survey. Since your metabolism is so near ours, I think this is where we shall deposit you for safekeeping."

"But without prey, Grraf-Commander, he will soon starve," said Apprentice Engineer.

The heavy look of the commander seemed full of ironic amusement. "No, he will not. Humans eat monkeyfood, remember? This specimen is a *kshat*."

Locklear colored but tried to ignore the insult. Any creature willing to eat vegetation was, to the kzinti, *kshat*, a herbivore capable of eating offal. And capable of little else. "You might leave me some rations anyway," he grumbled. "I'm in no condition to be climbing trees for food."

"But you soon may be, and a single monkey in this place could hide very well from a search party."

Apprentice Engineer, performing his extra duties proudly, waved a digit toward the screen. "Grraf-Commander, the gravity constant is exactly home normal. The temperature, too; solar flux, the same; atmosphere and micro-organisms as well. I suspect that the builders of this zoo planet have buried gravity polarizers with the force cylinder generators."

"No doubt those other compounds are equally equipped to surrogate certain worlds," the commander said. "I think, whoever they are—or were—the builders work very, very slowly."

Locklear, entertaining his own scenario, suspected the builders worked very slowly, all right—and in ways, with motives, beyond the understanding of man or kzin. But why tell his suspicions to Scarface? Locklear had by now given his own private labels to these infuriating kzin, after noting the commander's face-mark, the navigator's tremors of intent, the gunner's brutal stupidity and the engineer's abdominal patch: to Locklear, they had become Scarface, Brick-shitter, Goon, and Yellowbelly. Those labels gave him an emotional lift, but he knew better than to use them aloud.

Scarface made his intent clear to everyone, glancing at Locklear from time to time, as he gave his orders. Water and rations for eight duty watches were to be offloaded. Because every kzin craft has special equipment to pacify those kzinti who displayed criminal behavior, especially the Kdaptists with their treasonous leanings toward humankind, Scarface had prepared a *zzrou* for their human captive. The *zzrou* could be charged with a powerful soporific drug, or—as the commander said in this case—a poison. Affixed to a host and tuned to a transmitter, the *zzrou* could be set to inject its material into the host at regular intervals—or to meter it out whenever the host moved too far from that transmitter.

Scarface held the implant device, no larger than a biscuit with vicious prongs, in his hand, facing the captive. "If you try to extract this, it will kill you instantly. If you somehow found the transmitter and smashed it—again you would die instantly. Whenever you stray two steps too far from it, you will suffer. I shall set it so that you can move about far enough to feed yourself, but not far enough to make finding you a difficulty."

Locklear chewed his lip for a moment, thinking. "Is the poison cumulative?"

"Yes. And if you do not know that honor forbids me to lie, you will soon find out to your sorrow." He turned and handed a small device to Yellowbelly. "Take this transmitter and place it where no monkey might stumble across it. Do not wander more than eight-cubed paces from here in the process—and take a sidearm and a transceiver with you. I am not absolutely certain the place is uninhabited. Captive! Bare your back."

Locklear, dry-mouthed, removed his jacket and shirt. He watched Yellowbelly bound back down the short passageway and, soon afterward, heard the sigh of an airlock. He turned casually, trying to catch sight of him as Goon was peering through the viewport, and then he felt a paralyzing agony as Scarface impacted the prongs of the *zzrou* into his back just below the left shoulder blade.

His first sensation was a chill, and his second was a painful reminder of those *zzrou* prongs sunk into the muscles of his back. Locklear eased to a sitting position and looked around him. Except for depressions in the yellowish grass, and a terrifyingly small pile of provisions piled atop his shirt and jacket, he could see no evidence that a kzin lifeboat had ever landed here. "For all you know, they'll never come back," he told himself aloud, shivering as he donned his garments. Talking to himself was an old habit born of solitary researches, and made him feel less alone.

But now that he thought on it, he couldn't decide which he dreaded most, their return or permanent solitude. "So let's take stock," he said, squatting next to the provisions. A kzin's rations would last three times as long for him, but the numbers were depressing: within three flatlander weeks he'd either find water and food, or he would starve—if he did not freeze first.

If this was really a compound designed for kzin, it would be chilly for Locklear—and it was. The water would be drinkable, and no doubt he could eat kzin game animals if he found any that did not eat him first. He had already decided to head for the edge of that lake, which lay shining at a distance that was hard to judge, when he realized that local animals might destroy what food he had.

Wincing with the effort, he removed his light jacket again. They had taken his small utility knife but Yellowbelly had not checked his grooming tool very well. He deployed its shaving blade instead of the nail pincers and used it to slit away the jacket's epaulets, then cut carefully at the triple-folds of cloth, grateful for his accidental choice of a woven fabric. He found that when trying to break a thread, he would cut his hand before the thread parted. Good; a single thread would support all of those rations but the water bulbs.

His wristcomp told him the kzin had been gone an hour, and the position of that ersatz 61 Ursa Majoris hanging in the sky said he should have several more hours of light, unless the builders of this zoo had fudged on their timing. "Numbers," he said. "You need better numbers." He couldn't eat a number, but knowing the right ones might feed his belly.

In the landing pad depressions lay several stones, some crushed by the cruel weight of the kzin lifeboat. He pocketed a few fragments, two with sharp edges, tied a third stone to a twenty-meter length of thread and tossed it clumsily over a branch of a vine-choked tree. But when he tried to pull those rations up to suspend them out of harm's way, that thread sawed the pulpy branch in two. Sighing, he began collecting and stripping vines. Favoring his right shoulder, ignoring the pain of the *zzrou* as he used his left arm, he finally managed to suspend the plastic-encased bricks of leathery meat five meters above the grass. It was easier to cache the water, running slender vines through the carrying handles and suspending the water in two bundles. He kept one brick and one water bulb, which contained perhaps two gallons of the precious stuff.

And then he made his first crucial discovery, when a trickle of moisture issued from the severed end of a vine. It felt cool, and it didn't sting his hands, and taking the inevitable plunge he licked at a droplet, and then sucked at the end of that vine. Good clean water, faintly sweet; but with what subtle poisons? He decided to wait a day before trying it again, but he was smiling a ferocious little smile.

Somewhere within an eight-cubed of kzin paces lay the transmitter for that damned thing stuck into his back. No telling exactly how far he could stray from it. "Damned right there's some telling," he announced to the breeze. "Numbers, numbers," he muttered. And straight lines. If that misbegotten son of a hairball was telling the truth—and a kzin always did—then Locklear would know within a step or so when he'd gone too far. The safe distance from that transmitter would probably be the same in all directions, a hemisphere of space to roam in. Would it let him get as far as the lake?

He found out after sighting toward the nearest edge of the lake and setting out for it, slashing at the trunks of jungle trees with a sharp stone to blaze a straight-line trail. Not exactly straight, but nearly so. He listened hard at every step, moving steadily downhill, wondering what might have a menu with his name on it.

That careful pace saved him a great deal of pain, but not enough of it to suit him. Once, studying the heat-sensors that guided a captive rattlesnake to its prey back on Earth, Locklear had been bitten on the hand. It was like that now behind and below his left shoulder, a sudden burning ache that kept aching as he fell forward, writhing, hurting his right collarbone

again. Locklear scrambled backward five paces or so
and the sting was suddenly, shockingly, absent. That
part wasn't like a rattler bite, for sure. He cursed,
but knew he had to do it: moved forward again, very
slowly, until he felt the lancing bite of the *zzrou*. He
moved back a pace and the sting was gone. "But it's
cumulative," he said aloud. "Can't do this for a hobby."

He felled a small tree at that point, sawing it with
a thread tied to stones until the pulpy trunk fell,
held at an angle by vines. Its sap was milky. It stung
his finger. Damned if he would let it sting his tongue.
He couldn't wash the stuff off in lake water because
the lake was perhaps a klick beyond his limit. He
wondered if Yellowbelly had thought about that when
he hid the transmitter.

Locklear had intended to pace off the distance he
had moved from his food cache, but kzin gravity
seemed to drag at his heels and he knew that he
needed numbers more exact than the paces of a
tiring man. He unwound all of the thread on the
ball, then sat down and opened his grooming tool.
Whatever forgotten genius had stamped a five-
centimeter rule along the length of the pincer lever,
Locklear owed him. He measured twenty of those
lengths and then tied a knot. He then used that first
one-meter length to judge his second knot; used it
again for the third; and with fingers that stung from
tiny cuts, tied two knots at the five-meter point. He
tied three knots at the ten-meter point, then continued until he had fifteen meters of surveying line,
ignoring the last meter or so.

He needed another half-hour to measure the distance, as straight as he could make it, back to the
food cache: four hundred and thirty-seven meters.
He punched the datum into his wristcomp and rested,
drinking too much from that water bulb, noting that

the sunlight was making longer shadows now. The sundown direction was "West" by definition. And after sundown, what? Nocturnal predators? He was already exhausted, cold, and in need of shelter. Locklear managed to pile palmlike fronds as his bed in a narrow cleft of the promontory, made the best weapon he could by tying fist-sized stones two meters apart with a thread, grasped one stone and whirled the other experimentally. It made a satisfying whirr— and for all he knew, it might even be marginally useful.

The sunblaze fooled him, dying slowly while it was still halfway to his horizon. He punched the time into his wristcomp, and realized that the builders of this zoo might be limited in the degree to which they could surrogate a planetary surface, when other vast circular cages were adjacent to this one. It was too much to ask that any zoo cage be, for its specimens, the best of all possible worlds.

Locklear slept badly, but he slept. During the times when he lay awake, he felt the silence like a hermetic seal around him, broken only by the rasp and slither of distant tree fronds in vagrant breezes. Kzin-normal microorganisms, the navigator had said; maybe, but Locklear had seen no sign of animal life. Almost, he would have preferred stealthy footfalls or screams of nocturnal prowlers.

The next morning he noted on his wristcomp when the ersatz kzinti sun began to blaze—not on the horizon, but seeming to kindle when halfway to its zenith—rigged a better sling for his right arm, then sat scratching in the dirt for a time. The night had lasted thirteen hours and forty-eight minutes. If succeeding nights were longer, he was in for a tooth-chattering winter. But first: FIND THAT DAMNED TRANSMITTER. Because it was small enough to fit in a pocket. And then, ah then, he would not be held like a lap-dog on a leash. He pounded some kzin meat to soften it and took his first sightings while swilling from a water bulb.

The extension of that measured line, this time in the opposite direction, went more quickly except when he had to clamber on rocky inclines or cut one of those pulpy trees down to keep his sightings near-perfect. He had no spirit level, but estimated the inclines as well as he could, as he had done before, and used the wristcomp's trigonometric functions to adjust the numbers he took from his surveying thread. That damned kzin engineer was the kind who would be half-running to do his master's bidding, and an eight-cubed of his paces might be anywhere from six hundred meters to a kilometer. Or the hidden transmitter might be almost underfoot at the cache; but no more than a klick at most. Locklear was pondering that when the *zzrou* zapped him again.

He stiffened, yelped, and whirled back several paces, then advanced very slowly until he felt its first half-hearted bite, and moved back, punching in the datum, working backward using the same system to make doubly sure of his numbers. At the cache, he found his two new numbers varied by five meters and split the difference. His southwest limit had been 437 meters away, his northeast limit 529; which meant the total length of that line was 966 meters. It probably wasn't the full diameter of his circle, but those points lay on its circumference. He halved the number: 483. That number, minus the 437, was 46 meters. He measured off forty-six meters toward the northeast and piled pulpy branches in a pyramid higher than his head. This point, by God, *was* one point on the full diameter of that circle perpendicular to his first line! Next he had to survey a line at a right angle to the line he'd already surveyed, a line passing through that pyramid of branches.

It took him all morning and then some, lengthening his thread to be more certain of that crucial right-angle before he set off into the jungle, and he measured almost seven hundred meters before that bloody damned *zzrou* bit him again, this time not so painfully because by that time he was moving very slowly. He returned to the pyramid of branches and struck off in the opposite direction, just to be sure of the numbers he scratched in the dirt using the wristcomp. He was filled with joy when the *zzrou* faithfully poisoned him a bit over 300 meters away, within ten meters of his expectation.

Those first three limit points had been enough to rough out the circle; the fourth was confirmation. Locklear knew that he had passed the transmitter on that long northwest leg; calculated quickly, because he knew the exact length of that diameter, that it was a bit over two hundred meters from his pyramid; and measured off the distance after lunch.

"Just like that fur-licking bastard," he said, looking around him at the tangle of orange, green, and yellow jungle growth. "Probably shit on it before he buried it."

Locklear spent a fruitless hour clearing punky shrubs and man-high ferns from the soft turf before he saw it, and of course it was not where he had been looking at all. "It" was not a telltale mound of dirt, nor a kzin footprint. It was a group of three globes of milky sap, no larger than water droplets, just about knee-high on the biggest palm in the clearing. And just about the right pattern for a kzin's toe-claws.

He moved around the trunk, as thick as his body, staring up the tree, now picking out other sets of milky puncture marks spaced up the trunk. More kzin clawmarks. Softly, feeling the gooseflesh move down his arms, he called, "Ollee-ollee-all's-in-free," just for the hell of it. And then he cut the damned tree down, carefully, letting the breeze do part of the work so that the tree sagged, buckled, and came down at a leisurely pace.

The transmitter, which looked rather like a wrist-comp without a bracelet, lay in a hole scooped out by Yellowbelly's claws in the tender young top of the tree. It was sticky with sap, and Locklear hoped it had stung the kzin as it was stinging his own fingers. He wiped it off with vine leaves, rinsed it with dribbles of water from severed vines, wiped it off again, and then returned to his food cache.

"Yep, the shoulder hurts, and the damned gravity doesn't help but," he said, and yelled it at the sky, "now I'm loose, you rat-tailed sons of bitches!"

He spent another night at the first cache, now with little concern about things that went bump in the ersatz night. The sunblaze dimmed thirteen hours and forty-eight minutes after it began, and Locklear guessed that the days and nights of this synthetic arena never changed. "It'd be tough to develop a cosmology here," he said aloud, shivering because his right shoulder simply would not let him generate a fire by friction. "Maybe that was deliberate." If he wanted to study the behavior of intelligent species without risking their learning too much, and had not the faintest kind of ethics about it, Locklear decided he might imagine just such a vast enclosure for the kzinti. Only they were already a spacefaring race, and so was humankind, and he could have *sworn* the adjacent area on this impossible zoo planet was a ringer for one of the wild areas back on Earth. He cudgeled his memory until he recalled the lozenge shape of that lake seen from orbit, and the earthlike area.

"Right—about—there," he said, nodding to the southwest, across the lake. "If I don't starve first."

He knew that any kzinti searching for him could simply home in on the transmitter. Or maybe not so simply, if the signal was balked by stone or dirt. A cave with a kink in it could complicate their search nicely. He could test the idea—at the risk of absorbing one zap too many from that infuriating *zzrou* clinging to his back.

"Well, second things second," he said. He'd attended to the first things first. He slept poorly again, but the collarbone seemed to be mending.

Locklear admitted an instant's panic the next morning (he had counted down to the moment when the ersatz sun began to shine, missing it by a few seconds) as he moved beyond his old limit toward the lake. But the *zzrou* might have been a hockey puck for its inertness. The lake had small regular wavelets— *easy enough to generate if you have a timer on your gravity polarizer*, he mused to the builders—and a narrow beach that alternated between sand and pebbles. No prints of any kind, not even birds or molluscs. If this huge arena did not have extremes of weather, a single footprint on that sand might last a geologic era.

The food cache was within a stone's throw of the kzin landing, good enough reason to find a better place. Locklear found one, where a stream trickled to the lake (pumps, or rainfall? Time enough to find out), after cutting its passage down through basalt that was half-hidden by foliage. Locklear found a hollow beneath a low waterfall and, in three trips, portaged all his meagre stores to that hideyhole with its stone shelf. The water tasted good, and again he tested the trickle from slashed vines because he did not intend to stay tied to that lakeside forever.

The channel cut through basalt by water told him that the stream had once been a torrent and might be again. The channel also hinted that the stream had been cutting its patient way for tens of centuries, perhaps far longer. "Zoo has been here a long time," he said, startled at the tinny echo behind the murmur of water, realizing that he had begun to think of this planet as "Zoo." It might be untenanted, like that sad remnant of a capitalist's dream that still drew tourists to San Simeon on the coast of Earth's California. Cages for exotic fauna, but the animals long since gone. *Or never introduced?* One more puzzle to be shelved until more pieces could be studied.

During his fourth day on Zoo, Locklear realized that the water was almost certainly safe, and that he must begin testing the tubers, spiny nuts, and poisonous-looking fruit that he had been eyeing with mistrust. Might as well test the stuff while circumnavigating the lake, he decided, vowing to try one new plant a day. Nothing had nibbled at anything beyond mosslike growths on some soft-surfaced fruit. He guessed that the growths meant that the fruit was over-ripe, and judged ripeness that way. He did not need much time deciding about plants that stank horribly, or that stung his hands. On the seventh day on Zoo, while using a brown plant juice to draw a map on plastic food wrap (a pathetic left-handed effort), he began to feel distinct localized pains in his stomach. He put a finger down his throat, bringing up bits of kzin rations and pieces of the nutmeats he had swallowed after trying to chew them during breakfast. They had gone into his mouth like soft rubber capsules, and down his throat the same way.

But they had grown tiny hair-roots in his belly,

and while he watched the nasty stuff he had splashed on stone, those roots continued to grow, waving blindly. He applied himself to the task again and finally coughed up another. How many had he swallowed? Three, or four? He thought four, but saw only three, and only after smashing a dozen more of the nutshells was he satisfied that each shell held three, and only three, of the loathesome things. Not animals, perhaps, but they would eat you nonetheless. Maybe he should've named the place "Herbarium." The hell with it: "Zoo" it remained.

On the ninth day, carrying the meat in his jacket, he began to use his right arm sparingly. That was the day he realized that he had rounded the broad curve of the lake and, if his brief memory of it from orbit was accurate, the placid lake was perhaps three times as long as it was wide. He found it possible to run, one of his few athletic specialties, and despite the wear of kzin gravity he put fourteen thousand running paces behind him before exhaustion made him gather high grasses for a bed.

At a meter and a half per step, he had covered twenty-one klicks, give or take a bit, that day. Not bad in this gravity, he decided, even if the collarbone was aching again. On his abominable map, that placed him about midway down the long side of the lake. The following morning he turned west, following another stream through an open grassy plain, jogging, resting, jogging. He gathered tubers floating downstream and ate one, fearing that it would surely be deadly because it tasted like a wild strawberry.

He followed the stream for three more days, living mostly on those delicious tubers and water, nesting warmly in thick sheaves of grass. On the next day he spied a dark mass of basalt rising to the northwest, captured two litres of water in an empty plastic bag,

and risked all. It was well that he did for, late in the
following day with heaving chest, he saw clouds sweeping in from the north, dragging a gray downpour as a
bride drags her train. That stream far below and
klicks distant was soon a broad river which would
have swept him to the lake. But now he stood on a
rocky escarpment, seeing the glisten of water from
those crags in the distance, and knew that he would
not die of thirst in the highlands. He also suspected,
judging from the shredded-cotton roiling of cloud
beyond those crags, that he was very near the walls
of his cage.

Even for a runner, the two-kilometer rise of those
crags was daunting in high gravity. Locklear aimed
for a saddleback only a thousand meters high where
sheets of rain had fallen not long before, hiking beside a swollen stream until he found its source. It
wasn't much as glaciers went, but he found green
depths of ice filling the saddleback, shouldering up
against a force wall that beggared anything he had
ever seen up close.

The wall was transparent, apparent to the eye only
by its effects and by the eldritch blackness just beyond
it. The thing was horrendously cold, seeming to cut
straight across hills and crags with an inner border of
ice to define this kzin compound. Locklear knew it
only seemed straight because the curvature was so
gradual. When he tossed a stone at it, the stone
slowed abruptly and soundlessly as if encountering a
meters-deep cushion, then slid downward and back
to clatter onto the minuscule glacier. Uphill and
down, for as far as he could see, ice rimmed the
inside of the force wall. He moved nearer, staring
through that invisible sponge, and saw another line
of ice a klick distant. Between those ice rims lay bare

basalt, as uncompromisingly primitive as the surface of an asteroid. Most of that raw surface was so dark as to seem featureless, but reflections from ice lenses on each side dappled the dark basalt here and there. The dapples of light were crystal clear, without the usual fuzziness of objects a thousand meters away, and Locklear realized he was staring into a vacuum.

"So visitors to Zoo can wander comfortably around with gravity polarizer platforms between the cages," he said aloud, angrily because he could see the towering masses of ponderosa pines and blue spruce in the next compound. It was an Earth compound, all right—but he could see no evidence of animals across that distance, and that made him fiercely glad for some reason. He ached to cross those impenetrable barriers, and his vision of lofty conifers blurred with his tears.

His feet were freezing, now, and no vegetation grew as near as the frost that lined the ice rim. "You're good, but you're not perfect," he said to the builders. "You can't keep the heat in these compounds from leaking away at the rims." Hence frozen moisture and the lack of vegetation along the rim, and higher rainfall where clouds skirted that cold force wall.

Scanning the vast panoramic arc of that ice rim, Locklear noted that his prison compound had a gentle bowl shape, though some hills and crags surged up in the lowlands. *Maybe using the natural contours of old craters? Or maybe you made those craters.* It was an engineering project that held tremendous secrets for humankind, and it had been there for one hell of a long time. Widely spaced across that enormous bowl were spots of dramatic color, perhaps flowers. *But they won't scatter much without animal vectors to help the wind disperse seeds and such. Dammit, this place wasn't finished!*

He retraced his steps downward. There was no point in making a camp in this inclement place, and with every sudden whistle of breeze now he was starting to look up, scanning for the kzin ship he knew might come at any time. He needed to find a cave, or to make one, and that would require construction tools.

Late in the afternoon, while tying grass bundles at the edge of a low rolling plain, Locklear found wood of the kind he'd hardly dared to hope for. He simply had not expected it to grow horizontally. With a thin bark that simulated its surroundings, it lay mostly below the surface with shallow roots at intervals like bamboo. Kzinti probably would've known to seek it from the first, damn their hairy hides. The stuff—he dubbed it shamboo—grew parallel to the ground and arrow-straight, and its foliage popped up at regular intervals too. Some of its hard, hollow segments stored water, and some specimens grew thick as his thighs and ten meters long, tapering to wicked growth spines on each end. Locklear had been walking over potential hiking staffs, construction shoring, and rafts for a week without noticing. He pulled up one the size of a javelin and clipped it smooth.

His grooming tool would do precision work, but Locklear abraded blisters on his palms fashioning an axehead from a chertlike stone common in seams where basalt crags soared from the prairie. He spent two days learning how to socket a handaxe in a shamboo handle, living mostly on tuberberries and grain from grassheads, and elevated his respect for the first tool-using creatures in the process.

By now, Locklear's right arm felt almost as good as new, and the process of rediscovering primitive technology became a compelling pastime. He was so intent on ways to weave split shamboo filaments into cordage for a firebow, while trudging just below the basalt heights, that he almost missed the most important moment of his life.

He stepped from savannah grass onto a gritty surface that looked like other dry washes, continued for three paces, stepped up onto grassy turf again, then stopped. He recalled walking across sand-sprinkled tiles as a youth, and something in that old memory made him look back. The dry wash held wavelike patterns of grit, pebbles, and sand, but here and there were bare patches.

And those bare patches were as black and as smooth as machine-polished obsidian.

Locklear crammed the half-braided cord into a pocket and began to follow that dry wash up a gentle slope, toward the cleft ahead, and toward his destiny.

His heart pounding with hope and fear, Locklear stood five meters inside the perfect arc of obsidian that formed the entrance to that cave. No runoff had ever spilled grit across the smooth broad floor inside, and he felt an irrational concern that his footsteps were defiling something perfectly pristine, clean and cold as an ice cavern. But a far, *far* more rational concern was the portal before him, its facing made of the same material as the floor, the opening itself four meters wide and just as high. A faint flickering luminescence, as of gossamer film stretched across the portal, gave barely enough light to see. Locklear saw his reflection in it, and wanted to laugh aloud at this ragged, skinny, barrel-chested apparition with the stubble of beard wearing stained flight togs. And the apparition reminded him that he might not be alone.

He felt silly, but after clearing his throat twice he managed to call out: "Anybody home?"

Echoes; several of them, more than this little entrance space could possibly generate. He poked his sturdy shamboo hiking staff into the gossamer film and jumped when stronger light flickered in the distance. "Maybe you just eat animal tissue," he said, with a wavering chuckle. "Well—." He took his grooming pincers and cut away the dried curl of skin around a broken blister on his palm, clipped away sizeable crescents of fingernails, tossed them at the film.

Nothing but the tiny clicks of cuticles on obsidian, inside; *that's* how quiet it was. He held the pointed end of the staff like a lance in his right hand, extended the handaxe ahead in his left. He *was* right-handed, after all, so he'd rather lose the left one . . .

No sensation on his flesh, but a sudden flood of light as he moved through the portal, and Locklear dashed backward to the mouth of the cave. "Take it easy, fool," he chided himself. "What did you see?"

A long smooth passageway; walls without signs or features; light seeming to leap from obsidian walls, not too strong but damned disconcerting. He took several deep breaths and went in again, standing his ground this time when light flooded the artificial cave. His first thought, seeing the passageway's apparent end in another film-spanned portal two hundred meters distant, was, *Does it go all the way from Kzersatz to Newduvai?* He couldn't recall when he'd begun to think of this kzin compound as Kzersatz and the adjoining, Earthlike compound as Newduvai.

Footfalls echoing down side corridors, Locklear hurried to the opposite portal, but frost glistened on its facing and his staff would not penetrate more than a half-meter through the luminous film. He could

see his exhalations fogging the film. The resistance
beyond it felt spongy but increasingly hard, probably
an extension of that damned force wall. If his sense
of direction was right, he should be just about beneath the rim of Kzersatz. No doubt someone or
something knew how to penetrate that wall, because
the portal was there. But Locklear knew enough
about force walls and screens to despair of getting
through it without better understanding. Besides, if
he did get through he might punch a hole into vacuum. If his suspicions about the builders of Zoo were
correct, that's exactly what lay beyond the portal.

Sighing, he turned back, counting nine secondary
passages that yawned darkly on each side, choosing
the first one to his right. Light flooded it instantly.
Locklear gasped.

Row upon row of cubical, transparent containers
stretched down the corridor for fifty meters, some of
them tiny, some the size of a small room. And in
each container floated a specimen of animal life,
rotating slowly, evidently above its own gravity polarizer field. Locklear had seen a few of the creatures; had seen pictures of a few more; all, every last
one that he could identify, native to the kzin home-
world. He knew that many museums maintained
ranks of pickled specimens, and told himself he should
not feel such a surge of anger about this one. *Well,
you're an ethologist, you twit*, he told himself silently. *You're just pissed off because you can't study
behaviors of dead animals.* Yet, even taking that into
consideration, he felt a kind of righteous wrath toward builders who played at godhood without playing
it perfectly. It was a responsibility he would never
have chosen. He did not yet realize that he was
surrounded with similar choices.

He stood before a floating *vatach*, in life a fast-moving burrower the size of an earless hare, reputedly tasty but too mild-mannered for kzinti sport. No symbols on any container, but obvious differences among the score of *vatach* in those containers.

How many sexes? He couldn't recall. "But I bet you guys would," he said aloud. He passed on, shuddering at the critters with fangs and leathery wings, marveling at the stump-legged creatures the height of a horse and the mass of a rhino, all in positions that were probably fetal though some were obviously adult.

Retracing his steps to the *vatach* again, Locklear leaned a hand casually against the smooth metal base of one container. He heard nothing, but when he withdrew his hand the entire front face of the glasslike container levered up, the *vatach* settling gently to a cage floor that slid forward toward Locklear like an offering.

The *vatach* moved.

Locklear leaped back so fast he nearly fell, then darted forward again and shoved hard on the cage floor. Back it went, down came the transparent panel, up went the *vatach*, inert, into its permanent rotating waltz.

"Stasis fields! By God, they're alive," he said. The animals hadn't been pickled at all, only stored until someone was ready to stock Kzersatz. *Vatach* were edible herbivores—but if he released them without natural enemies, how long before they overran the whole damned compound? And did he really want to release their natural enemies, even if he could identify them?

"Sorry, fellas. Maybe I can find you an island," he told the little creatures, and moved on with an alertness that made him forget the time. He did not consider time because the glow of illumination did not dim when the sun of Kzersatz did, and only the growl of his empty belly sent him back to the cave entrance where he had left his jacket with his remaining food and water. Even then he chewed tuberberries from sheer necessity, his hands trembling as he looked out at the blackness of the Kzersatz night. Because he had passed down each of those eighteen side passages, and knew what they held, and knew that he had some godplaying of his own to ponder.

He said to the night and to himself, "Like for instance, whether to take one of those goddamned kzinti out of stasis."

His wristcomp held a hundred megabytes, much of it concerning zoology and ethology. Some native kzin animals were marginally intelligent, but he found nothing whatever in memory storage that might help him communicate abstract ideas with them. "Except the tabbies themselves, eighty-one by actual count," he mused aloud the next morning, sitting in sunlight outside. "Damned if I do. Damned if I don't. Damn if I know which is the damnedest," he admitted. But the issue was never very much in doubt; if a kzin ship did return, they'd find the cave sooner or later because they were the best hunters in known space. He'd make it expensive in flying fur, maybe—but there seemed to be no rear entrance. Well, he didn't have to go it alone; Kdaptist kzinti made wondrous allies. Maybe he could convert one, or win his loyalty by setting him free.

If the kzin ship didn't return, he was stuck with a neolithic future or with playing God to populate Kzersatz, unless—"Aw shitshitshit," he said at last, getting up, striding into the cave. "I'll just wake the smallest one and hope he's reasonable."

But the smallest ones weren't male; the females, with their four small but prominent nipples and the bushier fur on their tails, were the runts of that exhibit. In their way they were almost beautiful, with longer hindquarters and shorter torsos than the great bulky males, all eighty-one of the species rotating nude in fetal curls before him. He studied his wristcomp and his own memory, uncomfortably aware that female kzin were, at best, morons. Bred for bearing kits, and for catering to their warrior males, female kzinti were little more than ferociously protected pets in their own culture.

"Maybe that's what I need anyhow," he muttered, and finally chose the female that bulked smallest of them all. When he pressed that baseplate, he did it with grim forebodings.

She settled to the cage bottom and slid out, and Locklear stood well away, axe in one hand, lance in the other, trying to look as if he had no intention of using either. His Adam's apple bobbed as the female began to uncoil from her fetal position.

Her eyes snapped open so fast, Locklear thought they should have clicked audibly. She made motions like someone waving cobwebs aside, mewing in a way that he found pathetic, and then she fully noticed the little man standing near, and she screamed and leaped. That leap carried her to the top of a nearby container, *away* from him, cowering, eyes wide, ear umbrellas folded flat.

He remembered not to grin as he asked, "Is this my thanks for bringing you back?"

She blinked. "You (something, something) a devil, then?"

He denied it, pointing to the scores of other kzin around her, admitting he had found them this way.

If curiosity killed cats, this one would have died

then and there. She remained crouched and wary, her eyes flickering around as she formed more questions. Her speech was barely understandable. She used a form of verbal negation utterly new to him, and some familiar words were longer the way she pronounced them. The general linguistic rule was that abstract ideas first enter a lexicon as several words, later shortened by the impatient.

Probably her longer words were primitive forms; God only knew how long she had been in stasis! He told her who he was, but that did not reduce her wary hostility much. She had never heard of men. Nor of any intelligent race other than kzinti. Nor, for that matter, of spaceflight. But she was remarkably quick to absorb new ideas, and from Locklear's demeanor she realized all too soon that *he*, in fact, was scared spitless of *her*. That was the point when she came down off that container like a leopard from a limb, snatched his handaxe while he hesitated, and poked him in the gut with its haft.

It appeared, after all, that Locklear had revived a very, *very* old-fashioned female.

"You (something or other) captive," she sizzled, unsheathing a set of shining claws from her fingers as if to remind him of their potency. She turned a bit away from him then, looking sideways at him. "Do you have sex?"

His Adam's apple bobbed again before he intuited her meaning. Her first move was to gain control, her second to establish sex roles. A bright female; yeah, that's about what an ethologist should expect . . . "Humans have two sexes just as kzinti do," he said, "and I am male, and I won't submit as your captive. You people eat captives. You're not all that much bigger than I am, and this lance is sharp. I'm your benefactor. Ask yourself why I didn't spear you for lunch before you awoke."

"If you could eat me, I could eat you," she said. "Why do you cut words short?"

Bewildering changes of pace but always practical, he thought. Oh yes, an exceedingly bright female. "I speak modern Kzinti," he explained. "One day we may learn how many thousands of years you have been asleep." He enjoyed the almost human widening of her yellow eyes, and went on doggedly. "Since I have honorably waked you from what might have been a permanent sleep, I ask this: what does your honor suggest?"

"That I (something) clothes," she said. "And owe you a favor, if nakedness is what you want."

"It's cold for me, too." He'd left his food outside but was wearing the jacket, and took it off. "I'll trade this for the axe."

She took it, studying it with distaste, and eventually tied its sleeves like an apron to hide her mammaries. It could not have warmed her much. His question was half disbelief: "That's it? Now you're clothed?"

"As (something) of the (something) always do," she said. "Do you have a special name?"

He told her, and she managed "Rockear." Her own name, she said, was (something fiendishly tough for humans to manage), and he smiled. "I'll call you 'Miss Kitty.'"

"If it pleases you," she said, and something in the way that phrase rolled out gave him pause.

He leaned the shamboo lance aside and tucked the axe into his belt. "We must try to understand each other better," he said. "We are not on your home-world, but I think it is a very close approximation. A kind of incomplete zoo. Why don't we swap stories outside where it's warm?"

She agreed, still wary but no longer hostile, with a glance of something like satisfaction toward the massive kzin male rotating in the next container. And then they strolled outside into the wilderness of Kzersatz which, for some reason, forced thin mewling *miaows* from her. It had never occurred to Locklear that a kzin could weep.

As near as Locklear could understand, Miss Kitty's emotions were partly relief that she had lived to see her yellow fields and jungles again, and partly grief when she contemplated the loneliness she now faced. *I don't count*, he thought. *But if I expect to get her help, I'd best see that I do count.*

Everybody thinks his own dialect is superior, Locklear decided. Miss Kitty fumed at his brief forms of Kzinti, and he winced at her ancient elaborations, as they walked to the nearest stream. She had a temper, too, teaching him genteel curses as her bare feet encountered thorns. She seemed fascinated by his account of the kzin expansion, and that of humans, and others as well through the galaxy. She even accepted his description of the planet Zoo though she did not seem to understand it.

She accepted his story so readily, in fact, that he hit on an intuition. "Has it occurred to you that I might be lying?"

"Your talk is offensive," she flared. "My benefactor a criminal? No. Is it common among your kind?"

"More than among yours," he admitted, "but I have no reason to lie to you. Sorry," he added, seeing her react again. *Kzinti don't flare up at that word today; maybe all cusswords have to be replaced as they weaken from overuse.* Then he told her how man and kzin got along between wars, and ended by admitting it looked as if another war was brewing, which was why he had been abandoned here.

She looked around her. "Is Zoo your doing, or ours?"

"Neither. I think it must have been done by a race we know very little about: Outsiders, we call them. No one knows how many years they have traveled space, but very, very long. They live without air, without much heat. Just beyond the wall that surrounds Kzersatz, I have seen airless corridors with the cold darkness of space and dapples of light. They would be quite comfortable there."

"I do not think I like them."

Then he laughed, and had to explain how the display of his teeth was the opposite of anger.

"Those teeth could not support much anger," she replied, her small pink ear umbrellas winking down and up. He learned that this was her version of a smile.

Finally, when they had taken their fill of water, they returned as Miss Kitty told her tale. She had been trained as a palace *prret*; a servant and casual concubine of the mighty during the reign of *Rrawlrit* Eight and Three. Locklear said that the "Rrit" suffix meant high position among modern kzinti, and she made a sound very like a human sniff. *Rrawlrit* was the arrogant son of an arrogant son, and so on. He liked his females, lots of them, especially young ones. "I was (something) than most," she said, her four-digited hand slicing the air at her ear height.

"Petite, small?"

"Yes. Also smart. Also famous for my appearance," she added without the slightest show of modesty. She glanced at him as though judging which haunch might be tastiest. "Are you famous for yours?"

"Uh—not that I know of."

"But not unattractive?"

He slid a hand across his face, feeling its stubble. "I am considered petite, and by some as, uh, attractive." *Two or three are "some." Not much, but some . . .*

"With a suit of fur you would be (something)," she said, with that ear-waggle, and he quickly asked about palace life because he damned well did not want to know what that final word of hers had meant. It made him nervous as hell. Yeah, but what *did* it mean? Mud-ugly? Handsome? Tasty? *Listen to the lady, idiot, and quit suspecting what you're suspecting.*

She had been raised in a culture in which females occasionally ran a regency, and in which males fought duels over the argument as to whether females were their intellectual equals. Most thought not. Miss Kitty thought so, and proved it, rising to palace prominence with her backside, as she put it.

"You mean you were no better than you should be," he commented.

"What does that mean?"

"I haven't the foggiest idea, just an old phrase." She was still waiting, and her aspect was not benign. "Uh, it means nobody could expect you to do any better."

She nodded slowly, delighting him as she adopted one of the human gestures he'd been using. "I did too well to suit the males jealous of my power, Rockear. They convinced the regent that I was conspiring with other palace *prrets* to gain equality for our sex."

"And were you?"

She arched her back with pride. "Yes. Does that offend you?"

"No. Would you care if it did?"

"It would make things difficult, Rockear. You must understand that I loathe, admire, hate, desire kzintosh male kzin. I fought for equality because it was common knowledge that some were planning to breed *kzinrret*, females, to be no better than pets."

"I hate to tell you this, Miss Kitty, but they've done it."

"Already?"

"I don't know how long it took, but—" He paused, and then told her the worst. Long before man and kzin first met, their females had been bred into brainless docility. Even if Miss Kitty found modern sisters, they would be of no help to her.

She fought the urge to weep again, strangling her miaows with soft snarls of rage.

Locklear turned away, aware that she did not want to seem vulnerable, and consulted his wristcomp's encyclopedia. The earliest kzin history made reference to the downfall of a *Rrawlrit* the fifty-seventh—Seven Eights and One, and he gasped at what that told him. "Don't feel too bad, Miss Kitty," he said at last. "That was at least forty thousand years ago; do you understand eight to the fifth power?"

"It is very, very many," she said in a choked voice.

"It's been more years than that since you were brought here. How did you get here, anyhow?"

"They executed several of us. My last memory was of grappling with the lord high executioner, carrying him over the precipice into the sacred lagoon with me. I could not swim with those heavy chains around my ankles, but I remember trying. I hope he drowned," she said, eyes slitted. "Sex with him had always been my most hated chore."

A small flag began to wave in Locklear's head; he furled it for further reference. "So you were trying to swim. Then?"

"Then suddenly I was lying naked with a very strange creature staring at me," she said with that ear-wink, and a sharp talon pointed almost playfully at him. "Do not think ill of me because I reacted in fright."

He shook his head, and had to explain what *that* meant, and it became a short course in subtle nuances for each of them. Miss Kitty, it seemed, proved an old dictum about downtrodden groups: they became highly expert at reading body language, and at developing secret signals among themselves. It was not Locklear's fault that he was constantly, and completely unaware, sending messages that she misread.

But already, she was adapting to his gestures as he had to her language. "Of all the kzinti I could have taken from stasis, I got you," he chuckled finally, and because her glance was quizzical, he told a gallant half-lie: "I went for the prettiest, and got the smartest."

"And the hungriest," she said. "Perhaps I should hunt something for us."

He reminded her that there was nothing to hunt. "You can help me choose animals to release here. Meanwhile, you can have this," he added, offering her the kzinti rations.

The sun faded on schedule, and he dined on tuberberries while she devoured an entire brick of meat. She amazed him by popping a few tuberberries for dessert. When he asked her about it, she replied that certainly kzinti ate vegetables in her time; why should they not?

"Males want only meat," he shrugged.

"They would," she snarled. "In my day, some select warriors did the same. They claimed it made them ferocious and that eaters of vegetation were mere *kshauvat*, dumb herbivores; we *prret* claimed their diet just made them hopelessly aggressive."

"The word's been shortened to *kshat* now," he mused. "It's a favorite cussword of theirs. At least you don't have to start eating the animals in stasis to stay alive. That's the good news; the bad news is that the warriors who left me here may return at any time. What will you do then?"

"That depends on how accurate your words have been," she said cagily.

"And if I'm telling the plain truth?"

Her ears smiled for her: "Take up my war where I left it," she said.

Locklear felt his control slipping when Miss Kitty refused to wait before releasing most of the *vatach*. They were nocturnal with easily-spotted burrows, she insisted, and yes, they bred fast—but she pointed to specimens of a winged critter in stasis and said they would control the *vatach* very nicely if the need arose. By now he realized that this kzin female wasn't above trying to vamp him; and when that failed, a show of fang and talon would succeed.

He showed her how to open the cages only after she threatened him, and watched as she grasped waking *vatach* by their legs, quickly releasing them to the darkness outside. No need to release the (something) yet, she said; Locklear called the winged beasts "batowls." "I hope you know what you're doing," he grumbled. "I'd stop you if I could do it without a fight."

"You would wait forever," she retorted. "I know the animals of my world better than you do, and soon we may need a lot of them for food."

"Not so many; there's just the two of us."

The cat-eyes regarded him shrewdly. "Not for long," she said, and dropped her bombshell. "I recognized a friend of mine in one of those cages."

Locklear felt an icy needle down his spine. "A male?"

"Certainly not. Five of us were executed for the same offense, and at least one of them is here with us. Perhaps those Outsiders of yours collected us all as we sank in that stinking water."

"Not *my* Outsiders," he objected. "Listen, for all we know they're monitoring us, so be careful how you fiddle with their setup here."

She marched him to the kzin cages and purred her pleasure on recognizing two females, both *prret* like herself, both imposingly large for Locklear's taste. She placed a furry hand on one cage, enjoying the moment. "I could release you now, my sister in struggle," she said softly. "But I think I shall wait. Yes, I think it is best," she said to Locklear, turning away. "These two have been here a long time, and they will keep until—"

"Until you have everything under your control?"

"True," she said. "But you need not fear, Rockear. You are an ally, and you know too many things we must know. And besides," she added, rubbing against him sensuously, "you are (something)."

There was that same word again, *t'rralap* or some such, and now he was sure, with sinking heart, that it meant "cute." He didn't feel cute; he was beginning to feel like a Pomeranian on a short leash.

More by touch than anything else, they gathered bundles of grass for a bower at the cave entrance, and Miss Kitty showed no reluctance in falling asleep next to him, curled becomingly into a buzzing ball of fur. But when he moved away, she moved too, until they were touching again. He knew beyond doubt that if he moved too far in the direction of his lance and axe, she would be fully awake and suspicious as hell.

And she'd call my bluff, and I don't want to kill her, he thought, settling his head against her furry shoulder. *Even if I could, which is doubtful, I'm no longer master of all I survey. In fact, now I have a mistress of sorts, and I'm not too sure what kind of mistress she has in mind. They used to have a word for what I'm thinking. Maybe Miss Kitty doesn't care who or what she diddles; hell, she was a palace courtesan, doing it with males she hated. She thinks I'm t'rralap. Yeah, that's me, Locklear, Miss Kitty's trollop; and what the hell can I do about it? I wish there were some way I could get her back in that stasis cage* . . . And then he fell asleep.

To Locklear's intense relief, Miss Kitty seemed uninterested in the remaining cages on the following morning. They foraged for breakfast and he hid his astonishment as she taught him a dozen tricks in an hour. The root bulb of one spiny shrub tasted like an apple; the seed pods of some weeds were delicious; and she produced a tiny blaze by rapidly pounding an innocent-looking nutmeat between two stones. It occurred to him that nuts contained great amounts of energy. A pile of these firenuts, he reflected, might be turned into a weapon . . .

Feeding hunks of dry brush to the fire, she announced that those root bulbs baked nicely in coals. "If we can find clay, I can fire a few pottery dishes and cups, Rockear. It was part of my training, and I intend to have everything in domestic order before we wake those two."

"And what if a kzin ship returns and spots that smoke?"

That was a risk they must take, she said. Some woods burned more cleanly than others. He argued that they should at least build their fires far from the

cave, and while they were at it, the cave entrance
might be better disguised. She agreed, impressed
with his strategy, and then went down on all-fours to
inspect the dirt near a dry-wash. As he admired her
lithe movements, she shook her head in an almost
human gesture. "No good for clay."

"It's not important."

"It is vitally important!" Now she wheeled upright, impressive and fearsome. "Rockear, if any
kzintosh return here, we must be ready. For that,
we must have the help of others—the two prret. And
believe me, they will be helpful only if they see us as
their (something)."

She explained that the word meant, roughly, "paired
household leaders." The basic requirements of a household, to a kzin female, included sleeping bowers—
easily come by—and enough pottery for that household.
A male kzin needed one more thing, she said, her
eyes slitting: a wtsai.

"You mean one of those knives they all wear?"

"Yes. And you must have one in your belt." From
the waggle of her ears, he decided she was amused
by her next statement: "It is a—badge, of sorts. The
edge is usually sharp but I cannot allow that, and the
tip must be dull. I will show you why later."

"Dammit, these things could take weeks!"

"Not if we find the clay, and if you can make a
wtsai somehow. Trust me, Rockear; these are the
basics. Other kzinrret will not obey us otherwise.
They must see from the first that we are proper
providers, proper leaders with the pottery of a settled tribe, not the wooden implements of wanderers.
And they must take it for granted that you and I,"
she added, "are (something)." With that, she rubbed
lightly against him.

He caught himself moving aside and swallowed hard. "Miss Kitty, I don't want to offend you, but, uh, humans and kzinti do not mate."

"Why do they not?"

"Uhm. Well, they never have."

Her eyes slitted, yet with a flicker of her ears: "But they could?"

"Some might. Not me."

"Then they might be able to," she said as if to herself. "I thought I felt something familiar when we were sleeping." She studied his face carefully. "Why does your skin change color?"

"Because, goddammit, I'm upset!" He mastered his breathing after a moment and continued, speaking as if to a small child, "I don't know about kzinti, but a man can *not*, uh, mate unless he is, uh,—"

"Unless he is intent on the idea?"

"Right!"

"Then we will simply have to pretend that we do mate, Rockear. Otherwise, those two kzinrret will spend most of their time trying to become your mate and will be useless for work."

"Of all the," he began, and then dropped his chin and began to laugh helplessly. Human tribal customs had been just as complicated, once, and she was probably the only functioning expert in known space on the customs of ancient kzinrret. "We'll pretend, then, up to a point. Try and make that point, ah, not too pointed."

"Like your *wtsai*," she retorted. "I will try not to make your face change color."

"Please," he said fervently, and suggested that he might find the material for a *wtsai* inside the cave while she sought a deposit of clay. She bounded away on all-fours with the lope of a hunting leopard,

his jacket a somehow poignant touch as it flapped
against her lean belly.

When he looked back from the cave entrance, she
was a tiny dot two kilometers distant, coursing along
a shallow creekbed. "Maybe you won't lie, and I've
got no other ally," he said to the swift saffron dot.
"But you're not above misdirection with your own
kind. I'll remember that."

Locklear cursed as he failed to locate any kind of
tool chest or lab implements in those inner corridors.
But he blessed his grooming tool when the tip of its
pincer handle fitted screwheads in the cage that had
held Miss Kitty prisoner for so long. He puzzled for
minutes before he learned to turn screwheads a
quarter-turn, release pressure to let the screwheads
emerge, then another quarter-turn, and so on, nine
times each. He felt quickening excitement as the
cage cover detached, felt it stronger when he disassembled the base and realized its metal sheeting was
probably one of a myriad stainless steel alloys. The
diamond coating on his nailfile proved the sheet was
no indestructible substance. It was thin enough to
flex, even to be dented by a whack against an adjoining cage. It might take awhile, but he would soon
have his *wtsai* blade.

And two other devices now lay before him, ludi-
crously far advanced beyond an ornamental knife.
The gravity polarizer's main bulk was a doughnut of
ceramic and metal. Its switch, and that of the stasis
field, both were energized by the sliding cage floor
he had disassembled. The switches worked just as
well with fingertip pressure. They boasted separate
energy sources which Locklear dared not ˉassault;
anything that worked for forty thousand years with-

out harming the creatures near it would be more sophisticated than any fumble-fingered mechanic.

Using the glasslike cage as a test load, he learned which of the two switches flung the load into the air. The other, then, had to operate the stasis field—and both devices had simple internal levers for adjustments. When he learned how to stop the cage from spinning, and then how to make it hover only a hand's breadth above the device or to force it against the ceiling until it creaked, he was ecstatic. Then he energized the stasis switch with a chill of gooseflesh. Any prying paws into those devices would not pry for long, unless someone knew about that inconspicuous switch. Locklear could see no interconnects between the stasis generator and the polarizer, but both were detachable. If he could get that polarizer outside—. Locklear strode out of the cave laughing. It would be the damnedest vehicle ever, but its technologies would be wholly appropriate. He hid the device in nearby grass; the less his ally knew about such things, the more freedom he would have to pursue them.

Miss Kitty returned in late afternoon with a sopping mass of clay wrapped in greenish yellow palm leaves. The clay was poor quality, she said, but it would have to serve—and why was he battering that piece of metal with his stone axe?

If she knew a better way to cut off a *wtsai*-sized strip of steel than bending it back and forth, he replied, he'd love to hear it. Bickering like an old married couple, they sat near the cave mouth until dark and pursued their separate stone-age tasks. Locklear, whose hand calluses were still forming, had to admit that she had been wonderfully trained for domestic chores; under those quick four-digited hands of hers, rolled coils of clay soon became shallow bowls with thin sides, so nearly perfect they

might have been turned on a potter's wheel. By now
he was calling her "Kit," and she seemed genuinely
pleased when he praised her work. Ah, she said, but
wait until the pieces were sun-dried to leather hard-
ness; then she would make the bowls lovely with
talon-etched decoration. He objected that decoration
took time. She replied curtly that kzinrret did not
live for utility alone.

He helped pull flat fibers from the stalks of palm
leaves, which she began to weave into a mat. For
bedding, he asked? Certainly not, she said imperi-
ously: for the clothing which modesty required of
kzinrret. He pursued it: would they really care all
that much with only a human to see them? A human
male, she reminded him; if she considered him worthy of mating, the others would see him as a male
first, and a non-kzin second. He was half amused but
more than a little uneasy as they bedded down, she
curled slightly facing away, he crowded close at her
insistence, "—For companionship," as she put it.

Their last exchange that night implied a difference
between the rigorously truthful male kzin and their
females. "Kit, you can't tell the others we're mated
unless we are."

"I can ignore their questions and let them draw
their own conclusions," she said sleepily.

"Aren't you blurring that fine line between half-
truths and, uh, non-truths?"

"I do not intend to discuss it further," she said,
and soon was purring in sleep with the faint growl of
a predator.

He needed two more days, and a repair of the
handaxe, before he got that jagged slice of steel
pounded and, with abrasive stones, ground into something resembling a blade. Meanwhile, Kit built her

open-fired kiln of stones in a ravine some distance from the cave, ranging widely with that leopard lope of hers to gather firewood. Locklear was glad of her absence; it gave him time to finish a laminated shamboo handle for his blade, bound with thread, and to collect the thickest poles of shamboo he could find. The blade was sharp enough to trim the poles quickly, and tough enough to hold an edge.

He was tying crosspieces with plaited fiber to bind thick shamboo poles into a slender raft when, on the third day of those labors, he felt a presence behind him. Whirling, he brandished his blade. "Oh," he said, and lowered the *wtsai*. "Sorry, Kit. I keep worrying about the return of those kzintosh."

She was not amused. "Give it to me," she said, thrusting her hand out.

"The hell I will. I need this thing."

"I can see that it is too sharp."

"I need it sharp."

"I am sure you do. I need it dull." Her gesture for the blade was more than impatient.

Half straightening into a crouch, he brought the blade up again, eyes narrowed. "Well, by God, I've had about all your whims I can take. You want it? Come and get it."

She made a sound that was deeper than a purr, putting his hackles up, and went to all-fours, her furry tail-tip flicking as she began to pace around him. She was a lovely sight. She scared Locklear silly. "When I take it, I will hurt you," she warned.

"If you take it," he said, turning to face her, moving the *wtsai* in what he hoped was an unpredictable pattern. *Dammit, I can't back down now. A puncture wound might be fatal to her, so I've got to slash lightly.* Or maybe he wouldn't have to, when she saw he meant business.

But he did have to. She screamed and leaped toward his left, her own left hand sweeping out at his arm. He skipped aside and then felt her tail lash against his shins like a curled rope. He stumbled and whirled as she was twisting to repeat the charge, and by sheer chance his blade nicked her tail as she whisked it away from his vicinity.

She stood erect, holding her tail in her hands, eyes wide and accusing. "You—you insulted my tail," she snarled.

"Damn tootin'," he said between his teeth.

With arms folded, she turned her back on him, her tail curled protectively at her backside. "You have no respect," she said, and because it seemed she was going to leave, he dropped the blade and stood up, and realized too late just how much peripheral vision a kzin boasted. She spun and was on him in an instant, her hands gripping his wrists, and hurled them both to the grass, bringing those terrible ripping foot talons up to his stomach. They lay that way for perhaps three seconds. "Drop the *wtsai*," she growled, her mouth near his throat. Locklear had not been sure until now whether a very small female kzin had more muscular strength than he. The answer was not just awfully encouraging.

He could feel sharp needles piercing the skin at his stomach, kneading, releasing, piercing; a reminder that with one move she could disembowel him. The blade whispered into the grass. She bit him lightly at the juncture of his neck and shoulder, and then faced him with their noses almost touching. "A love bite," she said, and released his wrists, pushing away with her feet.

He rolled, hugging his stomach, fighting for breath, grateful that she had not used those fearsome talons with her push. She found the blade, stood over him, and now no sign of her anger remained. *Right; she's in complete control,* he thought.

"Nicely made, Rockear. I shall return it to you when it is presentable," she said.

"Get the hell away from me," he husked softly.

She did, with a bound, moving toward a distant wisp of smoke that skirled faintly across the sky. If a kzin ship returned now, they would follow that wisp immediately.

Locklear trotted without hesitation to the cave, cursing, wiping trickles of blood from his stomach and neck, wiping a tear of rage from his cheek. There were other ways to prove to this damned tabby that he could be trusted with a knife. One, at least, if he didn't get himself wasted in the process.

She returned quite late, with half of a cooked *vatach* and tuberberries as a peace offering, to find him weaving a huge triangular mat. It was a sail, he explained, for a boat. She had taken the little animal on impulse, she said, partly because it was a male, and ate her half on the spot for old times' sake. He'd told her his distaste for raw meat and evidently she never forgot anything.

He sulked awhile, complaining at the lack of salt, brightening a bit when she produced the *wtsai* from his jacket which she still wore. "You've ruined it," he said, seeing the colors along the dull blade as he held it. "Heated it up, didn't you?"

"And ground its edge off on the stones of my hot kiln," she agreed. "Would you like to try its point?" She placed a hand on her flank, where a man's kidney would be, moving nearer.

"Not much of a point now," he said. It was rounded like a formal dinner knife at its tip.

"Try it here," she said, and guided his hand so

that the blunt knifetip pointed against her flank. He hesitated. "Don't you want to?"

He dug it in, knowing it wouldn't hurt her much, and heard her soft miaow. Then she suggested the other side, and he did, feeling a suspicious unease. That, she said, was the way a *wtsai* was best used.

He frowned. "You mean, as a symbol of control?"

"More or less," she replied, her ears flicking, and then asked how he expected to float a boat down a drywash, and he told her because he needed her help with it. "A skyboat? Some trick of man, or kzin?"

"Of man," he shrugged. It was, so far as he knew, uniquely his trick—and it might not work at all. He could not be sure about his other trick either, until he tried it. Either one might get him killed.

When they curled up to sleep again, she turned her head and whispered, "Would you like to bite my neck?"

"I'd like to bite it off."

"Just do not break the skin. I did not mean to make yours bleed, Rockear. Men are tender creatures."

Feeling like an ass, he forced his nose into the fur at the curve of her shoulder and bit hard. Her miaow was familiar. And somehow he was sure that it was not exactly a cry of pain. She thrust her rump nearer, sighed, and went to sleep.

After an eternity of minutes, he shifted position, putting his knees in her back, flinging one of his hands to the edge of their grassy bower. She moved slightly. He felt in the grass for a familiar object; found it. Then he pulled his legs away and pressed with his fingers. She started to turn, then drew herself into a ball as he scrambled further aside, legs tingling.

He had not been certain the stasis field would

operate properly when its flat field grid was positioned beneath sheaves of grass, but obviously it was working. Indeed, his lower legs were numb for several minutes, lying in the edge of the field as they were when he threw that switch. He stamped the pins and needles from his feet, barely able to see her inert form in the faint luminosity of the cave portal. Once, while fumbling for the *wtsai*, he stumbled near her and dropped to his knees.

He trembled for half a minute before rising. "Fall over her now and you could lie here for all eternity," he said aloud. Then he fetched the heavy coil of fiber he'd woven, with those super-strength threads braided into it. He had no way of lighting the place enough to make sure of his work, so he lay down on the sail mat inside the cave. One thing was sure: she'd be right there the next morning.

He awoke disoriented at first, then darted to the cave mouth. She lay inert as a carven image. The Outsiders probably had good reason to rotate their specimens, so he couldn't leave her there for the days—or weeks! that temptation suggested. He decided that a day wouldn't hurt, and hurriedly set about finishing his airboat. The polarizer was lashed to the underside of his raft, with a slot through the shamboo so that he could reach down and adjust the switch and levers. The crosspieces, beneath, held the polarizer off the turf.

Finally, with a mixture of fear and excitement, he sat down in the middle of the raft-bottomed craft and snugged fiber straps across his lap. He reached down with his left hand, making sure the levers were pulled back, and flipped the switch. Nothing. Yet. When he had moved the second lever halfway, the raft began to rise very slowly. He vented a whoop—and suddenly the whole rig was tipping before he could snap the switch. The raft hit on one side and crashed flat like a barn door with a tooth-loosening impact.

Okay, the damn thing was tippy. He'd need a keel—a heavy rock on a short rope. Or a little rock on a long rope! He erected two short lengths of shamboo upright with a crosspiece like goalposts, over the seat of his raft, enlarging the hole under his thighs. Good; now he'd have a better view straight down, too. He used the cord he'd intended to bind Kit, tying it to a twenty-kilo stone, then feeding the cord through the hole and wrapping most of its fifteen-meter length around and around that thick crosspiece. Then he sighed, looked at the westering sun, and tried again.

The raft was still a bit tippy, but by paying the cordage out slowly he found himself ten meters up. By shifting his weight, he could make the little platform slant in any direction, yet he could move only in the direction the breeze took him. By adjusting the controls he rose until the heavy stone swung lazily, free of the ground, and then he was drifting with the breeze. He reduced power and hauled in on his keel weight until the raft settled, and then worked out the needed improvements. Higher skids off the ground, so he could work beneath the raft; a better method for winding that weight up and down; and a sturdy shamboo mast for his single sail—better still, a two-piece mast bound in a narrow A-frame to those goalposts. It didn't need to be high; a short catboat sail for tacking was all he could handle anyhow. And come to think of it, a pair of shamboo poles pivoted off the sides with small weights at their free ends just might make automatic keels.

He worked on that until a half-hour before dark, then carried his keel cordage inside the cave. First he made a slip noose, then flipped it toward her hands, which were folded close to her chin. He finally got the noose looped properly, pulled it tight, then moved around her at a safe distance, tugging the cord so that it passed under her neck and, with sharp tugs, down to her back. Then another pass. Then up to her neck, then around her flexed legs. He managed a pair of half-hitches before he ran short of cordage, then fetched his shamboo lance. With the lance against her throat, he snapped off the stasis field with his toe.

She began her purring rumble immediately. He pressed lightly with the lance, and then she waked, and needed a moment to realize that she was bound. Her ears flattened. Her grin was nothing even faintly like enjoyment. "You drugged me, you little *vatach*."

"No. Worse than that. Watch," he said, and with his free hand he pointed at her face, staring hard. He toed the switch again and watched her curl into an inert ball. The half-hitches came loose with a tug, and with some difficulty he managed to pull the cordage away until only the loop around her hand remained. He toed the switch again; watched her come awake, and pointed dramatically at her as she faced him. "I loosened your bonds," he said. "I can always tie you up again. Or put you back in stasis," he added with a tight smile, hoping this paltry piece of flummery would be taken as magic.

"May I rise?"

"Depends. Do you see that I can defeat you instantly, anytime I like?" She moved her hands, snarling at the loop, starting to bite it asunder. "Stop that! Answer my question," he said again, stern and unyielding, the finger pointing, his toe ready on the switch.

"It seems that you can," she said grudgingly.

"I could have killed you as you slept. Or brought one of the other *prret* out of stasis and made her my consort. Any number of things, Kit." Her nod was slow, and almost human. "Do you swear to obey me hereafter, and not to attack me again?"

She hated it, but she said it: "Yes. I—misjudged you, Rockear. If all men can do what you did, no wonder you win wars."

He saw that this little charade might get him in a mess later. "It is a special trick of mine; probably won't work for male kzin. In any case, I have your word. If you forget it, I will make you sorry. We need each other, Kit; just like I need a sharp edge on my knife." He lowered his arm then, offering her his hand. "Here, come outside and help me. It's nearly dark again."

She was astonished to find, from the sun's position, that she had "slept" almost a full day. But there was no doubting he had spent many hours on that airboat of his. She helped him for a few moments, then remembered that her kiln would now be cool, the bowls and water jug waiting in its primitive chimney. "May I retrieve my pottery, Rockear?"

He smiled at her obedient tone. "If I say no?"

"I do it tomorrow."

"Go ahead, Kit. It'll be dark soon." He watched her bounding away through high grass, then hurried into the cave. He had to put that stasis gadget back where he'd got it or, sure as hell, she'd figure it out and one fine day *he* would wake up hogtied. Or worse.

Locklear's praise of the pottery was not forced; Kit had a gift for handcrafts, and they ate from decorated bowls that night. He sensed her new deference when she asked, "Have you chosen a site for the manor?"

"Not until I've explored further. We'll want a hidden site we can defend and retreat from, with reliable sources of water, firewood, food—not like this cave. And I'll need your help in that decision, Kit."

"It must be done before we wake the others," she said, adding as if to echo his own warnings, "And soon, if we are to be ready for the kzintosh."

"Don't nag," he replied. He blew on blistered palms and lay full-length on their grassy bower. "We have to get that airboat working right away," he said, and patted the grass beside him. She curled up in her usual way. After a few moments he placed a hand on her shoulder.

"Thank you, Rockear," she murmured, and fell asleep. He lay awake for another hour, gnawing the ribs of two sciences. The engineering of the airboat would be largely trial and error. So would the ethology of a relationship between a man and a kzin female, with all those nuances he was beginning to sense. How, for example, did a kzin make love? Not that he intended to—*unless*, a vagrant thought nudged him, *I'm doing some of it already* . . .

Two more days and a near-disastrous capsizing later, Locklear found the right combination of ballast and sail. He found that Kit could sprint for short distances faster than he could urge the airboat, but over long distances he had a clear edge. Alone, tacking higher, he found stronger winds that bore him far across the sky of Kzersatz, and once he found himself drifting in cross-currents high above that frost line that curved visibly, now, tracing the edge of the force cylinder that was their cage.

He returned after a two-hour absence to find Kit weaving more mats, more cordage, for furnishings. She approached the airboat warily, mistrusting its magical properties but relieved to see him. "You'll be using this thing yourself, pretty soon, Kit," he confided. "Can you make us some decent ink and paper?"

In a day, yes, she said, if she found a scroll-leaf palm, to soak, pound, and dry its fronds. Ink was no problem. Then hop aboard, he said, and they'd go cruising for the palm. *That* was a problem; she was plainly terrified of flight in any form. Kzinti were fearless, he reminded her. Females were not, she said, adding that the sight of him dwindling in the sky to a scudding dot had "drawn up her tail"—a fear reaction, he learned.

He ordered her, at least, to mount the raft, sitting in tandem behind him. She found the position some-how obscene, but she did it. Evidently it was highly acceptable for a male to crowd close behind a female, but not the reverse. Then Locklear recalled how cats mated, and he understood. "Nobody will see us, Kit. Hang on to these cords and pull only when I tell you." With that, he levitated the airboat a meter, and stayed low for a time—until he felt the flexure of her foot talons relax at his thighs.

In another hour they were quartering the sky above the jungles and savannahs of Kzersatz, Kit enjoying the ride too much to retain her fears. They landed in a clearing near the unexplored end of the lake, Kit scrambling up a thick palm to return with young rolled fronds. "The sap stings when fresh," she said, indicating a familiar white substance. "But when dried and reheated it makes excellent glue." She also gath-ered fruit like purple leather melons, with flesh that smelled faintly of seafood, and stowed them for dinner.

The return trip was longer. He taught her how to tack upwind and later, watching her soak fronds that night inside the cave, exulted because soon they would have maps of this curious country. In only one particular was he evasive.

"Rockear, what is that thing I felt on your back under your clothing," she asked.

"It's, uh, just a thing your warriors do to captives. I have to keep it there," he said, and quickly changed the subject.

In another few days, they had crude air maps and several candidate sites for the manor. Locklear agreed to Kit's choice as they hovered above it, a gentle slope beneath a cliff overhang where a kzinrret could sun herself half the day. Fast-growing hardwoods nearby would provide timber and firewood, and the stream burbling in the throat of the ravine was the same stream where he had found that first waterfall down near the lake, and had conjectured on the age of Kzersatz. She rubbed her cheek against his neck when he accepted her decision.

He steered toward the hardwood grove, feeling a faint dampness on his neck. "What does that mean?"

"Why,—marking you, of course. It is a display of affection." He pursued it. The ritual transferred a pheromone from her furry cheeks to his flesh. He could not smell it, but she maintained that any kzin would recognize her marker until the scent evaporated in a few hours.

It was like a lipstick mark, he decided—"Or a hickey with your initials," he told her, and then had to explain himself. She admitted he had not guessed far off the mark. "But hold on, Kit. Could a kzin warrior track me by my scent?"

"Certainly. How else does one follow a spoor?"

He thought about that awhile. "If we come to the manor and leave it always by air, would that make it harder to find?"

Of course, she said. Trackers needed a scent trail; that's why she intended them to walk in the nearby stream, even if splashing in water was unpleasant. "But if they are determined to find you, Rockear, they will."

He sighed, letting the airboat settle near a stand of pole-straight trees, and as he hacked with the dulled *wtsai*, told her of the new weaponry: projectiles, beamers, energy fields, bombs. "When they do find us, we've got to trap them somehow; get their weapons. Could you kill your own kind?"

"They executed me," she reminded him and added after a moment, "Kzinrret weapons might be best. Leave it to me." She did not elaborate. Well, women's weapons had their uses.

He slung several logs under the airboat and left Kit stone-sharpening the long blade as he slowly tacked his way back to their ravine. Releasing the hitches was the work of a moment, thick poles thudding onto yellow-green grass, and soon he was back with Kit. By the time the sun faded, the *wtsai* was biting like a handaxe and Kit had prepared them a thick grassy pallet between the cliff face and their big foundation logs. It was the coldest night Locklear had spent on Kzersatz, but Kit's fur made it endurable.

Days later, she ate the last of the kzin rations as he chewed a fishnut and sketched in the dirt with a stick. "We'll run the shamboo plumbing out here from the kitchen," he said, "and dig our escape tunnel out from our sleep room parallel with the cliff. We'll need help, Kit. It's time."

She vented a long purring sigh. "I know. Things will be different, Rockear. Not as simple as our life has been."

He laughed at that, reminding her of the complications they had already faced, and then they resumed notching logs, raising the walls beyond window height. Their own work packed the earthen floors, but the roofing would require more hands than their own. That night, Kit kindled their first fire in the central room's hearth, and they fell asleep while she tutored him on the ways of ancient kzin females.

Leaning against the airboat alone near the cave, Locklear felt new misgivings. Kit had argued that his presence at the awakenings would be a Bad Idea. Let them grow used to him slowly, she'd said. Stand tall, give orders gently, and above all don't smile until they understand his show of teeth. *No fear of that*, he thought, shifting nervously a half-hour after Kit disappeared inside. *I don't feel like smiling*.

He heard a shuffling just out of sight; realized he was being viewed covertly; threw out his chest and flexed his pectorals. Not much by kzin standards, but he'd developed a lot of sinew during the past weeks. He felt silly as hell, and those other kzinrret had not made him any promises. The *wtsai* felt good at his belt.

Then Kit was striding into the open, with an expression of strained patience. Standing beside him, she muttered, "Mark me." Then, seeing his frown: "Your cheek against my neck, Rockear. *Quickly*."

He did so. She bowed before him, offering the tip of her tail in both hands, and he stroked it when she told him to. Then he saw a lithe movement of orange at the cave and raised both hands in a universal weaponless gesture as the second kzinrret emerged, watching him closely. She was much larger than Kit, with transverse stripes of darker orange and a banded tail. Close on her heels came a third, more reluctantly but staying close behind as if for protection, with facial markings that reminded Locklear of an

ocelot and very dark fur at hands and feet. They
were admirable creatures, but their ear umbrellas
lay flat and they were not yet his friends.

Kit moved to the first, urging her forward to
Locklear. After a few tentative sniffs the big kzinrret
said, in that curious ancient dialect, "I am (something truly unpronounceable), prret in service of
Rockear." She bent toward him, her stance defensive, and he marked her as Kit had said he must,
then stroked her tabby-banded tail. She moved away
and the third kzinrret approached, and Locklear's
eyes widened as he performed the greeting ritual.
She was either potbellied, or carrying a litter!

Both of their names being beyond him, he dubbed
the larger one Puss; the pregnant one, Boots. They
accepted their new names as proof that they were
members of a very different kind of household than
any they had known. Both wore aprons of woven
mat, Kit's deft work, and she offered them water
from bowls.

As they stood eyeing one another speculatively,
Kit surprised them all. "It is time to release the
animals," she said. "My lord Rockear-the-magician,
we are excellent herders, and from your flying boat
you can observe our work. The larger beasts might
also distract the kzintosh, and we will soon need
meat. Is it not so?"

She *knew* he couldn't afford an argument now—
and besides, she was right. He had no desire to try
herding some of those big critters outside anyhow,
and kzinti had been doing it from time immemorial.
*Damned clever tactic, Kit; Puss and Boots will get a
chance to work off their nerves, and so will I*. He
swept a permissive arm outward and sat down in the
airboat as the three kzin females moved into the
cave.

The next two hours were a crash course in zoology for Locklear, safe at fifty meter height as he watched herds, coveys, throngs and volleys of creatures as they crawled, flapped, hopped and galumphed off across the yellow prairie. A batowl found a perch atop his mast, trading foolish blinks with him until it whispered away after another of its kind. One huge ruminant with the bulk of a rhino and murderous spikes on its thick tail sat down to watch him, raising its bull's muzzle to issue a call like a wolf. An answering howl sent it lumbering off again, and Locklear wondered whether they were to be butchered, ridden, or simply avoided. He liked the last option best.

When at last Kit came loping out with shrill screams of false fury at the heels of a collie-sized, furry tyrannosaur, the operation was complete. He'd half-expected to see a troop of more kzinti bounding outside, but Kit was as good as her word. None of them recognized any of the other stasized kzinti, and all seemed content to let the strangers stay as they were.

The airboat did not have room for them all, but by now Kit could operate the polarizer levers. She sat ahead of Locklear for decorum's sake, making a show of her pairing with him, and let Puss and Boots follow beneath as the airboat slid ahead of a good breeze toward their tacky, unfinished little manor. "They will be nicely exhausted," she said to him, "by the time we reach home."

Home. My God, it may be my home for the rest of my life, he thought, watching the muscular Puss bound along behind them with Boots in arrears. *Three kzin courtesans for company; a sure 'nough cathouse! Is that much better than having those effing warriors to return? And if they don't, is there any*

way I could get across to my own turf, to Newduvai?
The gravity polarizer could get him to orbit, but he
would need propulsion, and a woven sail wasn't exactly de rigueur for travel in vacuum, and how the
hell could he build an airtight cockpit anyhow? Too
many questions, too few answers, and two more kzin
females who might be more hindrance than help,
hurtling along in the yellow sward behind him. One
of them pregnant.

And kzin litters were almost all twins, one male.
Like it or not, he was doomed to deal with at least
one kzintosh. The notion of killing the tiny male
forced itself forward. He quashed the idea instantly,
and hoped it would stay quashed. *Yeah, and one of
these days it'll weigh three times as much as I do,
and two of these randy females will be vying for
mating privileges.* The return of the kzin ship, he
decided, might be the least of his troubles.

That being so, the least of his troubles could kill
him.

Puss and Boots proved far more help than hindrance. Locklear admitted it to Kit one night, lying
in their small room off the "great hall," itself no larger
than five meters by ten and already pungent with
cooking smokes. "Those two hardly talk to me, but
they thatch a roof like crazy. How well can they
tunnel?"

This amused her. "Every pregnant kzinrret is an
expert at tunneling, as you will soon see. Except that
you will not see. When birthing time nears, a mother
digs her secret birthing place. The father sometimes
helps, but oftener not."

"Too lazy?"

She regarded him with eyes that reflected a dim
flicker from the fire dying in the next room's hearth,

and sent a shiver through him. "Too likely to eat the newborn male," she said simply.

"Good God. Not among modern kzinti, I hope."

"Perhaps. Females become good workers; males become aggressive hunters likely to challenge for household mastery. Which would *you* value more?"

"My choice is a matter of record," he joked, adding that they were certainly shaping the manor up fast. That, she said, was because they knew their places and their leaders. Soon they would be butchering and curing meat, making (something) from the milk of ruminants, cheese perhaps, and making ready for the kittens. Some of the released animals seemed already domesticated. A few *vatach*, she said, might be trapped and released nearby for convenience.

He asked if the others would really fight the returning kzin warriors, and she insisted that they would, especially Puss. "She was a highly valued *prret*, but she hates males," Kit warned. "In some ways I think she wishes to be one."

"Then why did she ask if I'd like to scratch her flanks with my *wtsai*," he asked.

"I will claw her eyes out if you do," she growled. "She is only negotiating for status. Keep your blade in your belt," she said angrily, with a metaphor he could not miss.

That blade reminded him (as he idly scratched her flanks with its dull tip to calm her) that the cave was now a treasury of materials. He must study the planting of the fast-growing vines which, according to Kit, would soon hide the roof thatching; those vines could also hide the cave entrance. He could scavenge enough steel for lances, more of the polarizers to build a whopping big airsloop, maybe even—. He sat up, startling her. "Meat storage!"

Kit did not understand. He wasn't sure he wanted

her to. He would need wire for remote switches,
which might be recovered from polarizer toroids if
he had the nerve to try it. "I may have a way to keep
meat fresh, Kit, but you must help me see that no
one else touches my magics. They could be dangerous." She said he was the boss, and he almost believed it.

Once the females began their escape tunnel,
Locklear rigged a larger sail and completed his mapping chores, amassing several scrolls which seemed
gibberish to the others. And each day he spent two
hours at the cave. When vines died, he planted
others to hide the entrance. He learned that polarizers and stasis units came in three sizes, and brought
trapped *vatach* back in large cages he had separated
from their gravity and stasis devices. Those clear
cage tops made admirable windows, and the cage
metal was then reworked by firelight in the main
hall.

Despite Kit's surly glances, he bade Puss sit beside him to learn metalwork, while Boots patiently
wove mats and formed trays of clay to his specifica-
tions for papermaking. One day he might begin a
journal. Meanwhile he needed awls, screwdrivers,
pliers—and a longbow with arrows. He was all thumbs
while shaping them.

Boots became more shy as her pregnancy advanced.
Locklear's new social problem became the casual
nuances from Puss that, by now, he knew were
sexual. She rarely spoke unless spoken to, but one
day while resting in the sun with the big kzinrret he
noticed her tailtip flicking near his leg. He had noticed previously that a moving rope or vine seemed
to mesmerize a kzin; they probably thought it fascinated him as well.

"Puss, I—uh—sleep only with Kit. Sorry, but that's the way of it."

"Pfaugh. I am more skilled at *ch'rowl* than she, and I could make you a pillow of her fur if I liked." Her gaze was calm, challenging; to a male kzin, probably very sexy.

"We must all work together, Puss. As head of the household, I forbid you to make trouble."

"My Lord," she said with a small nod, but her ear-flick was amused. "In that case, am I permitted to help in the birthing?"

"Of course," he said, touched. "Where is Boots, anyway?"

"Preparing her birthing chamber. It cannot be long now," Puss added, setting off down the ravine.

Locklear found Kit dragging a mat of dirt from the tunnel and asked her about the problems of birthing. The hardest part, she said, was the bower—and when males were near, the hiding. He asked why Puss would be needed at the birthing.

"Ah," said Kit. "It is symbolic, Rockear. You have agreed to let her play the mate role. It is not unheard-of, and the newborn male will be safe."

"You mean, symbolic like our pairing?"

"Not quite that symbolic," she replied with sarcasm as they distributed stone and earth outside. "Prret are flexible."

Then he asked her what *ch'rowl* meant.

Kit vented a tiny miaow of pleasure, then realized suddenly that he did not know what he had said. Furiously: "She used that word to you? I will break her tail!"

"I forbid it," he said. "She was angry because I told her I slept only with you." Pleased with this, Kit subsided as they moved into the tunnel again. Some kzin words, he learned, were triggers. At least one seemed to be blatantly lascivious. He was deflected from this line of thought only when Kit, digging upward now, broke through to the surface.

They replanted shrubs at the exit before dark, and lounged before the hearthfire afterward. At last Locklear yawned; checked his wristcomp. "They are very late," he said.

"Kittens are born at night," she replied, unworried.

"But—I assumed she'd tell us when it was time."

"She has not said eight-cubed of words to you. Why should she confide that to a male?"

He shrugged at the fire. Perhaps they would always treat him like a kzintosh. He wondered for the hundredth time whether, when push came to shove, they would fight with him or against him.

In his mapping sorties, Locklear had skirted near enough to the force walls to see that Kzersatz was adjacent to four other compounds. One, of course, was the tantalizing Newduvai. Another was hidden in swirling mists; he dubbed it Limbo. The others held no charm for him; he named them Who Needs It, and No Thanks. He wondered what collections of life forms roamed those mysterious lands, or slept there in stasis. The planet might have scores of such zoo compounds.

Meanwhile, he unwound a hundred meters of wire from a polarizer, and stole switches from others. One of his jury-rigs, outside the cave, was a catapult using a polarizer on a sturdy frame. He could stand fifty meters away and, with his remote switch, lob a heavy stone several hundred meters. Perhaps a series of the gravity polarizers would make a kind of mass driver—a true space drive! There was yet hope, he thought, of someday visiting Newduvai.

And then he transported some materials to the

manor where he installed a stasis device to keep
meat fresh indefinitely; and late that same day, Puss
returned. Even Kit, ignoring their rivalry, welcomed
the big kzinrret.

"They are all well," Puss reported smugly, pater-
nally. To Locklear's delighted question she replied in
severe tones, "You cannot see them until their eyes
open, Rockear."

"It is tradition," Kit injected. "The mother will
suckle them until then, and will hunt as she must."

"I am the hunter," Puss said. "When we build our
own manor, will your household help?"

Kit looked quickly toward Locklear, who realized
the implications. *By God, they're really pairing off
for another household*, he thought. After a moment
he said, "Yes, but you must locate it nearby." He
saw Kit relax and decided he'd made the right decision. To celebrate the new developments, Puss shooed
Locklear and Kit outside to catch the late sun while
she made them an early supper. They sat on their
rough-hewn bench above the ravine to eat, Puss
claiming she could return to the birthing bower in
full darkness, and Locklear allowed himself to bask
in a sense of well-being. It was not until Puss had
headed back down the ravine with food for Boots,
that Locklear realized she had stolen several small
items from his storage shelves.

He could accept the loss of tools and a knife; Puss
had, after all, helped him make them. What caused
his cold sweat was the fact that the tiny *zzrou* transmitter was missing. The *zzrou* prongs in his shoulder
began to itch as he thought about it. Puss could not
possibly know the importance of the transmitter to
him; maybe she thought it was some magical tool—
and maybe she would destroy it while studying it.

"Kit," he said, trying to keep the tremor from his voice, "I've got a problem and I need your help."

She seemed incensed, but not very surprised, to learn the function of the device that clung to his back. One thing was certain, he insisted: the birthing bower could not be more than a klick away. Because if Puss took the transmitter farther than that, he would die in agony. Could Kit lead him to the bower in darkness?

"I might find it, Rockear, but your presence there would provoke violence," she said. "I must go alone." She caressed his flank gently, then set off slowly down the ravine on all-fours, her nose close to the turf until she disappeared in darkness.

Locklear stood for a time at the manor entrance, wondering what this night would bring, and then saw a long scrawl of light as it slowed to a stop and winked out, many miles above the plains of Kzersatz. Now he knew what the morning would bring, and knew that he had not one deadly problem, but two. He began to check his pathetic little armory by the glow of his memocomp, because that was better than giving way entirely to despair.

When he awoke, it was to the warmth of Kit's fur nestled against his backside. *There was a time when she called this obscene*, he thought with a smile—and then he remembered everything, and lit the display of his memocomp. Two hours until dawn. How long until death, he wondered, and woke her.

She did not have the *zzrou* transmitter. "Puss heard my calls," she said, "and warned me away. She will return this morning to barter tools for things she wants."

"I'll tell you who else will return," he began. "No, don't rebuild the fire, Kit. I saw what looked like a ship stationing itself many miles away overhead, while you were gone. Smoke will only give us away. It might possibly be a Manship, but—expect the worst. You haven't told me how you plan to fight."

His hopes fell as she stammered out her ideas, and he countered each one, reflecting that she was no planner. They would hide and ambush the searchers—but he reminded her of their projectile and beam weapons. Very well, they would claim absolute homestead rights accepted by all ancient kzinti clans—but modern kzinti, he insisted, had probably forgotten those ancient immunities.

"You may as well invite them in for breakfast," he grumbled. "Back on earth, women's weapons included poison. I thought you had some kzinrret weapons."

"Poisons would take time, Rockear. It takes little time, and not much talent, to set warriors fighting to the death over a female. Surely they would still respond with foolish bravado?"

"I don't know; they've never seen a smart kzinrret. And ship's officers are very disciplined. I don't think they'd get into a free-for-all. Maybe lure them in here and hit 'em while they sleep . . ."

"As you did to me?"

"Uh no, I—yes!" He was suddenly galvanized by the idea, tantalized by the treasures he had left in the cave. "Kit, the machine I set up to preserve food is exactly the same as the one I placed under you, to make you sleep when I hit a foot switch." He saw her flash of anger at his earlier duplicity. "An ancient sage once said anything that's advanced enough beyond your understanding is indistinguishable from magic, Kit. But magic can turn on you. Could you get a warrior to sit or lie down by himself?"

"If I cannot, I am no *prret*," she purred. "Certainly I can *leave* one lying by himself. Or two. Or . . . "

"Okay, don't get graphic on me," he snapped. "We've got only one stasis unit here. If only I could get more but I can't leave in the airboat without that damned little transmitter! Kit, you'll have to go and get Puss now. I'll promise her anything within reason."

"She will know we are at a disadvantage. Her demands will be outrageous."

"We're *all* at a disadvantage! Tell her about the kzin warship that's hanging over us."

"Hanging magically over us," she corrected him. "It is true enough for me."

Then she was gone, loping away in darkness, leaving him to fumble his way to the meat storage unit he had so recently installed. The memocomp's faint light helped a little, and he was too busy to notice the passage of time until, with its usual sudden blaze, the sunlet of Kzersatz began to shine.

He was hiding the wires from Puss's bed to the foot switch near the little room's single doorway when he heard a distant roll of thunder. No, not thunder: it grew to a crackling howl in the sky, and from the nearest window he saw what he most feared to see. The kzin lifeboat left a thin contrail in its pass, circling just inside the force cylinder of Kzersatz, and its wingtips slid out as it slowed. No doubt of the newcomer now, and it disappeared in the direction of that first landing, so long ago. If only he'd thought to booby-trap that landing zone with stasis units! Well, he might've, given time.

He finished his work in fevered haste, knowing that time was now his enemy, and so were the kzinti in that ship, and so, for all practical purposes, was the traitor Puss. *And Kit? How easy it will be for her to switch sides! Those females will make out like bandits wherever they are, and I may learn Kit's decision when these goddamned prongs take a lethal bite in my back. Could be any time now.* And then he heard movements in the high grass nearby, and leaped for his longbow.

Kit flashed to the doorway, breathless. "She is coming, Rockear. Have you set your sleeptrap?"

He showed her the rig. "Toe it once for sleep, again for waking, again for sleep," he said. "Whatever you do, don't get near enough to touch the sleeper, or stand over him, or you'll be in the same fix. I've set it for maximum power."

"Why did you put it here, instead of our own bed?"

He coughed and shrugged. "Uh,—I don't know. Just seemed like—well, hell, it's *our* bed, Kit! I, um, didn't like the idea of your using it, ah, the way you'll have to use it."

"You are an endearing beast," she said, pinching him lightly at the neck, "to bind me with tenderness."

They both whirled at Puss's voice from the main doorway: "Bind who with tenderness?"

"I will explain," said Kit, her face bland. "If you brought those trade goods, display them on your bed."

"I think not," said Puss, striding into the room she'd shared with Boots. "But I will show them to you." With that, she sat on her bed and reached into her apron pocket, drawing out a *wtsai* for inspection.

An instant later she was unconscious. Kit, with Locklear kibitzing, used a grass broom to whisk the knife safely away. "I should use it on her throat," she snarled, but she let Locklear take the weapon.

"She came of her own accord," he said, "and she's a fighter. We need her, Kit. Hit the switch again."

A moment later, Puss was blinking, leaping up,

then suddenly backing away in fear. "Treachery," she spat.

In reply, Locklear tossed the knife onto her bed despite Kit's frown. "Just a display, Puss. You need the knife, and I'm your ally. But I've got to have that little gadget that looks like my wristcomp." He held out his hand.

"I left it at the birthing bower. I knew it was important," she said with a surly glance as she retrieved the knife. "For its return, I demand our total release from this household. I demand your help to build a manor as large as this, wherever I like. I demand teaching in your magical arts." She trembled, but stood defiant; a dangerous combination.

"Done, done, and done," he said. "You want equality, and I'm willing. But we may all be equally dead if that kzin ship finds us. We need a leader. Do you have a good plan?"

Puss swallowed hard. "Yes. Hunt at night, hide until they leave."

Sighing, Locklear told her that was no plan at all. He wasted long minutes arguing his case: Puss to steal near the landing site and report on the intruders; the return of his *zzrou* transmitter so he could try sneaking back to the cave; Kit to remain at the manor preparing food for a siege—and to defend the manor through what he termed guile, if necessary.

Puss refused. "My place," she insisted, "is defending the birthing bower."

"And you will not have a male as a leader," Kit said. "Is that not the way of it?"

"Exactly," Puss growled.

"I have agreed to your demands, Puss," Locklear reminded her. "But it won't happen if the kzin warriors get me. We've proved we won't abuse you.

At least give me back that transmitter. Please," he added gently.

Too late, he saw Puss's disdain for pleading. "So that is the source of your magic," she said, her ears lifting in a kzinrret smile. "I shall discover its secrets, Rockear."

"He will die if you damage it," Kit said quickly, "or take it far from him. You have done a stupid thing; without this manbeast who knows our enemy well, we will be slaves again. To males," she added.

Puss sidled along the wall, now holding the knife at ready, menacing Kit until a single bound put her through the doorway into the big room. Pausing at the outer doorway she stuck the *wtsai* into her apron. "I will consider what you say," she growled.

"Wait," Locklear said in his most commanding tone, the only one that Puss seemed to value. "The kzintosh will be searching for me. They have magics that let them see great distances even at night, and a big metal airboat that flies with the sound of thunder."

"I heard thunder this morning," Puss admitted.

"You heard their airboat. If they see you, they will probably capture you. You and Boots must be very careful, Puss."

"And do not hesitate to tempt males into (something) if you can," Kit put in.

"Now you would teach me my business," Puss spat at Kit, and set off down the ravine.

Locklear moved to the outer doorway, watching the sky, listening hard. Presently he asked, "Do you think we can lay siege to the birthing bower to get that transmitter back?"

"Boots is a suckling mother, which saps her strength," Kit replied matter-of-factly. "So Puss would fight like a crazed warrior. The truth is, she is stronger than both of us."

With a morose shake of his head, Locklear began to fashion more arrows while Kit sharpened his *wtsai* into a dagger, arguing tactics, drawing rough conclusions. They must build no fires at the manor, and hope that the searchers spread out for single, arrogant sorties. The lifeboat would hold eight warriors, and others might be waiting in orbit. Live captives might be better for negotiations than dead heroes— "But even as captives, the bastards would eat every scrap of meat in sight," Locklear admitted.

Kit argued persuasively that any warrior worth his *wtsai* would be more likely to negotiate with a potent enemy. "We must give them casualties," she insisted, "to gain their respect. Can these modern males be that different from those I knew?"

Probably not, he admitted. And knowing the modern breed, he knew they would be infuriated by his escape, dishonored by his shrewdness. He could expect no quarter when at last they did locate him. "And they won't go until they do," he said. On that, they agreed; some things never changed.

Locklear, dog-tired after hanging thatch over the gleaming windows, heard the lifeboat pass twice before dark but fell asleep as the sun faded.

Much later, Kit was shaking him. "Come to the door," she urged. "She refuses to come in."

He stumbled outside, found the bench by rote, and spoke to the darkness. "Puss? You have nothing to fear from us. Had a change of heart?"

Not far distant: "I hunted those slopes where you said the males left you, Rockear."

It was an obvious way to avoid saying she had reconnoitered as he'd asked, and he maintained the ruse. "Did you have good hunting?"

"Fair. A huge metal thing came and went and

came again. I found four warriors, in strange costume and barbaric speech like yours, with strange weapons. They are making a camp there, and spoke with surprise of seeing animals to hunt." She spoke slowly, pausing often. He asked her to describe the males. She had no trouble with that, having lain in her natural camouflage in the jungle's verge within thirty paces of the ship until dark. *Must've taken her hours to get here in the dark over rough country,* he thought. *This is one tough bimbo.*

He waited, his hackles rising, until she finished. "You're sure the leader had that band across his face?" She was. She'd heard him addressed as "Grraf-Commander." One with a light-banded belly was called "Apprentice Something." And the other two tallied, as well. "I can't believe it," he said to the darkness. "The same foursome that left me here! If they're all down here, they're deadly serious. Damn their good luck."

"Better than you think," said Puss. "You told me they had magic weapons. Now I believe it."

Kit, leaning near, whispered into Locklear's ear. "If she were injured, she would refuse to show her weakness to us."

He tried again. "Puss, how do you know of their weapons?"

With dry amusement and courage, the disembodied voice said, "The usual way: the huge sentry used one. Tiny sunbeams that struck as I reached thick cover. They truly can see in full darkness."

"So they've seen you," he said, dismayed.

"From their shouts, I think they were not sure what they saw. But I will kill them for this, sentry or no sentry."

Her voice was more distant now. Locklear raised his voice slightly: "Puss, can we help you?"

"I have been burned before," was the reply.

Kit, moving into the darkness quietly: "You are certain there are only four?"

"Positive," was the faint reply, and then they heard only the night wind.

Presently Kit said, "It would take both of us, and when wounded she will certainly fight to the death. But we might overpower her now, if we can find the bower."

"No. She did more than she promised. And now she knows she can kill me by smashing the transmitter. Let's get some sleep, Kit," he said. Then, when he had nestled behind her, he added with a chuckle, "I begin to see why the kzinti decided to breed females as mere pets. Sheer self-defense."

"I would break your tail for that, if you had one," she replied in mock ferocity. Then he laid his hand on her flank, heard her soft miaow, and then they slept.

Locklear had patrolled nearly as far as he dared down the ravine at midmorning, armed with his *wtsai*, longbow, and an arrow-filled quiver rubbing against the *zzrou* when he heard the first scream. He knew that Kit, with her short lance, had gone in the opposite direction on her patrol, but the repeated kzin screams sent gooseflesh up his spine. Perhaps the tabbies had surrounded Boots, or Puss. He notched an arrow, half climbing to the lip of the ravine, and peered over low brush. He stifled the exclamation in his throat.

They'd found Puss, all right—or she'd found them. She stood on all-fours on a level spot below, her tail erect, its tip curled over, watching two hated familiar figures in a tableau that must have been as old as kzin history. Almost naked for this primitive duel, ebony talons out and their musky scent heavy on the breeze, they bulked stupefyingly huge and ferocious. The massive gunner, Goon, and engineer Yellow-belly circled each other with drawn stilettoes. What boggled Locklear was that their modern weapons lay ignored in neat groups. Were they going through some ritual?

They were like hell, he decided. From time to time, Puss would utter a single word, accompanied by a tremor and a tail-twitch; and each time, Yellow-belly and Goon would stiffen, then scream at each other in frustration.

The word she repeated was *ch'rowl*. No telling how long they'd been there, but Goon's right forearm dripped blood, and Yellowbelly's thigh was a sodden red mess. Swaying drunkenly, Puss edged nearer to the weapons. As Yellowbelly screamed and leaped, Goon screamed and parried, bearing his smaller opponent to the turf. What followed then was fast enough to be virtually a blur in a roil of Kzersatz dust as two huge tigerlike bodies thrashed and rolled, knives flashing, talons ripping, fangs sinking into flesh.

Locklear scrambled downward through the grass, his progress unheard in the earsplitting caterwauls nearby. He saw Puss reach a beam rifle, grasp it, swing it experimentally by the barrel. That's when he forgot all caution and shouted, "No, Puss! Put the stock to your shoulder and pull the trigger!"

He might as well have told her to bazzfazz the shimstock; and in any case, poor valiant Puss collapsed while trying to figure the rifle out. He saw the long ugly trough in her side then, caked with dried blood. A wonder she was conscious, with such a wound. Then he saw something more fearful still, the quieter thrashing as Goon found the throat of

Yellowbelly, whose stiletto handle protruded from Goon's upper arm.

Ducking below the brush, Locklear moved to one side, nearer to Puss, whose breathing was as labored as that of the males. Or rather, of one male, as Goon stood erect and uttered a victory roar that must have carried to Newduvai. Yellowbelly's torn throat pumped the last of his blood onto alien dust.

"I claim my right," Goon screamed, and added a Word that Locklear was beginning to loathe. Only then did the huge gunner notice that Puss was in no condition to present him with what he had just killed to get. He nudged her roughly, and did not see Locklear approach with one arrow notched and another held between his teeth.

But his ear umbrellas pivoted as a twig snapped under Locklear's foot, and Goon spun furiously, the big legs flexed, and for one instant man and kzin stood twenty paces apart, unmoving. Goon leaped for the nearest weapon, the beam rifle Puss had dropped, and saw Locklear release the short arrow. It missed by a full armspan and now, his bloodlust rekindled and with no fear of such a marksman, Goon dropped the rifle and pulled Yellowbelly's stiletto from his own arm. He turned toward Locklear, who was unaccountably running *toward* him instead of fleeing as a monkey should flee a leopard, and threw his head back in a battle scream.

Locklear's second arrow, fired from a distance of five paces, pierced the roof of Goon's mouth, its stainless steel barb severing nerve bundles at the brain stem. Goon fell like a jointed tree, knees buckling first, arms hanging, and the ground's impact drove the arrow tip out the back of his head, slippery with gore. Goon's head lay two paces from Locklear's feet. He neither breathed nor twitched.

Locklear hurried to the side of poor, courageous, ill-starred Puss and saw her gazing calmly at him. "One for you, one for me, Puss. Only two more to go."

"I wish—I could live to celebrate that," she said, more softly than he had ever heard her speak.

"You're too tough to let a little burn," he began.

"They shot tiny things, too," she said, a finger migrating to a bluish perforation at the side of her ribcage. "Coughing blood. Hard to breathe," she managed.

He knew then that she was dying. A spray of slugs, roughly aimed at night from a perimeter-control smoothbore, had done to Puss what a beam rifle could not. Her lungs filling slowly with blood, she had still managed to report her patrol and then return to guard the birthing bower. He asked through the lump in his throat, "Is Boots all right?"

"They followed my spoor. When I—came out, twitching my best *prret* routine—they did not look into the bower."

"Smart, Puss."

She grasped his wrist, hard. "Swear to protect it with your life." Now she was coughing blood, fighting to breathe.

"Done," he said. "Where is it, Puss?"

But her eyes were already glazing. Locklear stood up slowly and strode to the beam rifle, hefting it, thinking idly that these weapons were too heavy for him to carry in one trip. And then he saw Puss again, and quit thinking, and lifted the rifle over his head with both hands in a manscream of fury, and of vengeance unappeased.

The battle scene was in sight of the lake, fully in the open within fifty paces of the creek, and he

found it impossible to lift Puss. Locklear cut bundles
of grass and spread them to hide the bodies, trembling
in delayed reaction, and carried three armloads of
weapons to a hiding place far up the ravine just
under its lip. He left the dead kzinti without stripping them; perhaps a mistake, but he had no time
now to puzzle out tightband comm sets or medkits.
Later, if there was a later . . .

He cursed his watery joints, knowing he could not
carry a kzin beam rifle with its heavy accumulator up
to the manor. He moved more cautiously now, re-
membering those kzin screams, wondering how far
they'd carried on the breeze which was toward the
lake. He read the safety legends on Goon's sidearm,
found he could handle the massive piece with both
hands, and stuck it and its twin from Yellowbelly's
arsenal into his belt, leaving his bow and quiver with
the other weapons.

He had stumbled within sight of the manor, planning how he could unmast the airboat and adjust its
buoyancy so that it could be towed by a man afoot to
retrieve those weapons, when a crackling hum sent a
blast of hot air across his cheeks. Face down, crawling for the lip of the ravine, he heard a shout from
near the manor.

"Grraf-Commander, the monkey approaches!" The
reply, deep-voiced and muffled, seemed to come
from inside the manor. So they'd known where the
manor was. Heat or motion sensors, perhaps, during
a pass in the lifeboat—not that it mattered now. A
classic pincers from down and up the ravine, but one
of those pincers now lay under shields of grass. They
could not know that he was still tethered invisibly to
that *zzrou* transmitter. But where was Kit?

Another hail from Brickshitter, whose tremors of
impatience with a beam rifle had become Locklear's

ally: "The others do not answer my calls, but I shall drive the monkey down to them." Well, maybe he'd intended merely to wing his quarry, or follow him.

You do that, Locklear thought to himself in cold rage as he scurried back in the ravine toward his weapons cache; *you just do that, Brickshitter.* He had covered two hundred meters when another crackle announced the pencil-thin beam, brighter than the sun, that struck a ridge of stone above him.

White-hot bees stung his face, back and arms; tiny smoke trails followed fragments of superheated stone into the ravine as Locklear tumbled to the creek, splashing out again, stumbling on slick stones. He turned, intending to fire a sidearm, but saw no target and realized that firing from him would tell volumes to that big sonofabitchkitty behind and above him. Well, they wouldn't have returned unless they wanted him alive, so Brickshitter was just playing with him, driving him as a man drives cattle with a prod. Beam weapons were limited in rate of fire and accumulator charge; maybe Brickshitter would empty this one with his trembling.

Then, horrifyingly near, above the ravine lip, the familiar voice: "I offer you honor, monkey."

Whatthehell: the navigator knew where his quarry was anyhow. Mopping a runnel of blood from his face, Locklear called upward as he continued his scramble. "What, a prisoner exchange?" He did not want to be more explicit than that.

"We already have the beauteous kzinrret," was the reply that chilled Locklear to his marrows. "Is that who you would have sacrificed for your worthless hide?"

That tears it; no hope now, Locklear thought. "Maybe I'll give myself up if you'll let her go," he called. *Would I? Probably not. Dear God, please*

don't give me that choice because I know there would
be no honor in mine . . .

"We have you caged, monkey," in tones of scorn.
"But Grraf-Commander warned that you may have
some primitive hunting weapon, so we accord you
some little honor. It occurs to me that you would
retain more honor if captured by an officer than by a
pair of rankings."

Locklear was now only a hundred meters from the
precious cache. *He's too close; he'll see the weapons*
cache when I get near it and that'll be all she wrote.
I've got to make the bastard careless and use what
I've got. He thought carefully how to translate a
nickname into kzin and began to ease up the far side
of the ravine. "Not if the officer has no honor, you
trembling shitter of bricks," he shouted, slipping the
safety from a sidearm.

Instantly a scream of raw rage and astonishment
from above at this unbelievably mortal insult, followed by the head and shoulders of an infuriated
navigator. Locklear aimed fast, squeezed the firing
stud, and saw a series of dirt clods spit from the
verge of the ravine. The damned thing shot low!

But Brickshitter had popped from sight as though
propelled by levers, and now Locklear was climbing,
stuffing the sidearm into his belt again to keep both
hands free for the ravine, and when he vaulted over
the lip into low brush, he could hear Brickshitter
babbling into his comm unit.

He wanted to hear the exchange more than he
wanted to move. He heard: ". . . has two kzin
handguns—of course I saw them, and heard them;
had I been slower he would have an officer's ears on
his belt now!—Nossir, no reply from the others.
How else would he have Hero's weapons? What do
you think?—I think so, too."

Locklear began to move out again, below brushtops, as the furious Brickshitter was promising a mansack to his commander as a trophy. *And they won't get that while I live*, he vowed to himself. In fact, with his promise, Brickshitter was admitting they no longer wanted him alive. He did not hear the next hum, but saw brush spatter ahead of him, some of it bursting into flame, and then he was firing at the exposed Brickshitter who now stood with brave stance, seven and a half feet tall and weaving from side to side, firing once a second, as fast as the beam rifle's accumulator would permit.

Locklear stood and delivered, moving back and forth. At his second burst, the weapon's receiver locked open. He ducked below, discarded the thing, and drew its twin, estimating he had emptied the first one with thirty rounds. When next he lifted his head, he saw that Brickshitter had outpaced him across the ravine and was firing at the brush again. Even as the stuff ahead of him was kindling, Locklear noticed that the brush behind him flamed higher than a man, now a wildfire moving in the same direction as he, though the steady breeze swept it away from the ravine. His only path now was along the ravine lip, or in it.

He guessed that this weapon would shoot low as well, and opened up at a distance of sixty paces. Good guess; Brickshitter turned toward him and at the same instant was slapped by an invisible fist that flung the heavy rifle from his grasp. Locklear dodged to the lip of the ravine to spot the weapons, saw them twenty paces away, and dropped the sidearm so that he could hang onto brush as he vaulted over, now in full view of Brickshitter.

Whose stuttering fire with his good arm reminded Locklear, nearly too late, that Brickshitter had other weapons beside that beam rifle. Spurts of dirt flew into Locklear's eyes as he flung himself back to safety. He crawled back for the sidearm, watching the navigator fumble for his rifle, and opened up again just as Brickshitter dropped from sight. More wasted ammo.

Behind him, the fire was raging downslope toward their mutual dead. Across the ravine, Brickshitter's enraged voice: "Small caliber flesh wound in the right shoulder but I have started brush fires to flush him. I can see beam rifles, close-combat weapons and other things almost below him in the ravine. —Yessir, he is almost out of ammunition and wants that cache. Yessir, a few more bolts. An easy shot."

Locklear had once seen an expedition bundle burn with a beam rifle in it. He began to run hard, skirting still-smouldering brush and grass, and had already passed the inert bodies of their unprotesting dead when the ground bucked beneath him. He fell to one knee, seeing a cloud of debris fan above the ravine, echoes of the explosion shouldering each other down the slopes, and he knew that Brickshitter's left-armed aim had been as good as necessary. Good enough, maybe, to get himself killed in that cloud of turf and stone and metal fragments, yes, and good wooden arrows that had made a warrior of Locklear. Yet any sensible warrior knows how to retreat.

The ravine widened now, the creek dropping in a series of lower falls, and Locklear knew that further headlong flight would send him far into the open, so far that the *zzrou* would kill him if Brickshitter didn't. And Brickshitter could track his spoor—but not in water. Locklear raced to the creek, heedless of the mis-step that could smash a knee or ankle, and began to negotiate the little falls.

The last one faced the lake. He turned, recognizing that he had cached his pathetic store of provis-

ions behind that waterfall soon after his arrival. It
was flanked by thick fronds and ferns, and Locklear
ducked into the hideyhole behind that sheet of water
streaming wet, gasping for breath.

A soft inquiry from somewhere behind him. He
whirled in sudden recognition. *It's REALLY a small
world,* he thought idiotically. "Boots?" No answer.
Well, of course not, to his voice, but he could see
the dim outline of a deep horizontal tunnel, turning
left inside its entrance, with dry grasses lining the
floor. "Boots, don't be afraid of me. Did you know
the kzin males have returned?"

Guarded, grudging it: "Yes. They have wounded
my mate."

"Worse, Boots. But she killed one,"—*it was her
doing as surely as if her fangs had torn out Yellowbelly's throat*—"and I killed another. She told me
to—to retrieve the things she took from me." It
seemed his heart must burst with this cowardly lie.
He was cold, exhausted, and on the run, and with
the transmitter he could escape to win another day,
and, and—. And he wanted to slash his wrists with
his *wtsai*.

"I will bring them. Do not come nearer," said the
soft voice, made deeper by echoes. He squatted
under the overhang, the splash of water now dwindling, and he realized that the blast up the ravine
had made a momentary check dam. He distinctly
heard the mewing of tiny kzin twins as Boots removed the security of her warm, soft fur. A moment
later, he saw her head and arms. Both hands, even
the one bearing a screwdriver and the transmitter,
had their claws fully extended and her ears lay so flat
on her skull that they might have been caps of skin.
Still, she shoved the articles forward.

Pocketing the transmitter with a thrill of undeserved success, he bade her keep the other items. He showed her the sidearm. "Boots, one of these killed Puss. Do you see that it could kill you just as easily?"

The growl in her throat was an illustrated manual of counterthreat.

"But I began as your protector. I would never harm you or your kittens. Do you see that now?"

"My head sees it. My heart says to fight you. Go."

He nodded, turned away, and eased himself into the deep pool that was now fed by a mere trickle of water. Ahead was the lake, smoke floating toward it, and he knew that he could run safely in the shallows hidden by smoke without leaving prints. And fight another day. And, he realized, staring back at the once-talkative little falls, leave Boots with her kittens where the cautious Brickshitter would almost certainly find them because now the mouth of her birthing bower was clearly visible.

No, I'm damned if you will!

"So check into it, Brickshitter," he muttered softly, backing deep into the cool cover of yellow ferns. "I've still got a few rounds here, if you're still alive."

He was alive, all right. Locklear knew it in his guts when a stone trickled its way down near the pool. He knew it for certain when he felt soft footfalls, the almost silent track of a big hunting cat, vibrate the damp grassy embankment against his back. He eased forward in water that was no deeper than his armpits, still hidden, but when the towering kzin warrior sprang to the verge of the water he made no sound at all. He carried only his sidearm and knife, and Locklear fired at a distance of only ten paces, actually a trifling space.

But a tremendous trifle, for Brickshitter was well-trained and did not pause after his leap before hopping aside in a squat. He was looking straight at Locklear and the horizontal spray of slugs ceased before it reached him. Brickshitter's arm was a blur. Foliage shredded where Locklear had hidden as the little man dropped below the surface, feeling two hot slugs trickle down his back after their velocity was spent underwater.

Locklear could not see clearly, but propelled himself forward as he broke the surface in a desperate attempt to reach the other side. He knew his sidearm was empty. He did not know that his opponent's was, until the kzin navigator threw the weapon at him, screamed, and leaped.

Locklear pulled himself to the bank with fronds as the big kzin strode toward him in water up to his belly. Too late to run, and Brickshitter had a look of cool confidence about him. *I like him better when he's not so cool.* "Come on, you *kshat,* you *vatach*'s ass," he chanted, backing toward the only place where he might have safety at his back—the stone shelf before Boots's bower, where great height was a disadvantage. "Come on, you fur-licking, brickshitting hairball, do it! Leaping and screaming, screaming and leaping; you stupid no-name," he finished, wondering if the last was an insult.

Evidently it was. With a howling scream of savagery, the big kzin tried to leap clear of the water, falling headlong as Locklear reached the stone shelf. Dagger now in hand, Brickshitter floundered to the bank spitting, emitting a string of words that doubled Locklear's command of kzinti curses. Then, almost as if reading Locklear's mind, the navigator paused a few paces away and held up his knife. And his voice, though quivering, was exceedingly mild. "Do you know what I am going to do with this, monkey?"

To break through this facade, Locklear made it

off-handed. "Cut your *ch'rowl*ing throat by accident, most likely," he said.

The effect was startling. Stiffening, then baring his fangs in a howl of frustration, the warrior sprang for the shelf, seeing in mid-leap that Locklear was waiting for exactly that with his *wtsai* thrust forward, its tip made needle-sharp by the same female who had once dulled it. But a kzin warrior's training went deep. Pivoting as he landed, rolling to one side, the navigator avoided Locklear's thrust, his long tail lashing to catch the little man's legs.

Locklear had seen that one before. His blade cut deeply into the kzin's tail and Brickshitter vented a yelp, whirling to spring. He feinted as if to hurl the knife and Locklear threw both arms before his face, seeing too late the beginning of the kzin's squatting leap in close quarters, like a swordsman's balestra. Locklear slammed his back painfully against the side of the cave, his own blade slashing blindly, and felt a horrendous fiery trail of pain down the length of his knife arm before the graceful kzin moved out of range. He switched hands with the *wtsai*.

"I am going to carve off your maleness while you watch, monkey," said Brickshitter, seeing the blood begin to course from the open gash on Locklear's arm.

"One word before you do," Locklear said, and pulled out all the stops. "*Ch'rowl* your grandmother. *Ch'rowl* your patriarch, and *ch'rowl* yourself."

With each repetition, Brickshitter seemed to coil into himself a bit farther, his eyes not slitted but saucer-round, and with his last phrase Locklear saw something from the edge of his vision that the big kzin saw clearly. Ropelike, temptingly bushy, it was the flick of Boots's tail at the mouth of her bower.

Like most feline hunters from the creche onward,

the kzin warrior reacted to this stimulus with rapt fascination, at least for an instant, already goaded to insane heights of frustration by the sexual triggerword. His eyes rolled upward for a flicker of time, and in that flicker Locklear acted. His headlong rush carried him in a full body slam against the navigator's injured shoulder, the *wtsai* going in just below the ribcage, torn from Locklear's grasp as his opponent flipped backward in agony to the water. Locklear cartwheeled into the pool, weaponless, choosing to swim because it was the fastest way out of reach.

He flailed up the embankment searching wildly for a loose stone, then tossed a glance over his shoulder. The navigator lay on his side, half out of the water, blood pumping from his belly, and in his good arm he held Locklear's *wtsai* by its handle. As if his arm were the only part of him still alive, he flipped the knife, caught it by the tip, forced himself erect.

Locklear did the first thing he could remember from dealing with vicious animals: reached down, grasped a handful of thin air, and mimicked hurling a stone. It did not deter the navigator's convulsive move in the slightest, the *wtsai* a silvery whirr before it thunked into a tree one pace from Locklear's breast. The kzin's motion carried him forward into water, face down. He did not entirely submerge, but slid forward inert, arms at his sides. Locklear wrestled his blade from the tree and waited, his chest heaving. The navigator did not move again.

Locklear held the knife aloft, eyes shut, for long moments, tears of exultation and vengeance coursing down his cheeks, mixing with dirty water from his hair and clean blood from his cheek. His eyes snapped open at the voice.

"May I name my son after you, Rockear?" Boots, just inside the overhang, held two tiny spotted kittens protectively where they could suckle. It was, he felt, meant to be an honor merely for him to see them.

"I would be honored, Boots. But the modern kzin custom is to make sons earn their names, I think."

"What do I care what they do? We are starting over here."

Locklear stuffed the blade into his belt, wiping wet stuff from his face again. "Not unless I can put away that scarfaced commander. He's got Kit at the manor unless she has him. I'm going to try and bias the results," he said grimly, and scanned the heights above the ravine.

To his back, Boots said, "It is not traditional, but—if you come for us, we would return to the manor's protection."

He turned, glancing up the ravine. "An honor. But right now, you'd better come out and wait for the waterfall to resume. When it does, it might flood your bower for a few minutes." He waved, and she waved back. When next he glanced downslope, from the upper lip of the ravine, he could see the brushfire dwindling at the jungle's edge, and water just beginning to carve its way through a jumble of debris in the throat of the ravine, and a small lithe orange-yellow figure holding two tiny spotted dots, patiently waiting in the sunlight for everything he said to come true.

"Lady," he said softly to the waiting Boots, "I sure hope you picked a winner."

He could have disappeared into the wilds of Kzersatz for months but Scarface, with vast advantages, might call for more searchers. Besides, running would be reactive, the act of mindless prey. Locklear opted to be *pro*active—a hunter's mindset.

Recalling the violence of that exploding rifle, he almost ignored the area because nothing useful could remain in the crater. But curiosity made him pause, squinting down from the heights, and excellent vision gave him an edge when he saw the dull gleam of Brickshitter's beam rifle across the ravine. It was probably fully discharged, else the navigator would not have abandoned it. But Scarface wouldn't know that.

Locklear doubled back and retrieved the heavy weapon, chuckling at the sharp stones that lay atop the turf. Brickshitter must have expended a few curses as those stones rained down. The faint orange light near the scope was next to a legend in Kzinti that translated as "insufficient charge." He thought about that a moment, then smeared his own blood over the light until its gleam was hidden. Shouldering the rifle, he set off again, circling high above the ravine so that he could come in from its upper end. Somehow the weapon seemed lighter now, or perhaps it was just his second wind. Locklear did not pause to reflect that his decision for immediate action brought optimism, and that optimism is another word for accumulated energy.

The sun was at his back when he stretched prone behind low cover and paused for breath. The zoom scope of the rifle showed that someone had ripped the thatches from the manor's window bulges, no doubt to give Scarface a better view. *Works both ways, hotshot,* he mused; but though he could see through the windows, he saw nothing move. Presently he began to crawl forward and down, holding the heavy rifle in the crooks of his arms, abrading his elbows as he went from brush to outcrop to declivity. His shadow stretched before him. Good; the sun would be in a watcher's eyes and he was dry-mouthed with awareness that Scarface must carry his own arsenal.

The vines they had planted already hid the shaft of their escape tunnel but Locklear paused for long moments at its mouth, listening, waiting until his breath was quiet and regular. What if Scarface were waiting in the tunnel? He ducked into the rifle sling, put his *wtsai* in his teeth, and eased down feet-first using remembered hand and footholds, his heart hammering his ribs. Then he scuffed earth with his knee and knew that his entry would no longer be a surprise if Scarface was waiting. He dropped the final two meters to soft dirt, squatting, hopping aside as he'd seen Brickshitter do.

Nothing but darkness. He waited for his panting to subside and then moved forward with great caution. It took him five minutes to stalk twenty meters of curving tunnel, feeling his way until he saw faint light filtering from above. By then, he could hear the fitz-rowr of kzin voices. He eased himself up to the opening and peered through long slits of shamboo matting that Boots had woven to cover the rough walls.

". . . Am learning, milady, that even the most potent Word loses its strength when used too often," a male voice was saying. Scarface, in tones Locklear had never expected to hear. "As soon as this operation is complete, rest assured I shall be the most gallant of suitors."

Locklear's view showed only their legs as modern warrior and ancient courtesan faced each other, seated on benches at the rough-hewn dining table. Kit, with a sulk in her voice, said, "I begin to wonder if your truthfulness extends to my attractions, milord."

Scarface, fervently: "The truth is that you are a warrior's wildest fantasies in fur. I cannot say how often I have wished for a mate I could actually talk to! Yet I am first Grraf-Commander, and second a kzintosh. Excuse me," he added, stood up, and strode to the main doorway, now in full view of Locklear. His belt held ceremonial *wtsai*, a sidearm and God knew what else in those pockets. His beam rifle lay propped beside the doorway. Taking a brick-sized device from his broad belt, he muttered, "I wonder if this rude hut is interfering with our signals."

A click and then, in gruff tones of frustrated command, he said, "Hunt leader to all units: report! If you cannot report, use a signal bomb from your beltpacs, dammit! If you cannot do that, return to the hut at triple time or I will hang your hides from a pennant pole."

Locklear grinned as Scarface moved back to the table with an almost human sigh. *Too bad I didn't know about those signal bombs. Warm this place up a little. Maybe I should go back for those beltpacs.* But he abandoned the notion as Scarface resumed his courtship.

"I have hinted, and you have evaded, milady. I must ask you now, bluntly: will you return with me when this operation is over?"

"I shall do as the commander wishes," she said demurely, and Locklear grinned again. She hadn't said "Grraf-Commander"; and even if Locklear didn't survive, *she* might very well wind up in command. Oh sure, she'd do whatever the commander liked.

"Another point on which you have been evasive," Scarface went on; "your assessment of the monkey, and what relationship he had to either of you." Locklear did not miss this nuance; Scarface knew of two kzinrret, presumably an initial report from one of the pair who'd found Puss. He did not know of Boots, then.

"The manbeast ruled us with strange magic forces, milord. He made us fearful at times. At any time he might be anywhere. Even now." *Enough of that crap*, Locklear thought at her, even though he felt she was only trying to put the wind up Scarface's backside. *Fat chance! Lull the bastard, put him to sleep.*

Scarface went to the heart of his question. "Did he act honorably toward you both?"

After a long pause: "I suppose he did, as a manbeast saw honor. He did not *ch'rowl* me, if that is—"

"Milady! You will rob the Word of its meaning, or drive me mad."

"I have an idea. Let me dance for you while you lie at your ease. I will avoid the term and drive you only a little crazy."

"For the eighth-squared time, I do not need to lie down. I need to complete this hunt; duty first, pleasure after. I—what?"

Locklear's nose had brushed the matting. The noise was faint, but Scarface was on his feet and at the doorway, rifle in hand, in two seconds. Locklear's nose itched, and he pinched his nostrils painfully. It seemed that the damned tabby was never completely off-guard, made edgy as a *wtsai* by his failure to contact his crew. Locklear felt a sneeze coming, sank down on his heels, rubbed furiously at his nose. When he stood up again, Scarface stood a pace outside, demanding a response with his comm set while Kit stood at the doorway. Locklear scratched carefully at the mat, willing Kit alone to hear it. No such luck.

Scarface began to pace back and forth outside, and Locklear scratched louder. Kit's ear-umbrellas flicked, lifted. Another scratch. She turned, and saw him move the matting. Her mouth opened slightly. *She's going to warn him,* Locklear thought wildly.

"Perhaps we could stroll down the ravine, milord," she said easily, taking a few steps outside.

Locklear saw the big kzin commander pass the doorway once, twice, muttering furiously about indecision. He caught the words, ". . . Return to the lifeboat with you now if I have not heard from them very soon," and knew that he could never regain an advantage if that happened. He paced his advance past the matting to coincide with Scarface's movements, easing the beam rifle into plain sight on the floor, now with his head and shoulders out above the dusty floor, now his waist, now his—his—his sneeze came without warning.

Scarface leaped for the entrance, snatching his sidearm as he came into view, and Locklear gave himself up then even though he was aiming the heavy beam rifle from a prone position, an empty threat. But a bushy tail flashed between the warrior's ankles, and his next bound sent him skidding forward on his face, the sidearm still in his hand but pointed away from Locklear.

And the muzzle of Locklear's beam rifle poked so near the commander's nose that he could only focus on it cross-eyed. Locklear said it almost pleasantly: "Could even a monkey miss such a target?"

"Perhaps," Scarface said, and swallowed hard. "But I think that rifle is exhausted."

"The one your nervous brickshitting navigator used? It probably was," said Locklear, brazening it out, adding the necessary lie with, "I broiled him with this one, which doesn't have that cute little light glowing, does it? Now then: skate that little shooter of yours across the floor. Your crew is all bugbait,

Scarface, and the only thing between you and kitty heaven is my good humor."

Much louder than need be, unless he was counting on Kit's help: "Have you no end of insults? Have you no sense of honor? Let us settle this as equals." Kit stood at the doorway now.

"The sidearm, Grraf-Commander. Or meet your ancestors. Your crew tried to kill me—and monkey see, monkey do."

The sidearm clattered across the rough floor mat. Locklear chose to avoid further insult; the last thing he needed was a loss of self-control from the big kzin. "Hands behind your back. Kit, get the strongest cord we have and bind him; the feet, then the hands. And stay to one side. If I have to pull this trigger, you don't want to get splattered."

Minutes later, holding the sidearm and sitting at the table, Locklear studied the prisoner who sat, legs before him, back against the doorway, and explained the facts of Kzersatz life while Kit cleaned his wounds. She murmured that his cheek scar would someday be *t'rralap* as he explained the options. "So you see, you have nothing to lose by giving your honorable parole, because I trust your honor. You have everything to lose by refusing, because you'll wind up as barbecue."

"Men do not eat captives," Scarface said. "You speak of honor and yet you lie."

"Oh, I wouldn't eat you. But *they* would. There are two kzinrret here who, if you'll recall, hate everything you stand for."

Scarface looked glumly at Kit. "Can this be true?"

She replied, "Can it be true that modern kzinrret have been bred into cattle?"

"Both can be true," he conceded. "But monk—

men are devious, false, conniving little brutes. How can a kzinrret of your intelligence approve of them?"

"Rockear has defeated your entire force—with a little help," she said. "I am content to pledge my honor to a male of his resourcefulness, especially when he does not abuse his leadership. I only wish he were of our race," she added wistfully.

Scarface: "My parole would depend on your absolute truthfulness, Rockear."

A pause from Locklear, and a nod. "You've got it as of now, but no backing out if you get some surprises later."

"One question, then, before I give my word: *are all my crew truly casualties?*"

"Deader than this beam rifle," Locklear said, grinning, holding its muzzle upward, squeezing its trigger.

Later, after pledging his parole, Scarface observed reasonably that there was a world of difference between an insufficient charge and *no* charge. The roof thatching burned slowly at first; slowly enough that they managed to remove everything worth keeping. But at last the whole place burned merrily enough. To Locklear's surprise, it was Scarface who mentioned safe removal of the *zzrou,* and pulled it loose easily after a few deft manipulations of the transmitter.

Kit seemed amused as they ate al fresco, a hundred meters from the embers of their manor. "It is a tradition in the ancient culture that a major change of household leadership requires burning of the old manor," she explained with a smile of her ears.

Locklear, still uneasy with the big kzin warrior so near and now without his bonds, surreptitiously felt of the sidearm in his belt and asked, "Am I not still the leader?"

"Yes," she said. "But what kind of leader would

deny happiness to his followers?" Her lowered glance toward Scarface could hardly be misunderstood.

The ear umbrellas of the big male turned a deeper hue. "I do not wish to dishonor another warrior, Locklear, but—if I am to remain your captive here as you say, um, such females may be impossibly over-stimulating."

"Not to me," Locklear said. "No offense, Kit; I'm half in love with you myself. In fact, I think the best thing for my own sanity would be to seek, uh, females of my own kind."

"You intended to take us back to the manworlds, I take it," said Scarface with some smugness.

"After a bit more research here, yes. The hell with wars anyhow. There's a lot about this planet you don't know about yet. Fascinating!"

"You will never get back in a lifeboat," said Scarface, "and the cruiser is now only a memory."

"You didn't!"

"I assuredly did, Locklear. My first act when you released my bonds was to send the self-destruct signal."

Locklear put his head between his hands. "Why didn't we hear the lifeboat go up?"

"Because I did not think to set it for destruct. It is not exactly a major asset."

"For me it damned well is," Locklear growled, then went on. "Look here: I won't release Kit from any pair-bonding to me unless you promise not to sabotage me in any way. And I further promise not to try turning you over to some military bunch, because I'm the, uh, mayor of this frigging planet and I can declare peace on it if I want to. Honor bound, honest injun, whatever the hell that means, and all the rigamarole that goes with it. Goddammit, I could have blown your head off."

"But you did not know that."

"With the sidearm, then! Don't *ch'r*—don't fiddle me around. Put your honor on the line, mister, and put your big paw against mine if you mean it."

After a long look at Kit, the big kzin commander reached out a hand, palm vertical, and Locklear met it with his own. "You are not the man we left here," said the vanquished kzin, eyeing Locklear without malice. "Brown and tough as dried meat—and older, I would say."

"Getting hunted by armed kzinti tends to age a feller," Locklear chuckled. "I'm glad we found peace with honor."

"Was any commander," the commander asked no one in particular, "ever faced with so many conflicts of honor?"

"You'll resolve them," Locklear predicted. "Think about it: I'm about to make you the head captive of a brand new region that has two newborn babes in it, two intelligent kzinrret at least, and over an eight-squared other kzinti who have been in stasis for longer than you can believe. Wake 'em, or don't, it's up to you, just don't interfere with me because I expect to be here part of the time, and somewhere else at other times. Kit, show him how to use the airboat. If you two can't figure out how to use the stuff in this Outsider zoo, I miss my—"

"Outsiders?" Scarface did not seem to like the sound of that.

"That's just my guess," Locklear shrugged. "Maybe they have hidden sensors that tell 'em what happens on the planet Zoo. Maybe they don't care. What I care about, is exploring the other compounds on Zoo, one especially. I may not find any of my kind on Newduvai, and if I do they might have foreheads a half-inch high, but it bears looking into. For that I need the lifeboat. Any reason why it wouldn't take me to another compound on Zoo?"

"No reason." After a moment of rumination, Scarface put on his best negotiation face again. "If I teach you to be an expert pilot, would you let me disable the hyperwave comm set?"

Locklear thought hard for a similar time. "Yes, if you swear to leave its local functions intact. Look, fella, we may want to talk to one another with it."

"Agreed, then," said the kzin commander.

That night, Locklear slept poorly. He lay awake for a time, wondering if Newduvai had its own specimen cave, and whether he could find it if one existed. The fact was that Kzersatz simply lacked the kind of company he had in mind. *Not even the right kind of cathouse*, he groused silently. He was not enormously heartened by the prospect of wooing a Neanderthal nymphet, either. Well, that was what field research was for. *Please, God, at least a few Cro-Magnons! Patience, Locklear, and earplugs*, because he could not find sleep for long.

It was not merely that he was alone, for the embers near his pallet kept him as toasty as kzinrret fur. No, it was the infernal yowling of those cats somewhere below in the ravine.

Here is an excerpt from the new novel by Timothy Zahn, coming in October 1988 from Baen Books:

TIMOTHY ZAHN

DEADMAN SWITCH

I was playing singleton chess in a corner of the crew lounge when we reached the Cloud.

Without warning, oddly enough, though the effect sphere's edge was supposed to be both stationary and well established. But reach it without warning we did. From the rear of the *Bellwether* came the faint *thunggk* of massive circuit breakers firing as the Mjollnir drive spontaneously kicked out, followed an instant later by a round of curses from the others in the lounge as the ultra-high-frequency electric current in the deck lost its Mjollnir-space identity of a pseudograv generator and crewers and drinks went scattering every which way.

And then, abruptly, there was silence. A dark silence, as suddenly everyone seemed to remember what was abut to happen.

A rook was drifting in front of my eyes, spiraling slowly about its long axis. Carefully, I reached out and plucked it from the air, feeling a sudden chill in my heart. We were at the edge of the Cloud, ten light-years out from Solitaire . . . and in a few minutes, up on the bridge, someone was going to die.

For in honor of their gods they have done everything detestable that God hates; yes, in honor of their gods, they even burn their own sons and daughters as sacrifices—

A tone from the intercom broke into my thoughts. "Sorry about that," Captain Jose Bartholomy said. Behind his carefully cultivated Starlit accent his voice was trying to be as unruffled as usual . . . but I don't think anyone aboard the *Bellwether* was really fooled. "Space-normal, for anyone who hasn't figured it out already. Approximately fifteen minutes to Mjollnir again; stand ready." He paused, and I heard him take a deep breath. "Mr. Benedar, please report to the bridge."

I didn't have to look to know that all eyes in the lounge had turned to me. Carefully, I eased out of my seat, hanging onto the arm until I'd adjusted adequately to the weightlessness and then giving myself a push toward the door. My movement seemed to break the others out of their paralysis—two of the crewers headed to the lockers for handvacs, while the rest suddenly seemed to remember there were glasses and floating snacks that needed to be collected and got to it. In the brisk and uncomfortable flurry of activity, I reached the door and left.

Randon was waiting for me just outside the bridge. "Benedar," he nodded, both voice and face tighter than he probably wanted them to be.

"Why?" I asked quietly, knowing he would understand what I meant.

He did, but chose to ignore the question. "Come in here," he said instead, waving at the door release and grabbing the jamb handle as the panel slid open.

"I'd rather not," I said.

"Come in here," he repeated. His voice made it clear he meant it.

Swallowing hard, I gave myself a slight push and entered the bridge.

Captain Bartholomy and First Officer Gielincki were there, of course: Gielincki because it was technically her shift as bridge officer, Bartholomy because he wasn't the type of man to foist a duty like this off on his subordinates. Standing beside them on the gripcarpet were Aikman and DeMont, the former with a small recorder hanging loosely from his hand, the latter with a medical kit gripped tightly in his. Flanking the helm chair to their right were two of Randon's shields, Daiv and Duge Ifversn, just beginning to move back . . . and in the chair itself sat a man.

The *Bellwether*'s sacrifice.

I couldn't see anything of him but one hand, strapped to the left chair arm, and the back of his head, similarly bound to the headrest. I didn't want to see anything more, either—not of him, not of anything else that was about to happen up here. But Randon was looking back at me. . . .

The days of my life are few enough: turn your eyes away, leave me a little joy, before I go to the place of no return, to the land of darkness and shadow dark as death . . .

Taking a deep breath, I set my feet into the gripcarpet and moved forward.

Daiv Ifversn had been heading toward Aikman as we entered; now, instead, he turned toward us. "The prisoner is secured, sir, as per orders," he told Randon, his face and voice making it clear he didn't care for this duty at all. "Further orders?"

Randon shook his head. "You two may leave."

"Yes, sir." Daiv caught his brother's eye, and the two of them headed for the door.

And all was ready. Taking a step toward the man in the chair, Aikman set his recorder down on one of the panel's grips, positioning it where it could take in the entire room. "Robern Roxbury Trembley," he said, his voice as coldly official as the atmosphere surrounding us, "you have been charged, tried, and convicted of the crimes of murder and high treason, said crimes having been committed on the world of Miland under the jurisdiction of the laws of the Four Worlds of the Patri."

From my position next to Randon and Captain Bartholomy, I could now see the man in profile. His chest was fluttering rapidly with short, shallow breaths, his face drawn and pale with the scent of death heavy on it . . . but through it all came the distinct sense that he was indeed guilty of the crimes for which he was about to die.

It came as little comfort.

"You have therefore," Aikman continued impassively, "been sentenced to death, by a duly authorized judiciary of your peers, under the laws of the Four Worlds of the Patri and their colonies. Said execution is to be carried out by lethal injection aboard this ship, the *Bellwether*, registered from the Patri world of Portslava, under the direction of Dr. Kurt DeMont, authorized by the governor of Solitaire.

"Robern Roxbury Trembley, do you have any last words?"

Trembley started to shake his head, discovered the headband prevented that. "No," he whispered, voice cracking slightly with the strain.

Aikman half turned, nodded at DeMont. Lips pressed tightly together, the doctor stepped forward, moving around the back of the helm chair to Trembley's right arm. Opening his medical kit, he withdrew a small hypo, already prepared. Trembley closed his eyes, face taut with fear and the approach of death . . . and DeMont touched the hypo nozzle to his arm.

Trembley jerked, inhaling sharply. "Connye," he whispered, lower jaw trembling as he exhaled a long, ragged breath.

His eyes never opened again . . . and a minute later he was dead.

DeMont gazed at the readouts in his kit for another minute before he confirmed it officially. "Execution carried out as ordered," he said, his voice both tired and grim. "Time: fifteen hundred twenty-seven hours, ship's chrono, Anno Patri date 14 Octyab 422." He raised his eyes to Bartholomy. "He's ready, Captain."

Bartholomy nodded, visibly steeled himself, and moved forward. Unstrapping Trembley's arms, he reached gingerly past the body to a black keyboard that had been plugged into the main helm panel. It came alive with indicator lights and prompts at his touch, and he set it down onto the main panel's front grip, positioning it over the main helm controls and directly in front of the chair. "Do I need to do anything else?" he asked Aikman, his voice almost a whisper.

"No," Aikman shook his head. He threw a glance at me, and I could sense the malicious satisfaction there at my presence. The big pious Watcher, forced to watch a man being executed. "No, from here on in it's just sit back and enjoy the ride."

Bartholomy snorted, a flash of dislike flickering out toward Aikman as he moved away from the body.

And as if on cue, the body stirred.

I knew what to expect; but even so, the sight of it was shattering. Trembley was *dead*—everything about him, every cue my Watcher training could detect told me he was dead . . . and to see his arms lift slowly away from the chair sent a horrible chill straight to the center of my being. And yet, at the same time, I couldn't force my eyes to turn away. There was an almost hypnotic fascination to the scene that held my intellect even while it repelled my emotions.

Trembley's arms were moving forward now, reaching out toward the black Deadman Switch panel. For a moment they hesitated, as if unsure of themselves. Then the hands stirred, the fingers curved over, and the arms lowered to the Mjollnir switch. One hand groped for position . . . paused . . . touched it—

And abruptly, gravity returned. We were on Mjollnir drive again, on our way through the Cloud.

With a dead man at the controls.

"Why?" I asked Randon again.

"Because you're the first Watcher to travel to Solitaire," he said. The words were directed to me; but his eyes remained on Trembley. The morbid fascination I'd felt still had Randon in its grip. "Hard to believe, isn't it?" he continued, his voice distant. "Seventy years after the discovery of the Deadman Switch and there still hasn't been a Watcher who's taken the trip in."

I shivered, my skin crawling. The Deadman Switch had hardly been "discovered"—the first ship to get to Solitaire had done so on pure idiot luck . . . if *luck* was the proper word. A university's scientific expedition had been nosing around the edge of the Cloud for days, trying to figure out why a Mjollnir drive couldn't operate within that region of space, when the drive had suddenly and impossibly kicked in, sending them off on the ten-hour trip inward to the Solitaire system. Busy with their readings and instruments, no one on board realized until they reached the system that the man operating the helm was dead—had, in fact, died of a stroke just before they'd entered the Cloud.

By the time they came to the correct conclusion, they'd been trapped in the system for nearly two months. Friendships, under such conditions, often grow rapidly. I wondered what it had been like, drawing lots to see who would die so that the rest could get home . . .

I shivered, violently. "The Watchers consider the Deadman Switch to be a form of human sacrifice," I told him.

Randon threw me a patient glance . . . but beneath the slightly amused sophistication there, I could tell he wasn't entirely comfortable with the ethics of it either. "I didn't bring you here to argue public morals with me," he said tartly. "I brought you here because—" he pursed his lips briefly— "because I thought you might be able to settle the question of whether or not the Cloud is really alive."

It was as if all the buried fears of my childhood had suddenly risen again from their half-forgotten shadows. To deliberately try and detect the presence of an entity that had coldly taken control of a dead human body . . .

THE MANY WORLDS OF
MELISSA SCOTT

*Winner of the John W. Campbell Award
for Best New Writer, 1986*

THE KINDLY ONES: "An ambitious novel of the world Orestes. This large, inhabited moon is governed by five Kinships whose society operates on a code of honor so strict that transgressors are declared legally 'dead' and are prevented from having any contact with the 'living.' . . . Scott is a writer to watch."—*Publishers Weekly*. A Main Selection of the Science Fiction Book Club.

65351-2 • 384 pp. • $2.95

The "Silence Leigh" Trilogy

FIVE-TWELFTHS OF HEAVEN (Book I): "Melissa Scott postulates a universe where technology interferes with magic. . . . The whole plot is one of space ships, space wars, and alien planets—not a unicorn or a dragon to be seen anywhere. Scott's space drive and description of space piloting alone would mark her as an expert in the melding of the [SF and fantasy] genres; this is the stuff of which 'sense of wonder' is made."—*Locus*

55952-4 • 352 pp. • $2.95

SILENCE IN SOLITUDE (Book II): "[Scott is] a voice you should seek out and read at every opportunity."
—*OtherRealms*.   65699-7 • 324 pp. • $2.95

THE EMPRESS OF EARTH (Book III):
65364-4 • 352 pp. • $3.50

A CHOICE OF DESTINIES: "Melissa Scott [is] one of science fiction's most talented newcomers. . . . The greatest delight of all is finding out how she managed to write a historical novel that could legitimately have spaceships on the cover . . . a marvelous gift for any fan."—*Baltimore Sun*   65563-9 • 320 pp. • $2.95

THE GAME BEYOND: "An exciting interstellar empire novel with a great deal of political intrigue and colorful interplanetary travel."—*Locus*

55918-4 • 352 pp. • $2.95